NEW WRITING FROM
BRITAIN'S OLDEST PUBLISHER

This is the fourth year of JM Originals,
a list from John Murray.
It is a home for fresh and distinctive new writing;
for books that provoke and entertain.

Also by Sam Thompson

Communion Town

Jott

Sam Thompson

JM ORIGINALS

First published in Great Britain in 2018 by JM Originals
An imprint of John Murray (Publishers)
An Hachette UK Company

1

© Sam Thompson 2018

Epigraph quotation from *How It Is* by Samuel Beckett, reproduced by permission
of Faber and Faber Ltd.

This novel is a work of fiction. In some cases true-life figures and places appear but
this is a literary device to create context and background. Any resemblance to actual
persons is purely coincidental.

A CIP catalogue record for this title is available from the British Library

ISBN 978-1-47367-505-6
Ebook ISBN 978-1-47367-506-3

Typeset in Minion Pro 11.5/14.5 pt by Palimpsest Book Production Limited,
Falkirk, Stirlingshire

Printed and bound by CPI Group (UK) Ltd, Croydon, CR0 4YY

John Murray policy is to use papers that are natural, renewable and
recyclable products and made from wood grown in sustainable forests.
The logging and manufacturing processes are expected to conform
to the environmental regulations of the country of origin.

John Murray (Publishers)
Carmelite House
50 Victoria Embankment
London EC4Y 0DZ

www.johnmurray.co.uk

To Caoileann, Oisín, Odhrán and Sadhbh
And to the family

that's how it was
Samuel Beckett

in actual fact it's not like that at all
Geoffrey Thompson

ONE

ONE

They walked in the grounds in silence. Meeting at the gate, it had been apparent that Louis was not in a talking mood, so Arthur, saying nothing, had fallen in step beside him, and in the time since then they had not spoken. Instead their shoes scraped on the path and the crows called in the trees. The Calvary might have been deserted.

The silence was not yet a long one, but the urge to speak was growing. He could ask after the work, reckless as that would be, or he could try Venn, or offer some morsel of medical life. The woman he had seen on admission this morning would appeal to Louis's taste, no doubt, having come here from a penitential retreat where after fasting and watching for three days and nights she had seen the devil scuttling for her along the floor of the dormitory. But he kept pace with Louis and said nothing, and the need eased. The discipline was meeting these moments when they came and passing through them into deeper silence.

They turned on to a path that led away from the main cluster of buildings, through stands of trees, past the nurses' houses and towards the woodland at the edge of the grounds. His fingers were numb, but he knew better than to suggest giving up the walk. The paradox was that for Louis to make the journey into the deep silence he craved, he needed a companion. To be silent alone just meant having no one to talk to, but to stay unspeaking with your friend beside you was to choose the silence, so that when you walked together wordlessly for hours, tracing and retracing these footpaths in cold mist, it became something achieved, and you grew to see that every conversation was the better for being unhad, because silence was more exacting than speech and more truly communicative. That they had often spent hours and even days together without exchanging a word was the mark of their friendship, its signature or proof. So it seemed to Arthur, though it was possible that Louis saw things differently. They had never actually discussed it.

As they passed the stone steps that led down to the croquet lawn, Louis stopped walking, arrested by some stray thought. Arthur continued a little further along the path, then waited. He blew on his fingernails. At this distance Louis cut a bedraggled figure, dark-headed and untidily tall, one hand gathering the lapels of his old tweed overcoat. There was no use in impatience, because it had never occurred to Louis to hurry himself on another person's account. All of his time was his own. Venn aside, he spent his days tramping around Battersea Park or hiding out in galleries, museums and pubs. When all else failed he'd go back to his digs and try to work, until the attempt brought him to such despair that he would trek out to the hospital, where Arthur would give him as long as he needed, saying no, of course it wasn't inconvenient and he wasn't too busy. In truth, though, he was always too busy. Arthur's time belonged to others.

They walked on, into the woodland that skirted the estate. Friendship was a word whose meaning grew less clear the more he said it to himself, but he knew that it was worth keeping. It was the work of many years. The longer a silence lasts the harder it becomes to break, and they would not now be capable of these rare silences if they hadn't shared the prehistory of schoolboy obsessions, student philosophising, angst of youth and all that. In his first term at Donard, he had been cornered in the library by two boys who snatched a letter he was writing to his mother and read it aloud in snivelling voices, until Louis appeared, levering himself up from an armchair and somehow, with a few casual and friendly-seeming words, causing the larger of the two boys to drop the letter on the table and hasten out of the library, snarling at his accomplice to keep up. Arthur couldn't remember how he'd felt about being rescued, whether he was glad or ashamed or in fact anything, because that was the era before he had been shaped into a thinking being with a point of view from which to make sense of what happened to him. As a new boy he hadn't so much minded a life regimented by early rising and cold baths, rules about where you could go when, morning chapel and cross-country runs. What had appalled him were the gaps in the timetable where you were left to fend for yourself. In the world that had swallowed him, he dimly understood, the trappings of the routine, with its hierarchies and rituals and organised violence, were only the visible signs of a deeper threat, which was invisible and nameless but which he had felt as it moved along the corridors and waited in the boot rooms. Even then he'd known the school wanted something from him that he was not prepared to give. Since those days he had thought of himself as hating institutional life and wanting only to be free, but then consider the evidence: after Donard, TCD, then more barrack life at Baggot Street, and now here he was, living and working in the Calvary and never going anywhere except to traipse up to Bloomsbury three times a week and pay his own tribute to Venn. And where was that supposed to lead?

Arthur still regularly lost his bearings when he walked around the hospital. The trees that grew throughout the grounds were disorienting, sometimes folding themselves aside to reveal one of the modern villas that housed most of the treatment rooms and offices, then a few paces later closing up so that nothing was visible but trunks rising from a mossy floor. Now, as they struck back towards the centre of the hospital, the greenery opened and two figures came towards them. A male nurse was escorting a male patient through the grounds. Louis stared frankly at the pair, but they passed by, keys clanking, as if they saw nothing. Some people could get on good easy terms with nurses with just a few words, a joke and a grin, which was an advantage, especially here, but Arthur had never had the knack.

The rims of his ears burned with the cold. A worse pain than his fingers. It was futile to be trailing around out here, putting on this pretence of companionable meditation when in truth he hated the cold waste of time and the pointless silence through which he always resigned himself to suffer until Louis decided it should end. He seemed to have no choice in this. It couldn't be fair, could it, to be made responsible for someone else, but at some turning point long forgotten he'd allowed it to happen. Certainly the tone had been set before they left Donard. Take that night in their last year when Louis had smuggled in a half-bottle of whiskey, necked the lot and slipped out of the school after lights out. Arthur had been furious and ready to break with him for good, but he had followed, deadly scared of getting caught out of bounds, to trail Louis across the playing fields and persuade him back inside.

Another screen of foliage shifted and the red brick of Creedy House was above them. Quiet Female One and Convalescent. The electric lamp over the entrance was lit. Arthur saw Celia Prentice with her face upturned at midnight in the light of a street lamp, her lips apart, waiting, beginning to laugh. Thanks be to Christ Louis doesn't know of that at least. But who could tell what Louis knew: perhaps he knew well that Arthur hated these silent walks, and perhaps he imposed them in a spirit of contempt, chuckling inwardly at Arthur putting up with it, Arthur squirming but not being honest enough to bring it to an end. Perhaps Louis was taking some form of revenge. But how much revenge did he need for all the miles of pavement Arthur had walked with him, and all the nights in dingy rooms spent sitting up until dawn? It was obvious by now that they would never reach the end of it. Whenever he thought he had discharged his duties they returned in a new guise, and he knew what the silence meant today. The book which Louis had been writing, in theory if not practice, ever since he had moved to London was in its customary state of crisis. The provisional title was *Jott*: beyond this cryptic syllable Louis had not revealed any of the details of what he was trying to write, though he would talk at length about the agonies involved in failing to write it. Arthur gathered that the book had been at death's door for months. It seemed likely that when it finally expired Louis would throw in his London life and limp back to Dublin, and that this would do him no good at all.

They passed the other ward blocks and the chapel, then cut

down an alley where the back wall of the kitchens vented steam and the smell of overcooked vegetables. The daylight was starting to go. If that was the meaning of the silence then it was Arthur's fault, of course, for talking too much about his own work in the first weeks. But Louis had led him into it by asking every time they met, and seeming so interested that Arthur could hardly be blamed if he'd shown off a little about his new responsibilities. Louis had asked all manner of questions about the hospital: about how wards were organised and what therapies were practised, about the attitudes of nurses to patients and of doctors to nurses, about the difficulties of caring for those who could not be held responsible for their words or actions. He wanted to hear about the patients themselves, and above all about the long-term cases, the hopeless ones, of whom there weren't many and whose presence was strictly against the rules, as the Calvary Royal Hospital was an institution for the curably insane. Why the chronic cases should have a special appeal for Louis Arthur did not want to ask, for fear of giving encouragement. If Arthur put Louis in a white coat and took him on a ward round then probably no one would give him a second glance, and really there could be no harm in it, but Arthur felt, without knowing quite why, that it must not happen.

Above all Louis wanted to meet Mr Walker, about whom he'd heard so much. He had only made the request once, on one of these walks in the hospital grounds: Arthur had mumbled something about it being an interesting idea and his having to see, and since then had been ever more conscious of Louis's irreproachable silence on the matter. Perhaps it was true that in some mysterious way going on the wards would help Louis get on with his book, and no doubt Arthur would be able to square it with his conscience well enough, telling himself it was a kindness to a friend and that putting the patients at the service of a struggling writer, doing them no harm, was no real betrayal. But he would know that in truth it was simpler than this, and that yet again he had been the weak one who gives way because the other will is stronger.

They were coming back towards the main gate, where the administration block, the junior doctors' accommodation and the reception ward faced one another across a courtyard. A purple tint had leaked into the air from among the branches of the trees, which were enormous, much taller than any of the hospital buildings: you could work here for weeks on end without registering them at all, and then at a moment like this you saw them for what they were, huge, ungraspable expressions of matter. And then, if you let them, they began to look like messengers, signifying perhaps that Arthur would never again be known in the way that Louis knew him, because no one he could hope to meet in his life from now on would get so deep a hold, because an association like this must begin before you are formed, because it's what forms you, and that can only happen once. Louis had stolen Arthur's chance to be other than what he was, now or ever; Louis had come here today for no other purpose than to torment him with silence until he surrendered; Louis was ruthless, and there was no escape. These were unreasonable thoughts but they were gaining now, so, close to giving himself away with some small noise or gesture, Arthur did the same thing he had done at this stage of every other visit that Louis had paid to the hospital, and challenged him to a game.

*

At Donard they had played all the time, Louis winning more often than not, though the outcome was unpredictable enough to make the game worthwhile. The oldest roots of their friendship were in shared enthusiasms of this kind. They had both been addicted to Conan Doyle, Wodehouse and M. R. James, and had amused one another by writing parodies and satires. They had gone through obsessions with piquet and whist and phases of inventing wordgames. Both being good at the books, they had become rival scholars: Louis was untouchable at languages ancient and modern, but Arthur sometimes edged him into second place in English and always beat him at the sciences. Arthur hated rugby, unlike Louis, who played fly half for the first fifteen, but both were decent cricketers and in the summer term of their fourth year they opened the batting. Their alliance had faced certain tests, too, as when they had decided they would refuse to join the Officer Training Corps, so that the deputy headmaster called them to his office and spoke with dangerous restraint about their duty to school and nation. While Louis observed that no rule compelled them to take part, Arthur stood tongue-tied and horrified that a bit of blustering talk after prep had led to this, so that the deputy head, spotting his target, leaned close, eyes bulging with the disfavour that would follow if Arthur did not betray his comrade, and invited him to change his mind. But somehow he held the line, and with a final snort the man dismissed them. As they escaped into the corridor they stifled laughter, Arthur not having known this kind of triumph was possible. They spent the Saturday afternoon lounging beside the tennis courts watching boys and masters march about, Arthur saying that patriotism was for asses, Louis adding that a nation was nothing more than a deceit practised on its people and both agreeing furthermore that religion was bosh and that society in its current form was rotten, though whereas Arthur took the view that science would eventually free humankind from all forms of unhappiness, Louis predicted that civilisation would stumble to a close before long and those left in the ashes would be better off. And one June Sunday they walked into the fields around the school, lay down under an oak tree and tried to learn 'Julian and Maddalo' by heart, Arthur soon forgetting all but a few lines of the poem but remembering the buzzing grasses and the glare of the sky.

Now Arthur pointed at Louis's left fist, which opened to reveal a white pawn. They had the junior doctors' common room to themselves. Ellis had been here, but as they came in he had swigged the last of his tea, shaken his newspaper shut and risen, nodding vaguely as he left. Now that they were alone they could draw a pair of low, threadbare armchairs up close to the electric fire, which was better than the one in Arthur's room. Louis set up the board with quick, sure movements and swivelled it to present him with White.

The set was a small boxwood Staunton which Louis had given Arthur when he began the Calvary job, saying he had found it in a Brompton junk shop and that it would give him an excuse to visit the hospital. Junk shop or not, it must have cost more than Louis could easily afford. Arthur liked the pieces, with their lead weighting and green felt bases, but as usual he couldn't think why he had let himself in for a game.

He slid the queen's pawn forward two squares, feeling reasonably sure that this did not amount to a howler. Playing White was worse because his opening move had nothing to guide it except his own incompetence. Louis moved his own queen's pawn out to meet White's, and at once the array of possible mistakes became overwhelming. Arthur advanced another pawn, the queen's bishop's, to stand beside the first. He could still remember one or two openings to a depth of a few moves, and he liked this one because it felt asymmetrical and surprising, as if he had a plan. If he could avoid disaster for two or three turns he might put up a respectable show.

Louis pushed the steel-rimmed spectacles up on his forehead, considering White's gambit. Arthur tried to concentrate. His second pawn was offering itself for capture, a lure to draw Black into a weaker position. Black could accept the gambit by taking the pawn, or decline it by moving up a second pawn to defend the first, but Louis did neither. He ignored the lure and brought out a knight to threaten White's pawn instead. Immediately at sea, Arthur stared at the board for too long, willing inspiration, and finally pushed another pawn forward. It was a purposeless move, but Louis brought his face closer to the board and pursed his lips as if searching for hidden brilliance.

At school it had never occurred to Arthur that chess was a waste of time, because, like cricket, cards and chemistry, like everything they did in those days, it was not so much itself as a promise of what was to come. Far from being trivial, those games had been their guarantees of what the future owed; but now it was today, and so much more had happened, and the only reason to play was to get it over with. Black having declined White's opening gambit, the pieces stayed where they were, blocking the middle of the board. All opening moves had been made, knights and bishops deployed and pawns locked into position, and Arthur could find nothing to do that would not expose him. Sooner or later in every game the pieces turned into dumb bits of wood, meaningless in relation to one another.

He had lost his taste for chess soon after going up to Trinity, where although they still played, most often in Louis's rooms with the foliage of Botany Bay screening the window, they were no longer a good match. Arthur had stopped improving, and any feeling he'd had for the game was leaving him. He needed to concentrate on other things. Arthur was reading medicine, Louis modern languages, and the fact of having come here together had introduced an intrepid note to their friendship. The first term in Dublin was solid rain, with light barely breaking the clouds each day before evening closed in, but Arthur was dizzy with discovering that all of this was his: O'Connell Street's decaying fronts, Stephen's Green, the reeling gulls and the river stinking of the sea, the Georgian slums, dank tea shops and pubs and the unkind faces that swarmed in the streets. He was falling towards the future, and if he was too smitten with his freedom to do much with it, that didn't seem to matter, because to be here was enough. It was enough that at chucking-out time he and Louis stumbled back to Front Arch, not feeling the cold though it had them shivering, to make it through before the porters locked up for the night. First thing in the morning Arthur hurried with shaking hands to the dissection room, then eight hours later called on Louis to find him still in bed but willing to rise for dinner in the chophouse on George Street, after which and a restorative in O'Neill's they would see a play at the Abbey, sitting in their favourite seats on the balcony aisle.

Louis castled on the kingside, picking up the king and the rook in one hand and switching them around with a fluent gesture. There seemed to be an essential difference between those prompt black pieces and the white ones that sat on this side of the board, refusing to cooperate. At school Arthur and

Louis had both liked the idea that it was in the nature of chess for the position to become, within a few moves, far too complex to understand, so that you had to play less against your opponent than against your own inadequacy to the task. It meant that the sensible approach was untroubled curiosity, watching the pattern unfold, learning from it and not minding the outcome, but Louis had always been better at that kind of detachment, and not only at the chessboard. When he wanted to he could take himself out of consideration, which accounted for his curious ability to go anywhere and speak to anyone. Once, walking through Rutland Square, Arthur had caught sight of Louis cross-legged on the pavement, deep in talk with the madman who sat there every day calling at passers-by. They looked as if they were thrashing out a serious matter, so Arthur kept his head down and continued along Frederick Street, unsure what he had learned about his friend. And the following spring Louis took him on a walk that lasted for most of a day, heading first into the rookeries of the north side, through foul alleys where Arthur saw foul sights – grown men squabbling like children, a small girl squatting naked, a doorway in which two maimed soldiers begged – and felt so conspicuous that putting one foot in front of the other became an unfamiliar operation, as in the dream where you trip yourself at every step.

Try telling mother and her friends about this, Louis had said as they walked along the canal towards the prison. Tell them about this down in Dalkey and they'll clench their nostrils like you've farted a goodun. Arthur, impressed, wanted to agree: it was true, the misery of the world was not to be tolerated. They went out as far as the racecourse and walked back through the Phoenix Park while the sky sifted into

14

rust-red, grey and old gold, getting back to college soon after dark, where, sitting up in Botany Bay, Louis talked until the small hours and Arthur slowly understood that he was hearing the story of a broken heart. There had been a young woman, a friend of the Molyneux family, known to Louis since they were small, whom he had loved for most of the time he had been at Donard. This was the first Arthur had heard of it. Louis had seen her in the summer vacations, but their mothers had found out about the attachment and separated them. Her name was Connie. He had not seen her alone for nearly three years, and not at all since coming up to Dublin, and now, yesterday, he had learned that she had died of tuberculosis, the news given as an aside in a letter from his mother. Arthur had not the faintest idea what to say. More confidences came out, quite casually, as Louis told the story: a liaison with a girl from the Modern Languages Society had come to an unpleasant end a fortnight ago; Louis had been paying night visits to Monto all the time he had been in the city. Arthur could think of nothing except to tell Louis that he should take a Wassermann test as soon as possible, and saying this he heard his own voice as that of a prim schoolboy, frightened and ignorant and trying to hide it. But why had Louis not let him in on that side of life: was it so plain that he had no business there? He had never had the chance, he'd barely spoken to a woman. No one could have been worse equipped to give counsel on these matters, but still, for some reason, Louis needed him to listen.

He noticed, too late, that Louis had set up a fork so that White was bound to lose either his queen or a bishop. He searched for a way out, wondering if perhaps an overlooked piece could spring into play and upset the scheme, but there was nothing. He moved the queen out of harm's way and the bishop was snapped up. It was an effort not to apologise for the weakness of his play now, and he knew the urge would grow with every move, as it did in every game. But saying sorry for a poor move was unsporting. A truly successful game would be one in which he made it all the way to defeat without apologising to Louis at all, but if he faltered once then successive apologies became harder to resist. There had been shameful encounters in which he had ended up mumbling his regrets every time he touched a piece. It had occurred to him that this struggle was more significant than the game itself, and a more important kind of victory to pursue, but the insight did not help either in the game itself or in the game outside the game. Louis moved a rook. The light caught softly on the pale wood and harder on the black. A sequence of five or six moves took place without Arthur thinking about them, at the end of which pawns were exchanged. He lost a rook through sheer inattention, and then, getting flustered, another pawn.

Louis was smiling in a foxy way that Arthur knew well. It meant he wanted something which Arthur would prefer not to give.

Louis dropped his gaze, keeping the smile to himself, and studied the board, in no hurry to make his next move. Arthur was pinned. He knew that when Louis asked again to go on the wards, asking here and now, face to face, with the weight of their friendship bearing down, he would weaken and agree. He was helpless to prevent it. It was no wonder Louis had taken so much from him over the years when he gave it so easily. In their third year at Trinity, when Louis was prone to nasty moods and was dropping his friends left and right, Arthur had carried on listening to his troubles. Sometimes, when Louis tired of saying wicked things against the world and himself, he would start saying them against Arthur, who would hear without complaint, cultivating his bedside manner and never once getting up and walking out. That he hadn't was incomprehensible, looking back. One night they sat up late in Arthur's room on Front Square, with the lights off and curtains open; the two of them sunk in the high-backed armchairs while Louis's voice, soft and vicious, explained that their association was a joke. You have your uses, but I have always despised you. Tomorrow, he added, he would take it back, as they both knew. He would ask forgiveness and beg Arthur to find out what was wrong with him that he could say such things to his oldest friend, but remember this: tomorrow he would be lying, and tonight he was telling the truth. His face was a livid shadow. A long silence followed, and then Louis asked: Do you want me to go? Arthur shook his head. He was being outplayed as always, but he wouldn't throw Louis out of the room. They sat on in silence instead.

The pieces were thinning out as White was forced into more frequent exchanges. Arthur thought of resigning, but it would be churlish not to let Black's triumph play out, so he occupied himself by advancing the last couple of pawns slowly down the rightmost files as if they believed they might reach the far side untaken. He had been too preoccupied with not losing his queen and had made bad moves to preserve her, so that now she was cornered and powerless. He glanced at the face above the chessboard. His life now would be quite different if, even once, he had walked away from Louis, pausing perhaps to suggest that his friend go and fuck himself.

But that had been the period in which, for the first time since school, Louis had started asking him to read things. Arthur had hardly known what to make of what he saw. There were clever, unfriendly poems, full of rain, rotting fruit, failed loves, dead animals and crippled children. There was a story, a few pages long, about a sensitive youth trying to escape the monstrous emotional demands of his mother through an encounter with a depraved girl in Amiens Street Station: after botching the transaction, the details of which remained shadowy, the youth returned to his dark family home never to leave again. There were essays, most of them appreciations of modern European poets and novelists whose names were unknown to Arthur. Louis apparently knew what he was talking about, but the style was an acid parody of scholarly prose, disfigured by self-contempt. It was obvious that the author wanted to slap the faces of the professors he was writing for. Arthur couldn't see that Louis would do himself any good like that, but no doubt he knew what would impress his audience.

Louis got the top first in his year and left Trinity swearing never to return to that boneyard of blathering cadavers. He borrowed money from his mother and moved to Paris, where he was to subsist giving English lessons, and write. Meanwhile, Arthur, free of all-day walks and night-long conversations, applied for a research fellowship in biochemistry at Guy's and St Thomas's, which he took up immediately after qualifying. It was the first time he had been outside Ireland, and London offered daunting freedoms. Each morning the young women went to work, swinging on to buses and striding through parks in the middle distance. One evening he attended a lecture by Edwin Webb at the Institute of Psychoanalysis, after which he walked into the night air thrilled that the secrets of human life could be exposed in a packed auditorium and examined without shame. He had discovered something, but, not knowing what to do about it, he finished the six months of the fellowship and returned to Dublin to take up a post as junior house physician at Baggot Street. So far it was an enviable career.

The letters that came from Paris bristled with parodies, puzzles, impersonations and sarcasm that cut in many directions at once, making slapstick of Louis's trials: the Sisyphean toil each morning of writing the sentence that he would spend the afternoon crossing out, the allergy to gainful employment and the persistent headaches that were, on the whole, less painful than his attempts at book reviewing and his efforts to get publishers to take an interest in the slim volume of stories he was preparing. Arthur put off replying, conscious that his own letters were dull things by comparison, but dreading that another would arrive from Paris before he had answered the previous. He tried, at least, to give Louis advice on his physical ailments, though in doing so he was plainly indulging a form of hypochondria. If he hadn't, perhaps none of the rest would have followed. But it makes no difference how far back you trace the causes: it only matters that once, long ago, he came and begged you to help him, and you helped, and now you owe him your care forever.

Black put White's king in check, and Arthur saw he could not prevent his queen from being captured on the next turn. He stared at the board for a while, seeking a single inspired move that would transform the position, freeing his king and in the same stroke setting up an irresistible offensive. He moved the king and Black took the queen. Louis never seemed shy about winning. The endgame worked itself through, and soon the white king was dodging behind his only surviving pawn, evading Black's queen and rook, but not for long. Arthur tipped the piece on its side.

19

'Ah well,' he said. 'I didn't suffer.'

'Tell me something now,' Louis said, still contemplating the board. He was smiling again. The moment was here and he was about to strike, but the surprise was that he had misjudged his move. Quite unexpectedly, Arthur had the resolve he needed. He would say that, regrettably, no, as it turned out it would not be possible for Louis to meet Walker or any other patient either now or in the future. He had decided it couldn't be done. This would be the end of it. Straightening his back, lifting his chin, finding that he was not so tired as he'd thought, he met Louis's eyes.

In his second year after qualifying, while he was still a houseman at Baggot Street, Arthur was involved in the treatment of a fifteen-year-old girl suffering from a congenital dislocation of the hip. The condition, which posed no threat to her life but which, left untreated, would in time cause increasing pain and incapacity, could be improved by a straightforward surgical procedure which she was therefore scheduled to undergo. The only unusual aspect, which would keep the case in Arthur's mind for some time afterwards, was the patient's unshakeable belief that if they operated on her she would die. At every consultation she told her mother and her doctors that this would happen, politely ignoring assurances to the contrary, not trying to dissuade them from the operation but seeming resigned to her fate. The mother was frightened by the girl's talk, but the registrar explained that there was no danger, the procedure being both safe and necessary. Her daughter was guilty only of a bit of excusable foolishness, and she would snap out of it once she was in recovery. Arthur observed the procedure, which went by the book in every respect except that after surgery the girl failed to recover consciousness, and some hours later did in fact die, no explanation for which could be found.

Arthur mentioned the case in a letter to Paris, and eleven months later Louis sent him a recent issue of a London little magazine, *The Margin*, in which he had published a story called 'A Routine Procedure'. The events were those of Arthur's anecdote, but in Louis's version it had become a horror tale, with the physicians and surgeons as pompous professional clowns who in treating the girl seemed instead of trying to correct a physical problem to be acting out strange, unacknowledged desires of their own. The story gave prominence to the youngest doctor, who in the fiction was the one responsible for sending the patient to perish on the operating table, and furthermore turned out in the final pages to have had some prior involvement with the girl's mother, his former schoolmistress, a fact which shaped the outcome, the story implied, though precisely how was not made clear. When the girl died she was the victim of her doctors and their self-deceits, but in a way she had also bested them, exposing them in some deep moral lack. The story finished by overplaying its irony, Arthur felt, with a scene of the mother humbly thanking the young doctor for everything he had done.

He tried to write a letter. He wanted to ask why Louis hadn't mentioned that he was working on the story and whether it was meant as the personal attack that it appeared to be, but such questions were out of bounds, he felt, and besides, what he really wanted to do was demonstrate that Louis had got it all wrong. The story had missed everything that mattered in the events it recounted. Certainly there was a question worth exploring here. Arthur had thought a good deal about the physical and psychological aspects of that case, asking himself whether the patient's delusional premonition had been pure coincidence or a causative factor of some sort that had yet to be understood. If Louis's story wanted to take a poor view of the medical profession, Arthur didn't mind: he was unhappy himself with the scorn of Dublin doctors for what the sick might have to say about their own ailments, and he had seen enough to think that the mental life of the patient, far from being ignored, should be viewed as integral to diagnosis and treatment. But Louis did not seem to be making any such argument, or suggesting that there was anything to be learned from the case at all. Instead the story played a trick. It appeared to take the side of the patient, showing how her life had been stolen by doctors who were complacent and sadistic – but how, actually, could Louis know the truth, and how could he presume to speak on the patient's behalf? Arthur could as easily accuse him of exploiting the case for his own ends, turning another person's misfortune into a pantomime of fancy words, and he could point out too that the story did not express the closeness of the room in which he had stood while the registrar spoke to the patient, or the way she lowered her head to show white scalp in her dark parting while she listened, rolling one of her small thumbs between the other thumb and forefinger. The story had none of this, but after reading it he was no longer sure that he knew what had really happened. If Louis's version hadn't displaced the reality, it had at least confused matters. Arthur wanted to say so, but he could not find the right way to begin the letter, and eventually, finding it too difficult and himself too tired and too busy, he gave up. And now it was hardly strange if he hesitated to bring Louis on the wards, however much he might want to trust that, given the chance, he would describe the hospital as it really was.

That question remained unresolved, because after check-mating him Louis had not asked the favour Arthur had been expecting. Instead he'd said: Come into town tonight, won't you? We're going boozing. Arthur, who had been planning to roost beside his bar heater and struggle through a number of the *International Journal of Psychoanalysis* that Venn had lent him, felt only weariness at the prospect of a night in the Lantern-Bearers with Louis's friends, but, caught unawares, he had promised to go. After seeing Louis to the gate he had found himself with just enough time to snatch his white coat from his room before hastening to Sinfield House for the evening round.

The charge nurse, Parry, was six feet four inches tall, with black curls and a handsome Roman face. Arthur had once overheard him telling a patient that he was born and bred in Bethnal Green. His movements were gentle, making you aware of how he would never use his big hands to pick you up and sling you into one of the quiet rooms where you would remain for as long as he chose. Arthur was pleased to find him on duty. On Parry's shifts the ward was calm, the patients co-operative and even likeable. There were other nurses, perfectly competent, whose presence would put a ward on the edge of insurrection. Outside the windows the lamps were coming on, setting up walls of darkness beyond. Parry whistled through his teeth as he shambled the length of the main corridor to collect the prescription book from the nurses' station.

It was slack time on the ward, the patients having been given tea an hour ago and another two hours remaining until bedtime. A few men moved along the corridor, some drifting, others restive. Beside the door to the latrine one spoke urgently to another, who paid him no attention. The rest were in the day rooms. Some read and some were listening to the concert on the wireless, but most just sat, ignoring the piano, the billiard table, the bookcases and one another. Someone out of sight was grumbling to himself without conviction. If Louis were to visit he would be disappointed by how pleasant it all was. The patients' rooms were clean and private, each with a Lloyd Loom chair and a window on the gardens. If the Calvary were a hotel, it would be a well-kept, comfortable one catering to two hundred and fifty guests at its full capacity. The worst one could say, on an evening like this, was that the heat from the radiators was stifling and that the whole place smelled excessively of paraldehyde: the walls, the furniture, the patients themselves steeped in a sweet, volatile odour like pear drops dissolved in ethyl alcohol, with a layer of rabbit-hutch rankness underneath.

Occasionally the Senior Assistant Physician might decide to gather the firm and lead a formal round of the wards, but daily rounds were left to the juniors, which was safe enough since the only medical decision that arose, or could possibly arise, was whether to increase a patient's paraldehyde or to keep him at his present dosage. Every patient in the Calvary was on a regime of paraldehyde. As he went around, Arthur introduced variation where he could: here, a measure of brandy to be given as an afternoon stimulant for a man tending to become depressed; there, hyoscine and a sulphonamide for one who had been picking at his scalp. Parry's pen scratched in the prescription book in a manner emphasising that he was nothing but an instrument of the doctor's will. In truth Parry knew the patients' needs better than Arthur, better than Ellis, better than the Physician-Superintendent himself. You could tell that a ward round had been successful if at no point the charge nurse stiffened for an instant before writing down the instruction with more than the usual servility. It couldn't be helped. Parry was probably younger than Arthur, but he had been working at the Calvary for seven years already and might stay for the next forty if he made no mistakes, whereas Arthur had been here for three months and would be finished by the end of the year. It was no wonder the hospital didn't trust its junior doctors to do anything on their own initiative, but it would have mattered more if there were really anything to be done. Everyone he had trained with must think he'd made a perverse choice, and there was no denying that he had side-tracked himself. By now he could have been well on the way to consultant physician at Baggot Street or the Rotunda, but instead he had chosen to come to London and become a junior house officer all over again, at a psychiatric hospital of all places, cut off from the advance of scientific medicine, with no real clinical work to speak of, only the unvaried round of sedation and caretaking, unambitious, underpaid and without hope of private practice in future. It was bewildering that his younger self could have dared to stake his prospects on this. Had he been so desperate to escape? But he still remembered that time as one of joy, the weather in Dublin clearing and himself becoming effectual as well as bold, writing letters to influential people, making the arrangements, keeping his plans to himself until it was time to announce them and then doing so without hesitation. Medical Dublin was a prison and he was not one to languish when a little enterprise could break him out. He'd laughed inside himself at how scandalised they would be when they heard that he who looked so promising and straight and had been appointed FRCPI less than a year ago was packing it in for psychological medicine, that unspeakable voodoo. He knew what they would think, but he defied them in his heart and made the voyage to Holyhead.

Waiting for Parry to let him out of the ward, Arthur wondered if it would be possible for them to become friends. Parry seemed a fair picture of what a friend should be. He would be a gentle, bearish one, to be relied on for strength and good humour. Arthur thanked him, and the clatter of the locks echoed in the stairwell. A friend you could rely on in any situation. Swinging around the turn with a hand on the iron banister, he thought of the time he had introduced Louis to his parents. For reasons lost to history Arthur had decided it would do Louis good to spend a weekend away, so they took the train to Wexford and soon found themselves sitting across the tea table from Arthur's mother and father. Mr and Mrs Bourne were baffled not so much by the ruinous state of Louis's overcoat, or by the fact that he refused to take it off for tea, as by his silence. He sat staring at the table top, his eyes blanked by his spectacles, and said nothing. At the offer of a scone he shook his head imperceptibly. Mr Bourne cleared his throat and asked whether Louis had noticed any of the new barns in the fields on the way in. Louis said that he was not interested in barns. Mrs Bourne suggested that Louis might like to walk up the hill later and see the town. Louis said that he was not interested in hills, or in towns. Mr Bourne said that he understood Louis was a literary man, and asked whether he could recommend any good books.

I'm not interested in books, Louis muttered. Arthur, not looking at his parents, drained his cup so fast that he got a mouthful of tea leaves.

26

That had been in the time after Louis gave up Paris. When life there had proved unsustainable he had come back to Dublin, still hoping to make a go of himself as a writer, or at least with no better idea: an old tutor at Trinity had invited him to apply for a temporary teaching post, making clear that the job was his for the asking, but Louis had refused to consider it, and, having no money, had no option but to go home to Dalkey. When Arthur met him in Doyle's or O'Neill's or Kennedy's, Louis would report that he had settled back into the maternal deadlock as if he'd never been away, and that he had now worked several of his short stories to a pitch of perfection such that no editor in the civilised world or the Irish Free State could be expected to read them to the end, let alone take them on. Most of all he complained about the headaches, which since he came home had grown monstrously in strength and could now leave him helpless for days on end. Then one afternoon Arthur finished a shift at Baggot Street and found Louis clinging to the railings outside the hospital, looking as if he had grown old overnight, his eyes bloodshot and the flesh of his face hanging like wetted paper. He smelled of vomit. He stumbled forward. Arthur caught him, helped him inside and checked him over while Louis clawed at his head, groaning. With a dose of tincture of opium he curled up shivering on an examination couch and slept.

That night Arthur took him back to the surgery. The days that followed would fix themselves in his memory, as in a bright gel, as a picture of happiness. He would leave Louis dosed in the room and come back from work to find him awake enough to submit to physical examination and talk again through the history of his complaint. Headache was no longer the word for it, he said shakily. Nowadays the skull

27

pains were only the main theme in a grand composition. To begin with, sparkling silver blotches would spread across his field of vision until he was almost blind; he would shiver, he couldn't get warm; he would be nauseous, then vomiting. Constipated also. As long as it lasts my bowels are like water but I can't move them for the life of me, he said, not a squirt however long I spend in the jakes cramping and retching and imploring the mercy of the Sainted Virgin Mother of Jesus. Then I know it's ending because it all pours out at once. My head clears and for about ten minutes I dance the Charleston, but I know I can expect another visitation in a week. Two if I'm lucky. I can't be doing with it any more, do you know?

As those days went by Arthur turned over a question in his mind, and by the time his patient was able to take a little sweetened tea and move around the surgery, he had reached a decision. He told Louis that he had found no signs of organic disease, that the complaint was psychosomatic in origin and that he recommended a course of psychoanalysis. The treatment was not to be undertaken lightly, and since it was out of the question in Dublin Louis would need to move to London. Louis stared at him with frightened eyes and nodded like a puppet. Arthur was in correspondence with Sebastian Venn at the Malet Clinic, and would try to interest him in Louis's case. Analysis was demanding, he warned. It would likely take years and there could be no promise of success. It was expensive, too. Louis pushed the heels of his hands into his eye sockets, and began to laugh unsteadily. Then there's one more thing you must do for me.

Arthur had never visited the Molyneux home before, though Louis had evoked it for him often enough as a cage of respectable piety. The atmosphere was uneasy, with Louis's brother

Tom, the wholesaler, hovering in the background as if he might need to intervene, and Ida Molyneux herself a kind of effigy, embalmed in disapproval. Later Arthur would wonder if his recollection of the meeting was to be trusted. He would remember the sea as a grey gesture in the window and the room half in darkness, with afternoon light thickening at the far end where Mrs Molyneux was fixed in place and somehow raised above the floor, as if she were standing on a chair throughout the interview, or hanging on the wall, glimmering in the dark, caught in the waxy glow, the skin of her face powdered and fragile and her hair made of cobwebs, all of which must be a trick of the memory. Arthur spoke at length but without making much sense, tripping himself up as he tried to explain psychoanalysis from first principles, while Louis sat deep in a sofa with his hands clasped and his head nearly touching his knees. At length Mrs Molyneux interrupted, calling him Doctor, and asked him if this treatment would get rid of Louis's complaint. Well, he said, trying to give a straight answer, I'm convinced it will help. I do not wish to hear any more about it, she said, now or in future, looking directly at Louis for the first time since they arrived. And as she leaned forward in Arthur's memory and thanked him, the image of Ida Molyneux as a frightful mummified thing gave way to the face of a woman who was afraid for her son.

Each day was the same for the patients of the Calvary, with every hour between waking and sleeping accounted for and tomorrow being no different from yesterday, so that fixity of routine in itself was the sedative, and no experience came that did not recur. Repetition was the rule. As Arthur took his seat in the cafeteria it struck him, as it did every day, that for a junior house officer, too, life in the hospital was a tissue of recurrence, and this was another of the moments that returned, sitting alone at the table with the window beside him so that at his elbow his reflection addressed itself to its own tray of sausages, beans and tea, with the lights of the wards spacing the dark beyond. Other members of staff, most of whom he knew by sight but not to speak to, were sitting in twos and fours in other parts of the room. He ate quickly, not looking around. The same thoughts always came at this time. You find yourself here as usual, too tired, eating this food, and yet again you realise that you are the laughing stock of this hospital and have been from the start without knowing it, so that everyone here is watching you sidelong as you eat your dinner and wipe your lips and get ready to go and make a show of yourself yet again.

Arthur rose and carried his tray to the counter.

The consulting room, which was at the end of a little used passage just outside Quiet Male Two, contained a pair of worn wingback chairs, a gothic radiator and a standard lamp. Arthur let himself in. He preferred to get here early to check the room and compose himself before Walker arrived.

William Walker had become Arthur's responsibility during his first days here, after he had asked Ellis, who was showing him the ropes, about the use of psychoanalytic methods in the hospital. When Ellis seemed not quite to understand, Arthur explained that while it was true that analysis was still more commonly thought of as a treatment for the neurotic, there was a view that it could also be beneficial to the class of patient that the Calvary took in. With Ellis looking increasingly puzzled, Arthur admitted that, although as yet he had no first-hand clinical experience to support his view, he had read one or two articles on the subject which had been interesting and which, he said, a sense of gentle disaster settling on him as he talked, he would be glad to look up if Ellis cared to see them. Ellis took a kindly breath and changed the subject, but the following day Arthur was invited to the Physician-Superintendent's office, where Julian Fletcher-Foxe, well tailored, freshly barbered and positioned at an imperturbable angle in the large leather chair behind his desk, put him at his ease by revealing that it was advisable to be fair but firm with the nurses and by sharing the knowledge of Ireland that he had gathered on a bicycling holiday. He then informed Arthur that, while the talking cure was a dubious notion at the best of times, being necessarily inimical to moral hygiene in the relation between doctor and patient, it was frankly absurd in cases of dementia praecox, it being the nature of that disease that the sufferer's thoughts and words lacked meaning. Being thus beyond communication, the hebephrenic was incapable of forming the understanding with the doctor upon which, if Fletcher-Foxe did not labour under a misapprehension, the talking cure was supposed to depend. These patients suffer from an illness caused by bacteria travelling from sites of organic infection to the brain, Fletcher-Foxe explained, and where we are able to help them it is by seeking out and extracting the physical causes of disease. However, he said, showing his palms like a conjurer, perhaps you will teach us otherwise.

Arthur adjusted the position of the chairs. He liked to have them at right angles so that he could keep Walker in his peripheral vision but gaze for relief at the peeling brown paint on the wall. Between the chairs, a ceramic ashtray stood on a small table. He closed the curtain, then stretched, rising on his toes to brush the ceiling with his fingertips. He dropped his chin to his chest and leaned forward to grasp his shins. He straightened up, rotated his shoulders, shook his fingers loose and exhaled. These gymnastics helped with the restlessness that would come over him as soon as the patient entered the room. Walker himself never fidgeted.

There had been an ironical twitch in Fletcher-Foxe's cheek as he nodded to a set of patient notes lying in the centre of his desk. Opening the file, Arthur had learned that William Walker was thirty-seven years old, the eldest son of a solicitor, born and brought up in a Hertfordshire cathedral town. After going up to Oxford he had tried at the age of twenty to drown himself in the Isis, since when he had been institutionalised. He had been in the Calvary for fifteen years, which, Fletcher-Foxe said, was somewhat outside the ordinary course of things: but the man was pliant and undemanding, and since he was also generously funded he could expect to stay here for the foreseeable future. This meant, in turn, that since there was no prospect of improving Walker's condition through the usual means, and since the Calvary did of course regard all its patients as curable, Arthur was in a position to put his theories to the test. Arthur began to explain that he was not yet a qualified analyst and that it was out of the question for him to attempt treatment with any patient, let alone one with Walker's difficulties, but Fletcher-Foxe raised a finger for silence. Then, with a gesture of the same clean hand, he conferred on Arthur the duty of carrying out the course of action on which the Physician-Superintendent had decided.

And what would they think, he asked himself, if he refused? Fletcher-Foxe must be trying to push him to feats of which he didn't yet know himself capable. Walking away from the Physician-Superintendent's office he began to imagine the article he would write up – 'A Successful Treatment by Psychoanalytic Psychotherapy in a Case of Dementia Praecox', perhaps, to be published in *Psychiatric Quarterly* – through which his name would start to be known, so that the way forward would become clear and he would make good on the gamble he had taken with the future. And that same evening he found himself in this consulting room for the first time, moving the chairs and trying to fix the neck of the lamp.

Those early Calvary days seemed a long time ago now. Hard to believe it had only been three months. He could already think with nostalgia of the November afternoon when he had tramped in the grounds with Louis, trying to describe his first evening with Walker. I'm not certain that it's not a practical joke, he said: maybe Fletcher-Foxe finds it amusing to have me try a talking cure with a patient who won't talk. I gave up after a while and just sat it out in silence. Maybe I should be a good sport, go back to him and say you certainly had me there, old boy. They're probably taking bets on how long I'll stick it.

Louis said nothing, and Arthur nodded and sighed. Now that he had started with Walker, it would be a long time before he could think of giving up. He'd accepted the task and it was part of the weave of things now, a thread that would not be picked free. As they were parting at the gate that afternoon, Louis opened his satchel and brought out a sheaf of typewritten pages held together with rubber bands. The top sheet was blank except for two words in the centre of the page: *Sham Abraham*.

It's far beyond perfection by now, Louis said. I can't be held responsible for the effects it may have either on the unsuspecting human reader or on the future course of literary history.

Your story collection, Arthur said. Finished?

If such they can be called, said Louis. And I'd rather thread my tenderest part through the typewriter than spend another instant working on the wretched thing, if that's what you mean.

I can't wait to read it, Arthur said.

Once Louis was on the bus back to Chelsea, Arthur took the typescript up to his room and put it on the table beside the chess set. He left it there while he went for dinner in the canteen, but when he got back there was no more reason to delay, so he switched on the desk lamp, drew the chair up to the table and turned over the first of the grubby foolscap sheets.

Sham Abraham contained twelve stories, each representing a separate episode in the life of a person called Leary, a university man with no visible means of subsistence who spent his time wandering around Dublin having encounters with various grotesques. The characters had names like Jenny Phlegm, Constable Gusto, Mickey Swollen, Father Phuckett, Professor Cockley, Malachy Febrile. In the first story Leary was bullied by his landlady, Mrs Mudd, into moving from a small, windowless room where he had been happy into a larger, well-appointed room where he was miserable; in the second he talked himself into a beating from some hearties on Pearse Street; in the third, he witnessed the leap of a would-be suicide from the O'Connell Bridge.

Arthur looked out at the lights of Sinfield, Creedy and Findlater. Louis's style had evolved since his Paris days. Those old stories had had a certain formality about them and a weakness for recondite vocabulary, but at least they had been simply expressed. They had seemed to intend the reader to follow what was happening, but the same could not be said of *Sham Abraham*. The next story, entitled 'Abcabcddee', began:

Good morrow to the day, thus Leary, recumbent resupine
on the public bench by the gentlemen's convenience on
College Green, and next, my gold: in media res yes but
whither hence I know not for this Leary idle young ghost
of a manikin will nowise lay shoulder to wheel nor neb to
the grinder urge him as I may. O pale youth, illfavoured
ephebe, my hopes of preferment rest with you and we must
away with haste for life is short and yet there he sits on his
ars longa. Rise, boy. Up, slave! It is well. And next my gold.
Leary plunged his hand to the wrist in the left front pocket
of his rustentinctured greasenfelted trousers, he groped and
delved but found not those sequins earmarked for the
matinal libation, found rather an aperture apt to admit
one solitary son of a stealer, found that is to say nothing,
and withdrawing ex nihilo fell into his nihil fit . . .

Gradually it turned out that Leary was knocking about town
trying to cadge money from his friends. In the end he managed
to get the price of a pint from one Dr Burke, a companion of
his student days, and Arthur pressed on through the book.
The longest story was the penultimate one, 'Uzwuzz'. Here
Leary found himself the unwilling object of the affections of
two young women, Miss Minerva Clamp and Miss Lucinda
De Frigg, bosom friends from earliest youth, between whom
there was nothing to choose, according to the character
sketches that opened the piece, for emptiness of mind, ampli-
tude of flesh, unbridlement of tongue, ungainliness of limb,
coarsity of feature or vanity of self-regard. Above all, there
was nothing to choose between them for the hotness with
which each young woman desired to make Leary her own

alone forever, although the story did not explain what they found so appealing about this man, who, the reader by now understood, was a heavy-drinking, penniless, sarcastic lay-about who had boils on his face and owned only one pair of trousers. Even so, they broke their hearts over him and he suffered amusingly from their attentions. Leary grew so harried that he fled to a seaside hotel, taking Dr Burke with him for moral support. The women followed implacably, but due to a misunderstanding about room numbers Lucinda insinuated herself into Burke's room in the dead of the night, while Minerva, in an access of mistaken jealousy, tripped and fell down three flights of hotel stairs. The closing paragraph skipped forward by a little more than nine months to show Leary, a bachelor as ever, visiting Burke at home and finding him well mired in domestic bliss with his wife Lucinda and their newborn, with the final sentence revealing that Burke, in his professional capacity, was daily at the sanatorial bedside of Minerva, who since the fateful night had experienced no sensation or movement in her body below the neck. As an ending Arthur felt this was more than enough, but there was still one story left: a final episode in which Leary got himself admitted to the Kilcarrick Lunatic Asylum on false pretences, fulfilling a lifelong ambition for free room and board and licence to say with impunity whatever came into his head at any time.

When he had finished the book Arthur squared up the typescript, fastened the elastic bands and pressed his palms to his temples. On their next walk around the hospital grounds Louis took back the script and denounced the stories as awful bootscrapings, pure bottled hypocrisy. Not at all, Arthur said: they were brilliant. To be perfectly honest, he added, they went over his head in places, but even to him their brilliance was obvious. Louis shook his head and mentioned that an editor at Gryphon, a nice young man called George Cope, wanted to read the book. This angel of the publisher's profession, the first and only to respond to Louis's letter of enquiry, had not only written back asking to see a sample story, but had then taken Louis for lunch at the Dorchester and made him promise that he would send the whole manuscript as soon as it was ready.

But this is thrilling news, Arthur said. I had no idea. Shows how much I know! Louis smiled at that, but he agreed he would send the book to Cope right away. Since then Arthur had heard no news, but he often wondered what had become of *Sham Abraham* when he was here in the consulting room, waiting for Walker. Those threads had twisted together in the weave.

Now he touched the cold radiator. He slid his wristwatch around so that it lay on the inside of his wrist. Despite this precaution it was impossible to glance at the watch without Walker knowing, and a portion of his energy in the hour to come would be spent resisting the urge to check the time. He yawned and sat down. It was quiet in here, but elsewhere in Sinfield and the other ward blocks the dark life of the hospital continued. Soon the patients would be medicated, washed, undressed and locked in their rooms until morning, and on the wards the nurses on night duty would make their first rounds, stopping at each room to flick the light switch, put an eye to the Judas and press the indicator. They would continue to do so every twenty minutes as the night wore on and the Calvary became more than ever a distorted image of schooldays: a tiny curled-up universe bound by routines which, absolute inside these walls, would be meaningless in any world beyond. He was swallowing another yawn when the door opened and a nurse led the patient into the room.

Arthur had grown up in a comfortable house on the edge of Wexford town. His parents had taken him to the Quaker meeting every Wednesday and Sunday. His father had been in charge of a small, prosperous firm specialising in the construction of iron sheds and barns throughout the county. His elder brother Thomas had died of diphtheria at the age of four. Arthur had been two years old at that time, and in adulthood had retained nothing that could be called a memory of his brother, which was perhaps why he had forgotten to mention Thomas's existence to Venn when they first went through his family history. He still had not found a chance to correct that omission, though now and then he wondered if he ought to bring it up, perhaps at a juncture like this, pausing at the kerb while a motor car went by.

They crossed the road into Russell Square and walked beside the railings. They always walked during analysis, because Venn liked to stretch his legs after a day in the clinic. He said that strolling in the evening with the lit streets to lull the mind and stimulate the senses was at least as apt an arrangement as the chair at the head of the couch. Venn was dressed as usual in brown brogues, hairy tweed suit and dickey bow, as if to conceal the fact that physically he was cut out for a navvy or a docker, a big, raw-boned man with a barrel chest and long legs, his features heavy but mobile, his Homburg seated high on his head. He was a decade older than Arthur and Louis, and had been decorated for his actions as an infantry commander in France, where he was supposed to have been wounded under heroic circumstances before coming home to qualify and going on to train at the Malet under Webb, no less. Altogether he was a figure of such daunting stature that they had no choice but to make fun of him in his absence. Louis, who had been seeing him three times a week for a year now, could imitate his soft, precise voice and his way of smoothing his moustache with his fingertips when he came to an analytical crux. But we dare not conspire against him, Louis said: he'd find us out, and what would happen to us then?

Venn brought out a large spotted handkerchief and blew his nose. By the time the handkerchief was folded away again they had turned the corner and crossed into Guilford Street. This evening they had begun by talking about Arthur's session with Walker, though there was nothing particular to report: he and his patient had sat for an hour in a silence broken by a single ironical chuckle from Walker at the forty-minute mark. Next they touched on Louis's visit to the Calvary in the afternoon, and discussed how peculiar it seemed to Arthur that, Venn being Louis's analyst as well, he must be hearing a contrasting account of the friendship from the other side. Or perhaps not – perhaps Louis never spoke about it. Here Arthur glanced at Venn, whose face was neutral. They discussed, as they often did, the sense in which Venn might appear as a father figure with Louis and Arthur as his sons, in competition for his favour but united in their desire to castrate him. I wouldn't bother with that part, you know, Venn liked to say, making his purse-lipped smile. More trouble than it's worth.

Perhaps he ought to put the question openly, Arthur thought: Louis wants to meet Walker and what should I do about it? But if he did ask, Venn would give no opinion and he would feel all the more compromised for having brought it up. Instead he told his dream of last night, an anxious affair set in a version of the Calvary muddled up with the court of an unhinged tyrant along the lines of Henry the Eighth. Walker had featured as an elegant, contemptuous figure lounging around a splendid apartment while Arthur pestered him with clumsy questions. In the dream it was plain that by doing this Arthur was breaching every social propriety, as well as exposing his own psychology in the most shameful fashion, but he could not make himself stop. He trailed Walker down long, cold corridors, pleading with him to take pity, despite knowing that this conduct would earn the tyrant's disfavour and bring terrible punishments. The dream had come back to him this evening as he sat on the upper deck of the bus, passing through the unfinished housing estates that lay between the hospital and the city proper.

It was bad manners for the dreamer to make the first incision, but as they passed Great Ormond Street Venn said nothing. He seemed to be thinking about something else. In Arthur's view, Venn could stand to show a little more enthusiasm for his analysand's dreams: often he was less interested in travelling the royal road into Arthur's unconscious than in going over professional gossip. He loved to complain about the follies of his colleagues in London and across two continents. He was involved in half a dozen major feuds, in person and by correspondence, and he was capable of lecturing for an entire session on the schisms and sects of psychoanalysis. Our profession wants to think of itself as a science, he had said once, and no one will admit that we are in fact an organised religion. Cults of personality, deference to authority, rampant factionalism, rule by doctrine and dogma. He had smiled serenely at Arthur. It's a preposterous enterprise and I advise you to get out while you can.

That had been at their first meeting in the flesh, in October, four months ago, in the disorderly office in the Malet. Venn had lifted a stack of books from the seat of one armchair and swept a pile of papers from the other. The room was so cramped that their knees touched as they sat down. Venn took off his spectacles, polished them with the end of his knitted-wool tie and resettled them on his nose. They had been corresponding for months about the possibility of a training analysis. Venn began to talk about the Malet, about the profession, about his colleagues and himself, and although Arthur understood that he was meant to interject in ways that would show he deserved to be admitted to this world, he couldn't think how to do it. Too much of his attention was taken up with Venn's big hands and the grey hairs that curled in his ears and nostrils. One lens of his spectacles had a thumb print on it. Arthur had not given much thought to what his correspondent would be like in person, but now, knee to knee in the crowded office, Venn's physical presence made the abstractions he spoke about sound less convincing than they had ever been on paper. Arthur nodded, made sounds of agreement and comprehension and threw in a few words of analytical vocabulary where he could, but he didn't know what the man was talking about. He had got himself into a false situation, and surely Venn would finish by saying there had been a misunderstanding and they would not be seeing one another again. Instead, though, he smiled, clapped his hands to his knees and suggested that they meet three times a week, starting tomorrow.

Now Venn smoothed his moustache and slowed his pace to a dawdle.

'Corridors,' he said. 'And cold.'

Arthur nodded. He wasn't sure what Venn was driving at.

'Tell me about the corridors. What were they like?'

'Cold,' Arthur said. 'The floor was hard.'

'You felt it, then. A cold, hard floor under your feet?'

'I believe so,' Arthur said. He was sounding recalcitrant, and he knew this was unwise. It would only give Venn the idea that he was hiding something.

'You don't often mention physical sensations in dreams,' Venn said. 'I wonder what we make of that.'

'I can't see that it matters.'

Venn considered this. Then he sniffed and began to get out his handkerchief again.

All at once Arthur was tired of tonight's analysis. He could predict the rest. Venn wanted to pull the dream inside out and subject it to the usual dreary party trick, the revelation that what you had thought was going on was not the real story at all. Arthur had been quite willing to discuss the dream as an allegory of his doubts about his analytical competence, and surely that was revealing enough, but it wasn't to be allowed. Instead, he was to be shown that behind the stage flats of the dream some other scene entirely had been taking place, no doubt featuring himself as a child in a dark passage, night-shirted and barefoot, at school or at home, about to glimpse something through a half-open door. He didn't believe it, though. It would be easy to take the lure and say yes, perhaps there was a night like that, and yes, perhaps I can remember, but Arthur baulked at being led down this particular passageway. Of course, as far as Venn was concerned that would only prove that it went somewhere significant, and so rebellion was useless, because the rules of analysis would always prevail, making denial into evidence more positive than confession. It could be that when he walked out of the Institute of Psychoanalysis that night after Webb's lecture, years ago, feeling the first stir of the excitement that had led him here, he had been making a strange and terrible mistake. He had stumbled into a world that, for all its institutes and clinics and conferences and learned publications and distinguished careers and bitter rivalries, might as well be the delusional system of a paranoid psychotic. Having no basis in anything real, it was only pretending to exist.

In any case, he wasn't going to cooperate tonight. He walked on, quickening the pace a little, and Venn did not press the point. He only followed, folding his hands behind his back, making the most of his evening stroll.

There was no sense in pretending, though, Arthur told himself half an hour later, walking alone down Gower Street, that it was anyone's fault but his own. He was in bad faith. The analysand's only duty was to speak freely, saying what came to mind without selection or censorship, but Arthur had never once spoken that way with Venn or with anyone else. He could not drop his guard. Tonight he had begun with the usual good intentions, but before long he had been hedging and hiding and jockeying, trying to placate Venn without giving himself away. He did want to be honest, in fact wanted nothing more than to confess, but it could not happen. He couldn't let Venn know his secret, and the longer they went on with the training analysis the easier it became to conceal.

His foot slipped off the kerb, nearly turning his ankle. His shoes had begun to rub. They were smart black Oxfords which he had bought the afternoon before his first day at the Calvary, spending too much because he had wanted them badly, unremarkable as they were, finding that he was comforted by the stiff cut of the leather, the discreet decorative patterns of punched holes on the toecaps and the smooth way the laces drew across his instep. The hard heels lifted his head and straightened his back, and when he walked they made a click on the floor. Really the shoes were a little too formal for the wards, and by the end of a day like today sore places were forming for tomorrow. More than that, these shoes all in themselves were an argument for the absurdity of what he was doing with Venn. What could be the point of undergoing a training analysis, seeking routes past all the barriers of social convention and psychic repression into the hot darkness of the self to confront the terror at the heart of things, when both parties making the journey insisted on wearing uncomfortable shoes decorated with lots of tiny little holes? Arthur and Venn, proceeding along the pavement with their collars snug around their clean-shaven throats, addressing one another in complete sentences, not quite sure what to do with their hands until the familiar route brought them back to the front steps of the Malet where they could shake firmly and wish each other well and part until their next appointment: if they believed their own doctrine, why not behave like apes instead, naked and shrieking and smeared with their own faeces? Why for that matter did Arthur not take a brick and bash in Venn's skull, free from the prison of himself, free from reason, free from free will? But he knew by now that analysis was not going to free him from anything. It could only bind him in new ways. That was the purpose of the training, subordinating him to Venn, who himself had been trained by Webb, who had been trained by Gerber, who had been trained by Hoffmann, who in turn was known to have drunk at the very fountainhead, so that what had once looked like an escape was the entrance to another institution. Arthur was to be inducted into a world of priestly secrets handed down a line of fathers: bald-headed and bespectacled ancestor gods who grew taller as they receded.

Tottenham Court Road was busy. Last week as he edged through the crowd here he had come chest to chest with a man whose collarless shirt was open to the breastbone, showing a triangle of raw skin. For an instant they blocked one another's way and Arthur murmured an apology. Then the man pushed past and Arthur moved on. Yer dead, wee man! The shout had come from behind, loud enough to carry over the traffic and set his pulse tripping, but he'd kept walking, careful not to speed up or slow down, with the back of his neck tingling in readiness for a physical blow and with the knowledge that he was hated with a hate that could not be contained. Nothing further had followed the shout, and perhaps it had not been meant for him – perhaps it had been someone else's rowdy joke, one friend calling to another up the street – so that perhaps he was not, after all, despised, in which case perhaps his heart could settle and he could carry on without his balance of mind having been spoiled. Odd how an encounter like that could touch you in such a deep place and then be forgotten. He hadn't mentioned it to Venn. They'd talked about Walker and about Louis instead, circling through the reliable anxieties to fill the time without straying into the regions that could not be approached.

Venn would not be so easily fooled in the end. Sooner or later Arthur would have to give more so that both of them could feel the analysis was making progress. Really, it was for this purpose that he had kept Thomas in reserve. He could recognise it now, though he hadn't known to begin with. The time would come when he'd need to let Venn draw that story out of him and demonstrate how it had made him the way he was. That he had held it back would only make the revelation the more convincing. Together, inevitably, they would come to understand that Arthur's whole personality was shaped by guilt for that missing other, by the feeling that his life belonged by rights to someone else and so on and so forth. It would fit the analytical bill. That it would not be true – that, embarrassingly enough, the loss of a sibling before he was old enough to know about it had not caused him a minute's unhappiness in his life, nor seriously occupied his thoughts – was beside the point, so long as it met Venn's requirements and kept the analysis safely away from what was really the matter with Arthur, which was that there was nothing much the matter with him, or nothing serious enough to excuse his secret: the creeping disaster of a secret that got worse with every day that passed and that he managed to forget about for much of the time, but choked him with panic when he was reminded, as he could be reminded by any glance, any word or any touch of a human hand, that he was two months from his thirtieth birthday and had not had a sexual experience.

There was no explaining it, as far as he could see. He had just always suffered from a kind of pathological innocence. At Donard there must have been intrigues among the boys – the wise ones practising the scales of bodies and hearts before they went out to play into the world – but Arthur hadn't known about it. Maybe he had been the only one left out. He bit off a corner of his thumbnail as he walked. Perhaps all this was no more than the predictable alarm of a man who, finding himself almost thirty and unmarried, realises that for the past fifteen years he has been spending altogether too much time on his work. But it was not that he wanted marriage for the sake of it, or even that he envied Louis his colourful personal history. What galled him was that all his life he had been sealed off like an egg from the very possibility of these things. Any other burden would be bearable. He wanted to suffer like Louis, with the kind of suffering that came from experience – experience painful and thrilling, experience illicit and unspoken, so that the real story of your life was not the one you could tell to friends and colleagues but the one that you wore inside your skin, next to your heart, and showed only by a certain canny composure around the eyes – so that you could regret what had happened instead of what had failed to, and you would not one day have to look back at a long and productive life in which you could not name one true thing you had done. But what came easily to Louis was forbidden to Arthur. It was as mystifying as ever, how at TCD the female students whom Arthur knew he could not go near were the same ones who would fall quite naturally into conversation with Louis, and who after a minute's chat would be laughing in his ear and shoving him in the shoulder.

He was sick of nursing his secret. He ought to make a clean breast of it with Venn, but he could no more say those words than he could wind back time to the midnight street lamp, weeks ago, where Celia Prentice had sighed and walked away. Any other failing he would gladly confess. Once at Donard, at the start of a new term, he had overheard a couple of boys in his year talking about what they had done over the break. They were harmless types, civil enough, he'd always thought.

But one was telling the other how all summer he and his mates had been having trouble with a gang of lads from his town, and that one night he'd sorted it once and for all by taking the ringleader's head and smashing it into a kerbstone. That lad hadn't walked away. Good enough for him, said the other boy. Arthur had not exactly believed what he was hearing, but he hadn't dared disbelieve it either, because, he felt, this must be what real young men were like: possessed of wild, dark lives, lives of muscle and chemical that they lived without consequences, never having learned how.

He was on Greek Street, and the people talked loud and loosely as they made for the pubs and restaurants, forming a procession conducting him towards the Lantern-Bearers. Because he could not tell Venn his secret, the analysis would never get to the root of the matter. Instead, Arthur would waste their sessions giving a passable imitation of an analysand, so that in due course they could decide the training was complete and he would qualify without once having spoken the truth. Then he would be trapped in his dishonesty forever, outwardly committed to a practice to which he had not dared give himself in spirit, and still nursing the shame that would ensure that any good thing he achieved was transformed into a sort of joke, because who could think without a smile and a snigger that the important names he seemed to want for himself – physician, psychiatrist, psychoanalyst – might apply to such a tongue-tied celibate? Or that he could in all seriousness appoint himself an expert on human desire, the world he had never dared to enter. Imagine if Louis knew his secret – but then, as he neared the tall mock-Tudor front of the Lantern-Bearers, glimpsing the red interior as someone barged into the street, he felt sure that Louis did know. How could he not? It must be transparent to him, and no doubt to Venn as well, so that when the two of them met they must exchange sympathetic smiles if the topic of Arthur came up. As he crossed the road he saw that he was a clown, balancing his idea of himself like a tall, unsteady stack of boxes beneath which he reeled here and there with a solemn expression on his face, relying on every single person he met not to give him the nudge that would send him tumbling. This was not the frame of mind he would have chosen for entering a pub crowded with the bohemians of Soho, but the door flapped wider as a party pushed ahead of him into the jumble of bodies, telling him that if he slowed even for a heartbeat now he would be hesitating, because it was time to wake up, be brave, banish thought, shake off the past and future and step into the present moment that was opening, offering all that was left to win or lose of tonight.

In the back of the saloon bar red glass lamps tinted the hands and faces of Violet Cornish, Celia Prentice and Myles MacDonagh. Louis was not with them. Naturally it was a mistake to have come. Arthur had known it as he stepped into the pub, his eyes filling with water and his shirt growing damp under his jacket as he threaded his way through the public bar, stung by the cigarette smoke and sweat and beer that hung in the air, edging past shoulders and backs and elbows that did not make way.

But it was too late to retreat, so, making noises to the effect that here he was, then, good evening – hello – he took a stool. Across the table Myles gave an easy nod. Myles, a black-haired Kerryman who had been just above them at Trinity but was living in London for years now, had dark-lashed, deep blue eyes. His corduroy trousers, soft shirt, loosened tie, undone waistcoat and vigorous black stubble meant that all the other men in the bar were dressed too formally. He sipped his pint. Violet's glass of red wine hung poised in mid-air as her face tried out a series of expressions and settled on a kind of secretive amusement. She was a slight young woman who this evening, as at every other time Arthur had seen her, had powdered her face dead white, setting this off with eyeshadow like two smudges of coal dust to match her black bob with its fringe cut straight across. She wore a black three-piece suit like a man's, complete with a white shirt buttoned to the throat and a black silk tie. She didn't return Arthur's greeting. She was an observer fascinated above all with her own responses. Beside her, Celia turned her profile to the room and blew a stream of smoke.

Their conversation had stopped. He gripped the edge of the table.

'Don't let me— That is, do by all means carry on with your—'

Myles pulled on his pint, waiting to see what Arthur hoped to accomplish with these words. Violet leaned in to Celia and murmured something in her ear. Arthur pushed back his stool.

'I'll just,' he said. 'Does anyone want another?'

The question evidently needed no answer. Celia's eyes strayed into the room, searching. Her copper hair, which hung down her back when she wore it loose, was presently coiled up like a turban, held in place by a pair of wooden chopsticks. Two long spiral strands of hair brushed her cheeks, and Arthur saw that her wide cheekbones were dusted with a substance that, even in this dim room, found the light and glowed.

As he joined the press waiting to be served, Arthur heard how he had sounded: like a schoolmaster or visiting uncle, hidebound and patronising, oblivious to the way these young ones lived. Over at the table they were talking again. None of them had ever uttered an inauthentic word. With Myles, Arthur always found himself asking those avuncular questions – How are things at the magazine? Reviewed anything interesting lately? – and forming as he did so a picture of himself as a creature riddled with hypocrisy and compromise, unable to justify his own life, ill at ease with his background, his education and the decisions he had made, constitutionally unable to say what he meant. Five minutes had passed since he walked into the pub and already the night was a failure. He could slip away now and save everyone the trouble. Or perhaps it would be better to take one drink before making his apologies. Either way, there was nothing to be salvaged. Celia glanced up. She was dressed as outlandishly as Violet but in a different mode, wearing a kimono of stiff gold silk embroidered with black willow trees, and yet he had once been alone with her under a street lamp. It had been another of Louis's boozing nights, and Arthur and Celia had straggled behind the others, talking about her preparations for the role of Dol Common, her shoulder bumping his once or twice as they walked. Then, as if they had come to an agreed place, she had stopped and turned and come so close that he could see into her dark pupils and taste the smoke and whiskey on her breath. If that seemed unlikely now, it was harder still to credit that after waiting long enough she had been obliged to laugh, detach her arm from around his neck and skip ahead of him along the street, so that by the time he caught up she was back in company and already there was no way to tell what, moments earlier, might have been possible. That night held a high place on the list of things for which he would never forgive himself. He should accept that it was his fate to become a funny little sexless elf: he could grow ever more virginal and eccentric and make a virtue of the fact that he had never personally entered into the mess of human life in which he claimed professional expertise. That might possibly be made to work.

As he carried his pint of stout back to the table a finger of froth eased down the side of the glass mug and Louis came up the staircase from the lavatories. His face brightened. He squeezed Arthur's elbow as if they had not seen one another for weeks, then clapped him between the shoulder blades and guided him over to the others.

'Now,' Louis said, taking a stool. He reached for the pint of mild standing on the table. As he drank his eyes darted foxily from Violet's face to Celia's. 'You fortunate women,' he said, putting down his pint, 'are now in the presence of *three* healthy specimens of what in my humility I will simply call the pinnacle of human development. I mean, of course, the modern Irishman.'

Celia and Violet looked at one another dubiously.

'To your kind, now,' Louis added, wagging a finger, 'the Irishman presents a mystery.'

'He does,' said Myles, 'bejaysis.'

'He entrances you but you will never comprehend him.'

Arthur recognised the tone. When they were together Louis and Myles liked to indulge in a kind of deadpan cross-talk, spinning out a lot of nonsense for as long as they could without ever actually saying anything. He drank and listened as they agreed that the English nation in its youth and naïveté could only gaze with wonder upon the ancient beauty of the

52

civilisation of Ireland. It was not the fault of the English that they had no culture of their own, Louis explained. Art, law, religion, poetry, philosophy, science: these were a few of Ireland's inventions which the English had taken up in their clumsy way. It was the tragedy of England that whatever its people created, they found it a faint and belated imitation of what Ireland had always possessed.

'That is why we, the flower of Irish youth, appeal so ineffably to you and all your compatriots,' said Louis.

Celia cocked an eyebrow.

'What my friend here means,' said Myles, stifling a belch, 'that's why ye love us so much.'

'You do talk an awful old load of cod,' said Violet, but Celia was chuckling, and as Arthur sipped his pint it dawned on him that although Louis and Myles were doing the talking, she was in charge of the conversation.

'But you three aren't *really* Irish, are you?' she said. 'You went to that posh college and everything.'

Louis and Myles gaped in outrage. Then: poor girl, they told each other, she understands so little. Tee See Dee, that platonic form of the seat of learning, which you English have aped as best you can – there now is an illustration of the theme. Cool shade in stone quadrangles, hidden gardens where the professors pace out their disputations, the xylophonic note of leather on willow in the summer heat of the field, young scholars and athletes exerting every cell of body and brain: it is in our alma mater that these traditions touch their origin and reach their fulfilment. When they had finished with Trinity they praised Dublin in general: our gracious grey mother city, they said, with her courts and towers, her monuments and theatres. Yes, take the theatres, said Louis. Like the

53

Greeks after us, we Irish have invented a form of civic life founded on poetry, for nightly at the Abbey language casts off its workaday disguise and walks in its glory, speaking golden truths into existence, joining art and justice in a phrase, while in the stalls the people bear witness to the spiritual life of their nation.

'Every Dublin man, woman and child is there once a week,' said Myles, 'at the bare minimum. They'd sooner miss the piece of fish and the pint of plain of a Friday night.'

'The English tried something similar a few centuries ago, but it didn't take,' Louis said. 'Poetry has never been much in their blood, I'm afraid.'

Violet snorted into her wine, while Celia cried out in protest and said something about Shakespeare.

'Shakespeare?' says Myles, glancing at Arthur and then at Louis. 'I seem to know the name, lads. Wasn't he a Donegal man?'

Arthur drained his pint. He was bored. He ought to join in with the blather, but he had delayed too long. He felt rebellious. By now, he felt, Celia must be thinking that all this meant nothing and wishing that someone would say something honest.

'We used to see everything at the Abbey when we were students,' he said.

There was a pause. Four faces turned to him. They were waiting for him to say more – it had not occurred to them that he might be dull enough to leave it at that – but it was no good. He had no punchline, he could not manage this kind of talk, and there was no choice, as the silence grew too long, but to press on with his excuse for an anecdote:

'Do you remember?' he said. 'If you got those seats at the

front of the balcony aisle, you could get a three-shilling view for the price of one and six.'

He didn't quite see why they all laughed so loudly, but after a moment he laughed with them. It seemed to signal the end of Louis's and Myles's performance, and shortly they began to argue with Celia about a novelist whose name Arthur did not catch. When Violet went up to the bar, he followed and helped her carry the drinks.

'At least someone here is a gent,' she said. Myles, accepting his fresh pint, waggled his brows at her but did not stop speaking. Arthur drank, and met Violet's sooty eyes.

'And now they're talking shop,' she told him. 'How dreary.'

The other three were indeed discussing books – in particular, the books that they themselves had not written but expected one day to write. Louis, swigging, slapped the table with his free hand. He wiped his lips.

'No,' he said. 'I reject your dead conventions. I require an art free of these fripperies. A mode of representation without sympathy and without beauty, whatever you mean by that. Absent anything that could be described as a character. None of your so-called human beings.' He jabbed a finger at Myles. 'I want the reader surrounded on all sides by stiff masks and false surfaces. I insist that the author make the only truthful gesture available to him, which is to state categorically that these figures in motion are no more than puppets jerking on strings.'

'It won't work,' Myles said.

'Of course it won't,' said Louis. 'It can only end in tears. But it's the only way left.'

Myles sucked air through his teeth and wished Louis the best of luck. Louis fitted a cigarette between his lips.

'You two can theorise all you like,' said Celia. 'It won't make any difference.'

Her eyes widened into the smoky space above, then found Arthur across the table.

'You understand me, don't you, Doctor?'

Arthur was saved by the fact that the glasses were empty. The bar was even busier now but he was content to wait for the crowd to part in its own time. It meant he could examine this new thought, that things had not gone so badly wrong after all. Celia's black-and-gold pump was dangling from her toe and her hands carved shapes in the air as she explained her views. The night with the street lamp had not ruined everything, because it had only been a moment in time, and finally no one can say what those mean except that they are always followed by more moments in which the meaning will change and keep on changing. He and Celia had once swum close together, and now here they were swimming again, he thought, feeling spruce and lively all of a sudden as he stepped up to the bar, finding coins in his trouser pocket. Celia's shoe bobbed with the beat of her talk. She was ribbing Louis about his peculiar literary notions.

As he paid for the round, Violet appeared beside him and lifted a couple of the drinks. She carried them over to the table, and he saw for the first time that she wore her extraordinary outfit not out of some complicated affectation but simply because it pleased her. Seeing this, he saw that there was a message in the precise way she set down the glasses. Taking his stool beside her, he found he could lean away from the other three and ask her how she was this evening. She did not respond at once, but then, turning her face to him in full, she smiled bravely, as if to say that it had been the right question, because he knew the answer already, and it was true what he had guessed: she was sad; much sadder than she would admit to him or to anyone. She touched the palm of her hand. There was nothing to be done about it. She did not need him to help her in her sadness, any more than she wanted it to make him sad in turn. She counted on his discretion. They both knew that sadness must be borne and that it must not trouble the decorum of life, and so, keeping it safe between them, her being sad, they would carry gallantly on and guide the night down its proper course.

He held up his pint and Violet tapped her glass against it, smiling with her eyes though not now with her mouth. They drank. The stout was smooth and cool and Arthur had a pleasant thirst. There had been no need for awkwardness. It had only been a matter of catching up. He took a long swallow and found that the glass was empty.

'The artist is a double traitor,' Louis was saying. 'Representation is betrayal. In the attempt he betrays his subject, and in the failure he betrays himself.'

He sounded a little plaintive. Myles and Celia were still teasing him about the book he had not yet written, interrogating him about his theories as if he were only playing the provocateur. They speculated on the chances of a publisher's editor buying the sort of book Louis was describing, and decided it would depend on whether the editor were sufficiently advanced in serious mental illness. They had failed to notice that Louis was not actually joking, and that the idea with which they were having their sport was the one on which he had staked his life. Louis kept his poise as they proved beyond doubt that his manifesto was absurd and that any book written to it would be unreadable, but Arthur could see that the blows were painful and the bruises would be deep, and – because everything flows, and the meaning keeps changing – that his friend needed his protection.

Arthur leaned across the table and began to speak, not sure what he was saying but knowing it must demonstrate that Louis was not so hopelessly on the wrong track as they supposed. He heard himself talking about the Calvary and about Walker, though he was relieved to note that even with the drink flushing through his brain he was leaving out names and identifying details: he spoke with humane professionalism about the isolation that a person like his anonymised patient suffered, an isolation so radical as to be unthinkable to most of us. He could not quite work out what this had to do with Louis and his writing, but still his words were enriching the discussion and setting it right, placing their talk in a more serious perspective. Another pint appeared on the table in front of him, fingertips brushed his shoulder, and in a burst of further insight he explained that just as his poor patient lived in a prison of the soul that the rest of us could not presume to attempt to begin to understand, so the art of alienation that Louis proposed might prove to be true in its own way: strange, yes, but true in its strangeness to some remote kind of human – he snatched at the air, seeking the phrase – some kind of human something-or-other.

Draining his pint as they looked at him with a new regard, he felt the happy unity of all things. He had helped Louis in his need and shown that always, all along, they had been working for the same purposes without knowing it, not just tonight but ever since school and through the years since, all of it flowing into this moment. Walker was in bed in his room in Quiet Male Two with the sheets drawn up to his chin, staring into the dark, listening for the tread of the nurse and the scrape of the Judas, but that too was all right. Arthur had done him no harm.

'Yes, yes,' Myles was saying. 'More of this.'

Violet nudged Arthur. 'You've done it now,' she said. 'You've only encouraged him.'

'Hush, woman!' said Myles. 'But first, my round.'

In the lavatory Arthur gasped with relief and stared for a long time at the standing wave on the porcelain. Climbing the stairs he met Myles coming down. They clapped one another on the shoulder, and as he took his stool again he grew a little distant from the room, closing his eyes to feel the life seethe around him and hear its voices as he began to slide away. Louis tapped his wrist and pushed a full pint towards him. They toasted one another, and as they drank the tide of the occasion took hold: Myles was here, Celia and Violet too, Louis was here, and they were all dissolving at the edges, their minds fizzing where they touched, breaking into one another just enough. They swam together and their bodies were joined in the rank heat of the public house. He looked around his friends at the table with a great love. Shame was gone, and envy too. Lust was gone and in its place a rich silent promise had been made. Nothing was lacking. All was well. They had Louis to thank for it, Arthur realised, because he had brought them here.

There was no need to speak. They drank, sensing the ripple of movement that went through the pub as the barmen began to call time, which also was as it should be, because now they would rise and be carried on the surge of people, not leaving too soon nor waiting too long. It would not do to linger, because the moment that had held them was already settling

59

and fading. It had not gone yet, but soon it would need to become something else, because time was running and soon, again, words would have to be found and actions taken if they were to keep hold of what they had discovered. Something was almost in his reach, Arthur knew, and, rubbing his eyes, he tried to find Celia through the spears of light. But she was putting on her coat and she did not hear him when he said her name.

Out in the street he discovered he was quite drunk. The patients would be getting up in a few hours and it was time to catch the late bus, but the others were setting off for Myles's flat and his bottle of Redbreast. Arthur followed. He'd be sorry in the morning, but he would be even sorrier if he gave up now, because surely tonight could not slip away: it must be leading towards a pool of light at which the world would stand still long enough for him to take hold, this time without hesitation. The others were stringing out ahead, weaving across the pavement, calling to one another. He hurried to catch up. Celia swayed over to him and caught his hand, letting her eyes roll sleepily and slipping him a smile. He racked his brain for what came next, but she hauled him sideways so that the two of them cannoned into Louis.

'There,' she said. 'You two can carry me home.'

Louis murmured something sardonic, and Celia pushed him away so that he stumbled off the kerb while she ended her movement in a dramatic pose, head dropped and arm out stiff. Louis regained his footing and doffed his hat to a trio of passing women. As students it had always been ticklish getting him home from the pub. One night on Dame Street, walking behind a party of Corkmen, Louis had mimicked them so accurately that he had been punched in the jaw, and Arthur, apologising over his shoulder, had hauled him the rest of the way to Front Arch at a healthy trot.

Celia told Arthur never to mind him. 'Myles,' she said, lunging forward and pulling Arthur with her. 'Here, I want you.'

Holding one another up, they staggered through the darkness and the blots of light.

Myles's flat was crammed with books, newspapers, rugs, overstuffed chairs and shaggy lampshades, barely leaving space for the five of them. Myles searched for glasses while Celia tipped backwards on the sofa and Louis eased himself to the floor beside the gramophone. Violet settled cross-legged in an armchair. Arthur perched on a corner of the paper-strewn desk that took up much of the room. Myles uncorked the whiskey and poured.

'Ah now,' he said, when Arthur protested that he'd had enough. 'The beautiful water of life never did anyone harm.'

Arthur sipped the drink while Myles shooed Celia's feet off the sofa and collapsed beside her. Louis achieved a sitting position against the fireplace, swallowed his drink in one go and filled his glass again. He passed the bottle on to Arthur, who gave in and topped himself up. Perhaps if they all kept going the night would come alive again. It didn't seem likely. Celia and Myles had started bickering in low voices, and Violet was ignoring them. Louis, sitting with his knees drawn up to his chin, was watching these events like a red-eyed vulture. Catching Violet's eye, Arthur made a sympathetic grimace, but she frowned and looked away.

Celia and Myles fell silent. She let him fill her glass. Arthur's head throbbed and his stomach was beginning to clench, but there must still be a way. Why shouldn't they walk out of here right now and find that same street, that very lamp, so that this time they could get it right? As the thought came to him, he noticed that he was squatting on his haunches beside the sofa with his face beside Celia's knee.

'I say,' he said.

She gazed down without interest or recognition. In the bathroom he held on to the sink and considered being sick. It would be a good idea but he couldn't face it. Go home, then, you gobshite.

When he came out of the bathroom Violet was asleep and Myles and Celia were alone with their thoughts at opposite ends of the sofa. Clambering to his feet, Louis slipped, landed on his tailbone and cursed. He looked set to remain there for the night, but when Arthur offered a hand he took the wrist in a sailor's grip and allowed himself to be hoisted upright. He nodded in answer to the unspoken suggestion.

Wind came off the river and Arthur turned his face to the cold. Tomorrow on the wards didn't bear thinking about and he didn't know how he was getting back to the Calvary, but it was too late to mind about that now. Having come to this last chamber of the night, it was better to forget the rest and attend to Louis, who was brooding as they walked, troubled about something.

At length he spoke.

'You've guessed, of course,' he said. 'About tonight.'

'What?'

'I didn't want to say it to the others,' Louis said. 'Feeble of me, but I couldn't be doing with the fuss. I just wanted to see you all once more before I go. A last hurrah.'

Arthur nodded, mystified.

'You know yourself it's no good. I've had my bellyful. Back to the bosom of the family, what?'

'You're going home?'

Louis squinted into the wind.

'I've nowhere else to go.'

Louis seemed to be searching through his overcoat pockets, but he gave up empty-handed. Fine sleet was in the air, visible only in the halos of the lamps.

'What about Venn?' Arthur said. 'You can't break off with him now. You've put in too much work.'

They passed a lamp post, and then another. As they approached the third, Louis explained that a week ago he had heard back from George Cope, the young editor at Gryphon who had been so enthusiastic about *Sham Abraham*. George Cope had masticated and digested, he had brooded on his judgments and communed with himself, and the decision had come that the stories were unpublishable.

'He considers the book a unique achievement,' Louis said, 'and he believes that to place it before the reading public would be the death of his career, and incidentally make a stillbirth of my own. He very much hopes that I will not be too disappointed, and that I will think of sending him anything I may write in the future.'

Arthur made noises of sympathetic exasperation.

'So now,' Louis said.

With heavy limbs and pounding head, Arthur saw the talk they would have. It would take them into the early hours and leave them unslept, footsore and shivering with cold in a distant part of the city. They would talk through Louis's predicament, his doubts about the analysis and his despair of the writing. Arthur would beg him to stick at the treatment and press on with *Jott*. He would argue that to go back to Dublin could only invite a relapse, not knowing whether he said it for Louis's good or for the sake of his own uneasy conscience, and in the end, Louis would agree. He would stay in London on condition that Arthur give him what he wanted. Arthur would be the one to suggest this, as if it were his own idea: he would have to manage it right, choose his moment, but he did not doubt that he would succeed. Perhaps, he would say, as if the idea were only now occurring to him, it might help Louis with his book if he could meet one or two of the patients at the Calvary? Perhaps William Walker. And by degrees Louis would be persuaded. Worn and weary, he would consent to give Arthur's prescription for his future one more try.

They had only to play out the last moves now. If they kept walking they could be at the hospital by morning.

TWO

Arthur shaved in cold water, in morning light. He had the washroom to himself. He had risen early and had been rewarded with a hush in the corridors of the junior doctors' residence that told him he was the first awake. The mirror behind the sink framed him from the waist up, the light from the high windows washing his skin bright white. He finished scraping away the stubble and splashed his face clean. He looked at his reflection: sparse hair on chest and stomach, ribs laced with blue veins, waist wrapped in a towel made rough by countless boilings in the Calvary laundry. He undid the towel and used it to dry his face and wipe the trails of shaving soap from his throat. He laid the towel beside the sink and leaned closer, craning forward as if peering into a window to see the whole of his body in the glass, blue-veined and bright.

Fifty minutes later he got off a bus and joined the pedestrians. They were clerks and shop assistants and secretaries, he guessed, still waking up as they left their lodgings and set off for work, sniffing with their summer colds. Living in the Calvary he seldom saw the morning rush. Buses swung in to the kerb, let out passengers and lurched away again. People darted between motor cars as reckless boys on bicycles shot past. Overhead the sky was clear. It was the first week of September.

He turned into a side road and then another. He walked the length of a high wall of yellow brick, and came to a set of iron gates through which he could see a gravelled forecourt and the severe front of the Carden High School for Girls. Carrying on past without breaking his pace, he crossed the street and found a position, leaning in the porch of a locked church, that felt reasonably discreet.

He was beginning to think he had missed her when she came around the corner. He ran across the road to catch up, touching her elbow and saying her name. When she turned, looking severe, he pulled her into the lee of one of the big brick gateposts of the school. She freed her hand from his, as if she were simply going to walk away – he glimpsed a prospect of apologies, explanations and amends for his ill-judged behaviour – but then she moved closer, glancing up and down the street. A crease appeared between her eyebrows.

'Shouldn't you be at the hospital?'

He could smell the shampoo that she got from Boots in a bottle with a green and white label. He wanted to tell her that as he stood in the church porch he had seen her walking past as a stranger might, and like a stranger had admired her stride, the twitch of her skirt and the strength of her Achilles tendons.

They had met five months ago at a public lecture by Franziska Bloch. Venn had said it would be worth Arthur's while to attend the series, as he had not heard Bloch speak before, although the lectures would contain little that was new to him, being aimed at a general audience. Bloch was doing her part to familiarise the public with the tenets of psychoanalysis in a form that would not cause panic and dismay. The title of the series was 'The Inner Life of Modern Men and Women', and on the night of the first lecture the main room of the Caxton Hall was full to capacity. Bloch, waiting behind her lectern and eyeballing the audience as it got into its seats, was a tiny, tough-looking woman who radiated the particular sort of glamour that Arthur had come to associate with leading figures in the British movement: shamanic but empiric, charismatic but withheld. Bloch was Austrian but had settled here decades ago and was now the foremost authority in Europe on the psychology of the child. The first talk was on the topic of weaning, and in spite of the anodyne title of the series it was strong enough stuff. The newborn infant is a crucible for violent, libidinal fantasies, Bloch explained, and the baby's relationship with its mother's breast cannot but be a tragedy which must form the structures of rage and grief that will persist in the adult, never to be escaped. The audience absorbed this news with every sign of enthusiasm, and when Bloch invited questions those who raised their hands were avid to learn more about what strange and monstrous lives they lived inside themselves.

The lecture was stimulating, in any case, and when Arthur and Sarah came face to face in the aisle on their way out perhaps it was some influence of Bloch's that caused them to smile at one another. The following week he noticed her in the high seats on the far side of the hall, and spent the whole lecture trying not to stare. At the last lecture of the series he could not see her anywhere, and he sunk low in his chair, struggling to stay awake, while Bloch explained how all forms of sexual and familial love are built on foundations of guilt and hatred. But as he left the building Sarah appeared beside him, asking, brisk and businesslike, what he had thought of it all, so that as they walked along Palmer Street in the thinning crowd of lecturegoers he found himself actually in discussion with this straight-backed, well-informed young woman who seemed to have appointed him defender of Bloch's theories even before he let slip that he had a professional interest. She told him that she knew nothing whatsoever about the subject – she taught dance and gymnastics, herself – but that she made a point of going to improving talks of all kinds. By the time she introduced herself, Arthur had shaken off enough of his bewilderment to tell her his name and return the handshake she offered.

I say, though, she said, a little later. I know it's your work and it's terribly important and modern and you must be fearfully brainy. But do you ever think—

What, he asked.

Well, do you ever think it might be a lot of bilge?

He laughed, not knowing quite why he was relieved at the question, or why now it seemed easy for him to ask whether she was hungry and for Sarah to reply that she knew a place for sandwiches nearby. They walked there together, and decided that the following week they should go to the pictures at the Granada Tooting. They saw *Werewolf of London* and agreed afterwards that they had enjoyed it, Arthur musing that the story of a man with a beast hidden inside him was a kind of allegory for the way that our own deepest motives are alien to us, and Sarah saying the woman had been useless in the last scene and should jolly well have kicked the monster down the stairs instead of standing there gawping until the chaps came to save her. Arthur hastened to agree. As they talked, they walked all the way back to Peckham where she lived in a room at the top of a house, and it seemed natural that standing in that small, cheap, clean room they should draw close, as they drew close now in the shelter of the gatepost of the Carden School.

70

Her hand was in the hollow of his back. She stepped away, straightening her jacket.

'Did you just come to make me late for assembly?'

He put his head on one side as if to give it serious consideration. Of course it was foolish to have come halfway across the city on a whim, but foolishness, he'd learned lately, was not a bad thing; not when it made you dashing and spirited and brought a look of fond exasperation to her face. She was working this morning, but she had the afternoon off, and the last time they met they had regretted that he couldn't get away from the hospital to spend the time with her. Now she tapped his hands away, but she was smiling.

'You should have told me sooner. Perhaps I have other plans now.'

'You finish at two, yes?' he said. 'We'll do whatever you like.'

She gave him a reproving look.

'Two o'clock, then.'

With that she walked through the gates, and he let his thoughts follow her, a thread that quickly drew out thin as she moved through school grounds he had never entered, into corridors he had never seen, where other voices must be speaking to her and claiming her attention in ways he could not guess, so that with every step she became less known to him until the thread parted and he was alone, leaning against the yellow bricks with his eyes closed, letting the sun warm him.

The sky was blue. The bricks were cool. He pushed away from the wall. It was time to get to work.

A figure was loitering by the entrance to the Calvary. It was Louis, balancing a walking-stick upright on the palm of his hand. He tossed and caught the stick, then swung the ferrule to his brow in a salute, looking for all the world like someone who expected to spend the next several hours strolling in the grounds of the hospital with a willing companion.

'Gallivanting about town, is it?'

He had a packet under his arm, an untidy oblong wrapped in brown paper and string.

'I'm late,' Arthur said. He sounded curt, he knew. But it was no more than Louis could expect, turning up here as if he could do what he liked, as if things were the same as ever.

'This afternoon, then,' Louis said, unruffled. 'Much to discuss.'

Arthur agreed he could probably manage that, wondering why he didn't say he was busy all day. They had not spoken for weeks, and Arthur had not felt inclined to get in touch. He couldn't excuse the way Louis had behaved.

It was six months since Louis had met Walker for the first time. After that night in the Lantern-Bearers Arthur had prevaricated for a week or two, but he could think of no way to go back on his promise, and in the event there had been no practical obstacles. The nurses must have noticed that he was bringing a stranger on the ward, but none of them raised an eyebrow: evidently Fletcher-Foxe's orders had licensed him to make whatever therapeutic moves he thought best, even if this included exposing the patient to a gangly Irishman in a shabby overcoat and a wide-brimmed artistic hat. One afternoon in the consulting room, therefore, Arthur had made the introductions. Mr Walker, this is Mr Louis Molyneux; Louis, Mr William Walker. Mr Molyneux would like to sit in with us today. Do you have any objection?

Do *you*? Walker replied, but he sounded good-natured about

it, and didn't seem to mind when Arthur gave Louis a chair in the corner. That session was much as usual, with Walker laughing and fencing and occasionally repeating Arthur's enquiries back to him word for word, although with Louis for an audience the performance was all the more laborious. Arthur was a Punch-and-Judy man, waggling his puppets and trying to convince the spectator that something more or less lifelike was taking place. Louis kept in the background and said nothing, but at the end of the hour, as they were getting up to leave, Walker spoke.

Next time you come, leave him outside.

Hearing this, Arthur was pleased. It was a lucid request and Louis would have to acknowledge it. The patient had made his wishes clear. It meant that Arthur had kept his promise to Louis by bringing him on the ward, but that this was an end to the business. It was a good sign in other ways too, because surely Walker was recognising some value to their time together, even admitting to some involvement in the therapeutic project. These thoughts came as the nurse led Walker out of the room, and it was only as the door closed that he realised the words had not been addressed to him at all. Walker had been talking to Louis.

After that there seemed to be no choice, and each week Arthur gave up one of the sessions so that Louis could visit Walker in his place. After all, it might have a therapeutic value. It must be beneficial to encourage the patient in any impulse towards social contact, and spending time with a third party might be his way of beginning the communication that he was not ready to attempt with the therapist. At the very least, Arthur told himself, Louis would emerge from the room with new respect for the rigours of the analyst's work.

He was taken aback when Louis came out looking as chipper as anything. He's an interesting man, he said. I think we'll get on.

They returned to the subject a few days later, on a Friday afternoon. Arthur had an hour to spare before his training analysis, so they were walking around the Wallace Collection, to which Louis was devoted. Walker was going to be a great help to his work, he said. After the meeting he had gone back to the novel and found it not half so hopeless as he had remembered. Speaking to Walker had made him feel for the first time since he'd given up *Sham Abraham* as a bad job that he had something to write about. Good, said Arthur, I'm glad to hear it – and it was true, he was pleased. He brimmed with goodwill. On previous visits he had found the Wallace cloying, with its rooms decorated in tissue-paper pinks and greens, its chandeliers like great twists of gold foil, the gleaming caramel of the eighteenth-century writing desks and toilet tables and the paintings in which the fondant flesh of cherubs was cushioned by sugary clouds, but today he understood what Louis saw in the place. It was touching to see the passion that had been worked into these dainty things by their dead makers, and if this change in his disposition might have something to do with events in his private life he didn't mind admitting it. By now he had paid several visits to Peckham, as well as meeting Sarah for walks, for tea and for trips to the pictures, and getting into states of breathlessness whenever they could find a private place. He had not yet mentioned these developments to Louis, but now seemed as good a time as any, and so, shyly, as they contemplated the Strawberry Girl, he said that he was hoping he might soon introduce a friend.

Louis chuckled. Oh, he said, is that it? I thought it must be. I didn't think the psychotics alone could be taking up quite so much of your attention.

Arthur remembered how easily Louis had deflated him that day, showing him that nothing he did could possibly be a surprise. And now, instead of telling Louis that he would not come for a pint later, that today belonged to Sarah alone, he was standing here at the gate of the Calvary agreeing to meet at the Cross Keys at six o'clock although he knew very well that this would cut the afternoon with her short. It was the same as ever: Louis demanded, he gave.

'What's your news, then?' he asked.

Louis took a slow step backwards, then another, with exaggerated caution, beating a comic retreat. He gave his stick a twirl as he walked away.

William Walker was dressed in black silk pyjamas, scarlet leather slippers and a dressing-gown of yellow silk trimmed with black braid. He always wore some version of this outfit, though sometimes the gown was claret-red, mahogany-brown or peacock-blue. His hair was rather long, neatly combed and parted, darkened with oil. He wore a signet ring on the little finger of his left hand.

He had been brought here every weekday for eight months now, but, as usual, he looked around as if the room were quite new to him. It evidently fell short of his expectations. He made a languid gesture of dismissal to the nurse, and strolled towards his chair, swaying his hips and trailing his hands through the air as if through water. He always put Arthur in mind of an undergraduate, the sort of young man who tries to seem sophisticated by adopting a decadent pose. He settled himself in his favourite position, crossing his left knee over the right and then hooking his left toe behind his right ankle, so that his small legs were not so much crossed as entwined. In spite of the sallow skin and yellow eyes he had a youthful look, with his unlined face and his smooth chin. According to the file he was four feet ten inches tall.

Arthur liked to think that in the matter of height he could sympathise with his patient. In his early schooling Arthur had been small for his age, and although he had caught up to a respectable degree by the time he got to Donard he had retained the sense of being, in spirit, one of the shrimps. However unlike they might be in other respects, at least he and Walker had shared that much. Walker, too, must know what it was to be surrounded by larger boys who saw you as a more trivial creature than themselves, and this was valuable knowledge, as Arthur had once tried to explain to Louis – six-foot-one-inch Louis – on a Sunday ramble around Dublin, years ago. The small person is sensitive to all manner of social vibrations, he had said: the small male can judge the character of larger men, because you can always spot those who look down at you from their height. Even the kindliest of tall men can be this way. They may not mean to, but they can't help believing in their hearts that they are the aristocrats of nature. Arthur had expected Louis to chuckle at his theory, which he didn't mean very seriously, but Louis did not laugh. Instead he asked: And what about me? What kind of subjugator am I? I don't know, Arthur said, finding himself outside the text of his conceit. I think you're different.

Walker let his head tilt until his temple rested against the wing of the chair. His mouth curled at the corner. His eyes strayed towards Arthur, then darted away. He liked to take his time at the beginning of a session and it was best not to hurry him. He was a reserved sort, and his fifteen years in the Calvary had not been eventful: he was on a suicide tab, but that was done on the flimsiest of grounds, on the principle that it was better to be safe than sorry, and although the notes mentioned episodes of agitation in the past, the most recent of these had been six years ago. His record was unblemished since then.

Arthur cleared his throat.

Walker fished in the pocket of his dressing-gown and brought out his silver cigarette case. He took a cigarette between his lips and snapped the case shut. Then he produced his matchbox in its silver cover. He lit the cigarette, shook out the match and tossed it into the ashtray.

He took a long drag and exhaled smoke through his nose. He smiled as if an amusing thought had come to him out of nowhere. Arthur was seven years younger than his patient, but Walker's schoolboy postures made him feel like an exasperated elder, wanting to say buck up, come on, make a bit of effort – you know perfectly well that we'll only get anywhere if you return the ball once in a while. None of that could be allowed to show.

What would Louis say to Walker now? Arthur couldn't imagine. Louis had kept up his weekly calls on Walker for almost three months, but he had never volunteered any information about what went on between them. Louis would turn up punctually at the hospital gate, often with his travelling chess set under his arm; Arthur would escort him to the consulting room and pace in the corridor for an hour, resisting the temptation to listen at the door. It was apparent that the two of them had struck up a friendship which was founded, somehow, on Arthur's exclusion.

Walker watched the smoke unwind from his cigarette. When he was in the mood he could be almost chatty in his supercilious manner, an imprisoned nobleman passing the time of day with his jailer. At other times it was hard work to coax even a single cryptic utterance from him, as it had been yesterday, when after half an hour of careful encouragement Walker had leaned forward and, like someone delivering a weighty piece of wisdom, had declared Honesty is a pattern, not a position. And then there were the evenings when he said nothing but kept going into fits of laughter, and those when he simply sat in silence. If Arthur had really expected Louis to have a therapeutic influence, he knew better now. Walker had only grown more impenetrable since the visits.

Now he gave Arthur a slow, considering look. The smile grew sly; he had come to a judgment. He sat back in the chair, saying nothing. Silence it was, then. Arthur could hear Walker's breathing and his own. Venn's advice was to trust the flow of one's own thoughts in the analysis. Especially with a patient who gives you such sparse material to work with, he said, you must attend to the associations that come, relying on intuition to lead you to some shared idea through which you can begin to make contact. Arthur tried to clear his thoughts, to rest in the silence in such a way that his mind and Walker's might draw close together. Certainly Walker was alert to unspoken signals, and in fact his sensitivity could be unnerving. In one session, weeks ago now, they had sat in silence for twenty minutes while Arthur allowed his thoughts to drift along an ill-advised path, beginning with the futility of the analysis and wandering into familiar puzzles about his life in the hospital,

78

whether he should have come at all or whether it had been an irreparable mistake, whether they saw him as the impostor he knew himself essentially to be, sinking deep and circling back to reflect on how much easier it would be to live like Walker, with all your needs taken care of and none of the problems of a life in the outside world. As this thought came to him, Walker spoke. Well, if you like, we can change places. For an instant Arthur wondered whether he had said something aloud by mistake, but Walker only sat in his chair, giving nothing away.

Now he took a last drag on his cigarette, ground the butt into the ashtray and chuckled to himself. He never gave anything away. In the first weeks Arthur had tried inviting him to tell some part of the story of his life, asking for memories of his childhood and adolescence, his mother and father, but the response to such questions was always the same. However cooperative Walker had seemed at the beginning of the hour, his face would stiffen into the classic mask – the eyes as flat as enamel buttons, the mouth twisted into a cunning smirk – and he would not speak for the rest of the session. After eight months, Arthur knew precisely nothing about how his patient saw the world.

His wristwatch ticked, soft as an insect. Of course Walker's resistance made analytical sense. When Arthur had discussed it with Venn, they had agreed that the silences, riddles and mocking laughter were forms of expression in themselves. They signalled Walker's hostility towards Arthur, which was all to the good, because hostility was a necessary preliminary phase, correlating with the patient's anxiety at the prospect of establishing a close, dependent relationship with his analyst. If Arthur held steady, Venn assured him, there was every reason to expect that Walker would soon be ready to move forward into meaningful communication. But he must be allowed to do it in his own time, and it was a slow business. Sometimes in the middle of a session Arthur would get the feeling that he was alone in the room, as if the limp little figure in the other chair were a heap of abandoned clothes that he had mistaken for a person.

Walker was sitting up straighter in his chair now. He leaned fractionally in Arthur's direction and took a long draught of air, his nostrils flaring. He sniffed again, then settled back as if a suspicion had been confirmed. He was observant, and he sometimes liked to make a game of it, letting you know that he could guess what you had been doing outside the consulting room from the traces he detected on your person. It was another aspect of his youthfulness. Arthur remembered a period at Donard when he and Louis had been in a Holmesian phase and had done the same thing, deducing that a boy had been mitching by the brick dust on his blazer, or drawing conclusions about the French master's state of mind from the condition of his fingernails.

'You notice something?' Arthur said.

Surely this was beyond reproach as a therapeutic move – he was following a cue that the patient had given, but gently, asking no explicit question, only inviting him to develop a thought if he cared to. But it was no good. It was a false move, because however gently he might pose the question he didn't want to hear the answer. He was too conscious of where it could lead. Perhaps his clothes smelled of his early morning errand across the city: perhaps he trailed the scents of exhaust and parks and bread and Sarah's shampoo, so that Walker's preternatural senses could trace the whole story of how he had been spending his time. It was not desirable for the analyst to share any substantial information about his private life with the patient, but some leakage was impossible to avoid. He had never mentioned Sarah to Walker, of course, but Walker was free to look out of the windows of his ward and might easily have caught sight of her on a visit. For that matter, nurses and patients were always gossiping. Once you began, it was only too easy to invent ways that Walker might know anything he cared to know about your private affairs. Perhaps Louis and Walker had spent their hours together chuckling over Arthur's infatuation, comparing notes on his behaviour and wondering wryly what he would do next.

The session was turning treacherous. He'd have to report this to Venn, he supposed. A moment's paranoia could be fodder for a whole hour's perambulation, although it would reveal nothing that he didn't already know. He really ought to stop approaching the training analysis in this way, collecting up scraps that he thought would please and laying them like birds on Venn's doormat. He was still choosing what to give away, still failing in the analysand's duty to be an open book. Not that he hadn't made some progress. He had told Venn about Sarah, and had even confessed that she was the first woman really to take an interest in him in that way. Leaving the Malet after that session he'd been euphoric at having thrown off the burden of his secret: at least now he had something to talk about, so that there was no need to conjure up homosexual affections for Louis, dig around for Greek tragedies in his relations with his parents or press poor old Thomas into service. And yet, as the training analysis went on, nothing much seemed to have changed. Venn still paced beside him, listening, commenting, advising, asking questions, but always waiting with infinite patience, it seemed, for him to get around to saying something that was true.

Small shivers went through his hands. Some psychosomatic discomfort was not necessarily a bad thing: it meant that significant events were taking place at the unconscious level of the analysis. Sweat crawled inside his shirt. The trick, as ever, was to turn the interaction to therapeutic ends. Take Walker's antics and use them to guide him towards the health that he did not yet know he was seeking.

Somewhere in Walker there *was* a desire to communicate, Arthur thought. That basic healthy urge had not been lost. When you glimpsed him on the ward he could appear almost sociable, drifting around in one of his gorgeous gowns, not speaking to the other patients but tolerating them amiably enough. He had seemed positively to enjoy himself at the Fancy Dress Ball. This was an important event in the calendar of the Calvary, held between Christmas and the new year and taken very seriously by all concerned: the theme last time had been characters of Shakespeare's plays, with identities assigned at the luck of the draw and costumes supplied from the hospital's excellent dressing-up box. Arthur, self-conscious in the yellow stockings he had been given, had watched doctors and nurses mingling with patients in the Recreation Hall. Fletcher-Foxe, swathed in a starry cloak and carrying a staff and a leather-bound book, leaned down so that Ellis, in a toga and laurel wreath, dagger in hand, could murmur in his ear. Parry, looking handsome despite the donkey's ears he wore, danced a step with Cleopatra, made a joke with Henry V, wagged a finger at Juliet. Many of the patients stood rooted to the spot, nonplussed by the proceedings, but Walker was not one of these. Tiny and elegant, dressed in a black silk suit, equipped with a toy rapier and a skull, he strolled around like a host among his guests, bowing to the partygoers now and then. He looked in such good form that Arthur went over and asked how he liked the ball. Walker did not answer: instead he fell into a meditative stance, staring into the eye sockets of the skull, which, Arthur noticed, was a real human skull, presumably on loan from someone's office. The upper part of the cranium had been sawn across and was secured by tiny brass catches. When Walker finally seemed to notice Arthur, a faint, pained smile touched his lips. He was a prince whose contemplations had been interrupted by some gadfly courtier, some sycophant. He turned and strolled away.

The fever chills eased and Arthur was calm again. Therapeutic ends. Don't become defensive. If you assume that silence is hostility, that's what it will become. Think instead that sitting here in silence may be the only form of communication open to Walker today. Never forget what an enormous task it is for someone in his situation to speak in a way that others can understand. Remember that even an hour of unbroken silence has its meaning.

Walker was slouching in his chair, his gaze dissolving into the space of the room. He deserved admiration, actually. Who knew what an effort he was making at this very moment to convey his message through the silence. So help him. Don't say anything; don't break the flow of these thoughts, yours and his; simply listen and be patient, follow the thoughts flowing together, and wait for him to tell you what the silence means.

And, indeed, as Arthur waited, some slow change was coming over Walker. He did not look up, but his hands began to tremble, then his shoulders. At first he was silent, but then a snort escaped him. Then a giggle, and another, and then a full-throated laugh. The laughter built in waves, as if he kept seeing new and more diverting sides of the joke. Soon he was cackling wildly, rocking in his seat, unable to help himself.

Eventually the laughter ebbed. He gave an apologetic shake of the head and wiped the corner of his eye. He glanced up. When he spoke, it was in a flawless imitation of Arthur's own accent.

'If I could tell you that,' he said, 'we wouldn't be here, now, would we?'

She stepped through the gates of the Carden High School for Girls at three minutes past two. They greeted one another at arm's length and began to walk side by side, their feet swinging in step. Voices of girls and mistresses clamoured behind them. When they came to the corner, they linked hands and ran a good fifty yards before falling into a bright alleyway. When they drew apart she was smiling, making fun of him for being out of breath. One of her upper front incisors was a different shade of ivory from the others, because it was artificial. She had lost the tooth a year ago, when one of the girls threw a netball in her face in a gym class. Pure accident, poor thing, Sarah had said when she told the story, but Arthur had wished worse than broken teeth on the little blister who had done it.

The sun grew brighter in the street.

As they walked to the bus stop it occurred to him that now was the time to mention that he'd promised to meet Louis. But blast Louis: it couldn't be the first thing he said to her, and put a damper on the whole afternoon. It would be easier to confess later on. For now let him walk along the street with his hand in Sarah's hand.

He had introduced the two of them on a wet March evening over supper at L'Étoile. Sitting at the small table in the crowded room, crumbling bread, waiting, Sarah was nervous, which was Arthur's fault for having described Louis in exaggerated terms, making him a caricature of a brilliant, erratic, unconventional type. I'm sure I shan't be able to keep up, she said, but they got on well from the moment Louis stooped into the restaurant like a drenched crow, grinning through his misted spectacles, rainwater running from the hem of his overcoat. Arthur barely had to contribute to the conversation. He could not remember having seen Louis so animated yet so easy, nor had he realised that Sarah was so articulate on subjects from sex to eugenics to the future of Europe. After the plates were cleared they got on to the fad for keep-fit and physical hygiene. Sarah mentioned that she was a member of the Women's Health and Beauty Association, and Louis pretended to be shocked. Oh, I've seen them on the newsreels, he said. Marching up and down, shouldering their legs like rifles. He put on a crisp English newsreel voice and, making a view-finder of his thumbs and forefingers, framed Sarah: Yes, she's a picture of health, and she's a charming member of the Women's Health and Beauty Association, an organisation that's caught the imagination of young women up and down the country. These girls believe in exercising *every* part of the body. The ancient ceremony of showing a leg was never more gracefully demonstrated. These girls may bend the knee but they yield to no one in physical fitness and complete harmony of mind and body. There are no strenuous movements, just rhythmical exercises that bring Grace, to say nothing of Maud and Phyllis and the rest, as near to physical perfection as possible . . .

Stop that! Sarah laughed, but Louis shook his head. I'm not fooled, he said. They're not so innocent as they want us to believe. This sinister confederation of female supremacists is reaching its tendrils across the globe, and who knows what they're really up to when they claim to be bending and stretching? Who knows what plans they've laid?

Wouldn't you like to know, Sarah said. But I'm afraid you'd be disappointed. It's all thoroughly wholesome. You pay three shillings for your badge, you pledge to take regular exercise, and then you go along to the local centre for callisthenics, dance and rhythmic movement classes. It helps you keep fit, and it's a way to meet other women. On second thoughts, that's probably what you don't like – the idea of us all getting together behind your back. What if we're talking about *you*?

Jesus, what if you're *not*? said Louis.

They laughed and Arthur tasted his wine. It didn't matter if he couldn't keep up. He was content to bask in the honour of having brought them together, because tonight he was the one who had made it happen: the ordinary marvel of three people eating and talking and liking one another while the rain streaked the windows and the crowds passed outside.

Days later he met Louis for a pint, standing at the bar of an underground dive somewhere south of the river, each resting a foot on the rail. The choice of venue was Louis's but the urge to meet had been Arthur's. Since the night in L'Étoile he felt that he knew Sarah better: introducing her to Louis had helped him to see her as not simply a miraculous visitation but, more than that, a person he had hardly begun to know. As they stood side by side at the bar he couldn't understand why Louis was so unwilling to talk, why he sighed and sucked on his pint, ignoring Arthur's attempts to introduce the topic. Eventually he asked whether Arthur really wanted to know what he thought of the girl.

As he listened, Arthur kept his face composed and did not try to interrupt. If Louis had the nerve to tell him these things, then he could hear them as bravely. You have to beware, Louis said. Hadn't Arthur felt the falsity of everything that had been said at supper the other night? I must be blunt, he said. I know her kind. Her consciousness amounts to a single imperative. She'll sink into matrimony the first chance she gets, because she believes that afterwards no exertion will be required of her ever again. Oh, she may work up a little charm in aid of her ambition, but once it's achieved she grows bovine and permits you to spend the ensuing decades working yourself to death for her comfort, for which your reward will be that she turns bitter as time passes and she discovers that wedded bliss is not, after all, the solution to all the little wants and dissatisfactions of her life – a state of affairs for which you, of course, are to blame.

Louis looked glum. I can only tell you the truth, he said. I wouldn't have told it if you hadn't asked. Arthur had thanked him for his candour and left his pint unfinished on the bar. And why should it matter, he asked himself, if Louis thinks I'm a fool? They were free to take different views. That Sunday he and Sarah went on an outing to the new lido at Ruislip, and as they walked along the artificial beach, battered by gusts of wind at the lake's edge where tiny waves ran to their feet, he took her hand in defiance. The gulls fought over sandwich crusts, shivering thigh-deep bathers splashed water on their chests, and Arthur and Sarah walked along the path into the woods surrounding the lake. Soon they were alone under the trees. She let go of his hand so that she could pass ahead of him through a kissing gate. They were tongue-tied, but if they didn't have much to say just now, so what? Not everyone could be like Louis, burning with conviction to the fingertips, living by a hunger that would not be satisfied, incapable of doing a dull or conventional thing. Arthur grabbed Sarah's hand again and pushed through a screen of willow leaves. He pulled her on to a bench and brought her face close to his. Their noses and teeth bumped; their mouths kept meeting at the wrong angle. Her hands were chapped. The air was cold and smelled faintly of dog shit. He fumbled at the buttons of her coat, at the stiff fabric, but after a minute she stopped him. They walked on, Arthur thinking that if she was angry she should say so, but as they rounded the farthest point of the lake she told him that three years ago she had been engaged to a man who after seven months had broken it off without any warning. He was a gastric surgeon and had married a nurse. Oh, well, I'll have to do, then, will I? Arthur had not understood why he said this, or why they said the things they went on to say as they walked back towards the bathers' beach: why it had so suddenly become clear that she knew nothing of his true needs, or why in the end he gestured wildly back towards the bench by the willow tree and said at least now I know why we never get anywhere, do we, because you know just how much you need to give to get what you want. Sarah looked away from him, her eyes pink and sore, her face plain with dislike, and said that they had better not see one another again. Arthur could only agree.

Now they walked along the King's Road with their hands linked. September felt like full summer. The longer the good weather lasted, the stronger the illusion that it would go on forever. Arthur didn't yet want to give up the hot days and long bright evenings that he and Sarah had known, but walking through the hospital this morning he'd caught a taste of earth and leaves in the air and had known that autumn was already here, waiting behind the warmth. Sarah had had her current winter coat for three years and it was practically worn out, so to find a new one they were going to the flagship branch of Parker and Vance on Sloane Square.

The shop was a severe modernist palace as tall as a cliff, its facade a curtain wall of curved glass six storeys high. They passed through heavy glass doors and were disoriented in a world of dark wood counters, moving staircases and lifts opening and closing without a whisper. He followed Sarah, natural light giving way to electric as they went into the groves of hanging fabric among perspectives tricked by dim pools of glass. Arthur had been in here once before, trying to buy a hat, but had left empty-handed. The place was beyond him. He understood the ordinary shops in the smaller streets, where the shopkeepers kept their goods out of reach and the customer must petition for a new collar or an ounce of tea, but here everything was on display and the shoppers were comfortably in charge, going where they liked, rubbing cloth between fingers, picking up dishes, examining ornaments, giving a bedside clock a shake. The shopworkers scurried to fetch them what they lacked, approved their choices and admired their taste, not only ministering to their desires but cooing over those desires as over so many new babies. At Parker and Vance the customer was to be congratulated for wanting things. When Arthur had come here by himself the real customers had frowned at him, so obvious was it that he did not belong in this universe where every wish had its immediate satisfaction. But with Sarah it was different. She moved along the

89

aisles as expertly as the other shoppers, pausing now and then to touch a fabric or consider the hang of a skirt on a mannequin, then continuing, never losing her bearings – but she was nothing like those others, because all she wanted here was a new coat for the winter and to get it she was not going to give in to Parker and Vance's inducements. She was wise to this place, so that when she showed him a bolt of rich purple-and-silver tartan she might as well have been pointing out a bank of heather on a hillside, and when she turned and half-echoed the mannequin's pose for him, there was a joke in the gesture and a glint of rebellion. Louis would have noticed none of this, because he was incapable of seeing what Sarah was like.

A fortnight after the day at the lido, Arthur had admitted to Louis that he was no longer meeting her. He supposed that some commiseration might not be out of the question, but Louis kept his eyes on the path at his feet and barely seemed to hear. Arthur pressed the point, worrying aloud about why it had all gone wrong, and when they reached the hospital gate Louis turned on him. I strongly advise you to forget about it, he said. I should imagine that by now she's in the arms of some burly Blackshirt she found at a rally. When he was gone, Arthur took an extra turn around the hospital grounds by himself, wondering what on earth Louis meant. Whatever he thought of Sarah, that slander made no sense. He claimed to think that the Women's Health and Beauty Association was a militaristic organisation, but that had been a joke and a silly one; Arthur should have noticed the hostility it concealed. It was obvious now that Louis had nothing but contempt for Sarah's wish to meet like-minded people, to take good care of herself and to find satisfaction in straightforward physical pursuits. Louis who had never joined a club in his life.

Sarah had once invited Arthur to an outdoor display by her chapter of the Association. They were putting it on in Hyde Park to demonstrate their activities to the public and recruit new members. Arthur stood with a small crowd of spectators and watched as a platoon of young women dressed in white sleeveless blouses, black knickers and white gym pumps marched around the perimeter of the field in an approximation of lockstep, four abreast. They formed a square and went through their routines: marching on the spot, bending and stretching, sitting down to rotate their ankles, lying down to raise their legs. It was a curious sight, a hundred young women on their backs on the grass and two hundred bare legs waving in the air. Finally they made a ring with linked hands and high-stepped in a circle, like an army of nymphs in a painting on a classical theme. They moved in less than perfect synchronisation: for all the marching and the uniforms, the impression was reassuringly amateurish. A young woman in a white dress stood at the front, calling out instructions and conducting the exercises with large motions of her arms.

Watching, Arthur felt like a peeping tom, in spite of the fact that the crowd was made up of women and children and respectable men. The performing women themselves appeared quite sure that there could be nothing unwholesome about their display, but there was a strange, unbalanced mood among the spectators, expressed only through restless shifting of feet and shrugging inside raincoats, in uneasy grinning and giggling and glancing. By the end of the display he was exhilarated in a way he could not have explained if Sarah had asked. As the event broke up she came over and found him, bringing another young woman whom she introduced as her friend Cicely. They were still in their identical brief uniforms, and

Arthur felt himself redden. If it was flustering to see the women going through their routines, it was all the more so to find that they were allowed to come and talk to him afterwards. Sarah and Cicely stood side by side in their outfits, quite at ease, as if it would never in a million years have occurred to them that there might be anything discomfiting about their display of healthy young womanhood.

Cicely smiled and shook his hand.

Did you enjoy the demonstration? she said.

Oh, it was marvellous, he said. That is – he searched for the right words – it was . . . most edifying.

Cicely looked at Sarah and the two women gave an identical snort.

Which was as it should be, Arthur thought as he walked around the hospital grounds. It was a wonderful thing. As he walked, Louis's portrait of Sarah as a Blackshirt-loving fascist crumbled to pieces in his mind. He saw how ridiculous Louis could be – how histrionic, how superior, how wrong – and he told himself that he had been duped for the last time.

Sarah led him past home furnishings, kitchen wear, pharmacy and men's clothing, up the moving staircases towards the particular region of ladies' clothing that they were seeking. She had a coat in mind but wanted his opinion before she decided. As they went higher and deeper, shoppers and shopworkers made way for her and their eyes followed her as she passed. She was immune to the power of the department store because it wanted her far more than she wanted anything it could give her in return. Submitting gladly, the shop arranged itself around her, stairs rising under her feet and doors gliding open to guide her through the maze at whose heart was the gift that had been prepared for her since time immemorial, waiting for her to find it, choose it, put it on. He held her jacket while she took the coat from its hanger. She was doubtful, not only because it was on the expensive side but also maybe because it was a bit too showy, too modish and conspicuous, because don't forget it had to last several seasons and it was bound to go out of fashion. But she tried it on, and as she did so shop girls turned their heads, clerks peered around the doors of their offices and a ginger cat leapt up to a counter. Two grandmothers agreed that they approved. The mannequins and mirrors themselves had gathered like handmaids and witnesses to Sarah, who accepted the tributes without pride. Arthur was proud, though, to be the one chosen from the congregation to tell her that the coat was just the thing and that she must have it, and at the till he stood to one side like a simple groom while the clerk accepted the money, folded the garment in an arcane manner, wrapped it in tissue paper and then in brown packing paper, and slid it into a stiff card carrier bag with cotton ropes for handles. The bag was decorated with a monotone print showing an elfin woman admiring her face in a hand mirror, beside the words *Parker & Vance Ltd*, and below that, *Blouses and Jumpers in the Latest Styles*. The ropes were long enough for Arthur to sling the bulky package over his shoulder.

On the way out they stopped in the Food Hall, where Arthur bought lemonade, iced buns, cheddar, biscuits, bread rolls, egg mayonnaise and a pork pie. Then, remembering something he had spotted on the way up, he ran back to another department and bought a blanket and a small Opinel clasp knife. The extravagance didn't matter, because now they were stepping from the shop's cool interior on to the street where the heat of the sun was the universe kissing him on the brow. This is what it means not to believe your luck.

After that day at the lido he had spent a grim week of nights in his room trying to write her a letter, searching for some way of taking back what he had said. He wanted to prove to her that she had misunderstood him, that he hadn't meant what she thought, but sitting over the paper with a pen in his hand he had only known how to write in complete sentences that made too much sense to express what he needed to say. In the end he went to Peckham uninvited. She let him into the narrow hallway but would not bring him up to her room, never mind what the other tenants heard over the banisters. She waited for him to explain himself, but he could only stumble and sigh and stop. He had nothing to plead in mitigation. He could only tell her that he was a fool, a bounder and generally beyond the pale, that he was not asking her to take any further interest in him – she watched him fumble for the words he needed – and that now he would go away and never trouble her again. Having defeated himself as fully as possible, he slunk back to the hospital, knowing that now he would always have to remember her face as it had looked that afternoon, altered by pain and disappointment.

But two days later, as he and Venn were walking back to the Malet at the end of a session, he recognised the figure standing at the foot of the clinic's steps, glancing up and down the street as if she were about to hurry away. She knew the times of his meetings. In the spring twilight he could not make out her expression, but he ran forward to meet her before she could disappear, and when she turned and recognised him her face was no longer changed. Only a little drawn, it seemed to him: a little hurt, but still the face he felt he'd always known.

Now they passed the Lister and crossed the Chelsea Bridge into the park. Walking along by the river, they stopped to look over the parapet at what the low tide had revealed: a mudflat, a gravel verge, a massive bank of stone steps green with weed. Clouds covered the sun and it was chilly, so they stopped to unpack the new coat. Arthur watched her fasten the buttons and tighten the belt. He stood away to admire the outline.

They left the river and walked deeper into the park. Leaves blew and settled on paths already plastered with the damp yellow tissues. They passed the bandstand, then came to the boating lake and followed its shoreline to a rustic bridge made of logs. Crossing it, they found a sheltered bank beside a second, smaller lake, on the far side of which a crowd of trees with veined and bulbous trunks rose directly from the water on a mass of exposed roots. A swan drifted. Arthur spread the blanket. While Sarah unpacked the picnic things he opened his knife, with which he was very pleased. He liked its shape, its smallness, the near weightlessness of the beech-wood handle, the scrape of the stainless steel blade across the pad of his thumb and the clever mechanism that locked it open. He sliced the cheese and the pork pie, tore open the rolls and spread the mayonnaise. He stuck the knife in the ground up to the hinge to clean the blade, then wiped it on his hand-kerchief and folded it away. They ate. They drank the lemonade from the bottle. They wiped their hands in the grass.

They were only a few feet from the path, but it was screened by low branches, and no human activity was visible on the lake below. Only the drifting swan, the strange trees and the thicker woods beyond. She sat cross-legged and straight-backed with the skirts of the coat spread around her. He leaned on one hand while with the other he parted the strands of her hair to find the shape of the back of her skull.

'Do you remember this morning?'

An asinine question. He didn't know what he meant by it, but she didn't seem to mind. He felt her face move as she smiled, and, noticing what was now possible, he unbuttoned the coat – she helped him when he couldn't get the knack – and opened the lapels. It took him a long time to find the edges of the skirts of her dress and sort his way through the layers of fabric. She was shifting her position to make it easier when they heard voices on the path behind them, and he snatched his fingers away. But the walkers passed and his hand found its way back as Sarah settled and held quite still, turning her face so that her breath warmed his cheek.

Another walker went by, with a dog that snuffled along the low branches. When they were gone the quiet of the park returned. Water was trickling nearby. Somewhere a rope beat a slow, regular rhythm against a flagpole. Arthur's hand was tingling, twisted at a difficult angle. They sat side by side, growing deeply calm as now she lowered her eyelids and looked out at the trees across the lake, then leaned back, bracing her arms behind, and, with tiny, exact movements, began to guide him.

Knowing Sarah was like living in a new country, he thought. Whenever he followed her into the room in Peckham he was surrounded by beguiling foreign sights and customs: her hair-grips on the shelf, her keep-fit kit pegged to dry over the sink, the leaflets for improving talks and activities that she pinned to a bit of cork on the back of the door, the stack of paperback novels that she kept on the bedside cabinet. She liked John Buchan and Sax Rohmer. Arthur had once let slip to Louis that she was reading *The Lair of Fu Manchu*. Quite right, quite right, Louis had said, chuckling: every blossom of English womanhood should read that stuff. Arthur had shaken his head, not seeing why Louis was so amused. It was impossible to explain to Louis how being with Sarah made things new. She gave him everything to discover again. Even his own past was different. He found that he could tell her stories about himself where before there had been nothing to tell. She wanted to hear about the Quaker meetings, for instance: about child-Arthur sitting quietly on the wooden bench, hoping that the worship would pass in silence because it was always so uncomfortable when one of the Friends stood up to minister. As he described this to her, he remembered a strange time when one of the Friends had begun to weep and tremble, and the tears had spread through the whole meeting until even his parents on either side of him were wiping their faces, leaving Arthur the only one untouched.

In June they had gone out of London together for the first time. They took the train as far as Wareham and caught a bus that carried them along narrow hedged-in lanes towards the fishing village on the south coast where Sarah had grown up. Her father and sister still lived there. The lanes and villages were unlike Irish lanes and villages, and here too he was learning the ways of an unfamiliar country, making a journey into the history and hinterland of the culture in which he was an immigrant: Sarah's life. They left the bus and walked the last half-mile to a village whose main street ran steeply down to a cove. She took him straight to the beach, where streams ran across pebbles and the waves sucked on the shingle. Every time she came home, she said, the first thing she did was come down and see the sea. There were holidaymakers buying ice creams, men fixing lobster pots, gulls, hotels, beached rowing boats, thatched cottages. They walked back up the street to the low stone house where Sarah's family lived, across from a row of coastguards' cottages. At the garden gate she hesitated, began to say something and stopped. There was some obstacle here, some ugly shape that was invisible to him, blocking the way into the house. Not knowing what to do about it, he laid his hand on top of hers where it rested on the gate. She led on.

Inside, the house was a dark jumble of stairs and passages with ceilings so low that Arthur sometimes had to duck. Louis would have been stooping continually. She led him through a stone-flagged dining room and up uneven stairs to a cramped kitchen, where a young woman with no resemblance to Sarah turned from the sink and told them they had not been expected for another hour at least. She walked past them, sighing, and told Arthur he was in the back bedroom. They followed her down to a sitting room where a thickset man with a few licks of hair across his pate was pushing himself out of his arm-chair. When he saw Sarah and Arthur his hands began to clench and unclench, and Arthur wondered if the visit was to open with the intimidations that suitors were traditionally meant to receive from patriarchs. But instead Sarah's father grunted, turned his back on them and got down to tinker with the fireplace, cursing as it coughed smoke and coal dust into the room.

Sarah took him out for a walk, first around to the tip of the cove, balancing along big rocks under the clay cliffs, then back up a hillside to the top of another cliff. They looked down to where the sea exploded through a natural archway in the rock, over and over. When they got back to the house Sarah's father and sister were already at the dinner table, staring at their empty plates and at the congealing dishes of boiled bacon, cabbage and Brussels sprouts. Once apologies had been made and the food served, the conversation became slow. Mary restricted herself to one or two ironical comments about Sarah's life in London, ignoring Arthur entirely. Mr Beamish, though, was interested in his prospects, asking why he wanted to be a zookeeper for loonies instead of a real doctor, and wasn't he worried that it would send him bats himself sooner rather than later, and why was it that they had to be kept in the lap of luxury anyhow when anyone knew they'd be better off out of their misery. Arthur listened to these points and tasted the sour brown ale that had been poured for him. He was glad the discussion was staying away from the topic of his friendship with Sarah. She kept her eyes down, pushing at a bit of meat on her plate, as her father went on to talk about the blights that were eating away at the nation, the communists, socialists, Jews and homosexuals. Arthur looked across at her and said nothing. Her cutlery scraped on the china. Mr Beamish's thoughts circled back towards Arthur's odd choice of profession. It's all the same thing, he said. Stamp them out. If we don't do it, there's others that will, and then where'll we be? Once the meal was finished it was time to sit by the fire, but after a perfunctory silence Mr Beamish stumped off to bed, which meant the rest had to go too. Sarah wished Arthur a formal goodnight in front of Mary. Undressing alone in the back bedroom, he felt a bodily disgust at being here in the bosom of an alien family with its alien habits and alien flesh. He climbed between the clammy sheets and tried to read, but he kept nodding off and waking again to see the enormous doll's house, as large and solid as a wardrobe, that stood at the foot of the bed, its windowpanes clogged with dust. Was this what Sarah wanted for them, then: to lie staring at sagging ceilings at opposite ends of the house where she had been born? Perhaps she couldn't help but want it. By now they had often lain with their clothes loosened on her bed in her room in Peckham, moving clumsily together, but by bringing him to this place she was telling him that nothing more could happen, because of the existence of the father and the sister and the house and the village and the past. If so, he could only agree. How could they go further with all this against them? The cliffs were full of dinosaur bones.

And she was telling him, too, that if he wanted to go further it was easily done. He need only buy a cheap ring from Woolworth's. But if he offered it and she accepted, what would that mean except that they had surrendered? They would be able to lie down together naked, but it would be with the approval of her father and her sister and all the miserable generations that had gone before, and that, even he could see, was no way to be naked. Whatever they had that was precious would be lost if they needed the permission of the rotten old world. Perhaps that was what she wanted – you don't say, whispered Louis in his mind's ear – but at least she was telling him the truth. Balanced on the cusp of sleep, he saw her gallantry. She had warned him that if they continued, the path they followed would not take them deeper into the bright places they had known so far, but would end in this house. She had told him, so that he could turn back if he chose. The book fell from his hands.

He was woken by a tap on the bedroom door, and Sarah slipped in. He sat up in bed, confused, but she squeezed his hands – hers were hot and dry – and whispered at him not to make any noise. She wore a heavy old salt-stained overcoat.

He pulled on clothes and shoes and she led him down to the kitchen, where a storm lantern was flickering on the table. She picked it up, stepped into a pair of crusted boots standing by the back door, lifted the latch and led him outside.

I'll show you, she said, when he asked what was going on. It's not far.

They went up stone steps, past a chicken cage and along the back of the house, which was built into the side of a steep hill so that the thatch touched the ground. They were at the bottom of a trench formed by sloping roof on one hand and hillside on the other. Light was still dying in the sky. A pale rowing boat stood in an open shed. Sarah led him down beside the shed and into a pathway like a tunnel, with a roof of entangled branches. The storm lantern lit a stone wall on one side and an unkempt hedge on the other. After a steep climb the ground levelled and they crossed a patch of long grass that wetted the legs of Arthur's trousers. Look up there, she said, and further up the hillside, almost hidden by vegetation, he saw a window that seemed to be lodged in the treetops. We call it the Shingle House, she said. No one uses it. A still narrower tunnel of trunks and undergrowth led them higher, until without warning they were at the door of the shack. It's a kind of summer house, she said, struggling with the catch, or it used to be. They don't come up here. She got the door open and carried the lantern into a windowless room crammed with junk. The smell of dry rotten wood was edged with paraffin. They picked their way through stacks of mouldy books and rotten clothes, worm-eaten furniture, long-dead toys and rusted bits of chandlery, into a larger and clearer room beyond. The floorboards had been swept and a cream silk scarf had been hung across the window. Sarah put the lantern down on the floor.

A Valor stove stood in the corner, giving off a smell of burned dust. I came up here just now, she said, to get everything ready. She checked the grate and rubbed her hands on the old overcoat.

The only furniture was a straight-backed chair on which a bottle stood beside two glasses. A thick pile of blankets, eiderdowns, sheets and pillows lay on the floor. Her father wouldn't miss the sherry, Sarah said. She poured the thick brown stuff, gave him one of the glasses and drank off the other in one swallow. Ugh, she said. Quick, it's too cold. She stepped out of the boots and took off the overcoat. Underneath, she was in her nightclothes. She dived into the pile of blankets, shivered and held them open to him, so he prised off his shoes and joined her, still in his trousers and sweater. They laid their heads on pillows that smelled dusty but were less damp than the ones in his bedroom.

I hope this is all right, she said. I've imagined it. I don't know why. They lay with their hands at one another's faces. He moved closer and soon they were getting tangled up in their attempts to remove clothes under blankets. Sitting up to free his ankles, Arthur paused and reached over to pour more of the nasty sherry. They rested on their elbows in the makeshift bed, Sarah holding the top of the sheet to her throat. She touched the skin of his chest. Men are soft, she said.

A few minutes later, Arthur asked: Is it all right? I don't— I mean, obviously I haven't got—

We're quite safe, she said. It's the right time. They dived down again, and as he rolled on top of her he found that it was simpler than he had thought. She was more wonderful than he had reckoned on, the world was more wonderful, and now the chance had come, not as a promise that he lacked the nerve to make real but as a woman who was here and had imagined this. His head swam a little. He tasted sherry and dust and paraffin and her skin. Sarah. Now it was time to make it all right and undo the failure of the past many years, but now that it was time at last, now that everything was simple and clear and there was no further possibility of misunderstanding, why, then, was he uncomfortably aware of the mechanical movement of their bodies, which did not seem to know quite how to fit together, and why instead of plunging into the flow that should come now and show them naturally what to do was he conscious of himself trying to do it, conscious of the blood beating in his head and of his body labouring to pretend that it was responding as it should? Trying to force himself to be ready, he moved heavily, too roughly, and she caught her breath and told him to be gentle, as if he were a virile brute liable to lose his self-control in his passion. At that he nearly started laughing.

By the time they gave up, the silk scarf was screening a dark sky. They lay in the blankets for a while, Arthur too ashamed to move. Soon, he knew, he would grow angry with himself, and no doubt Sarah was mortally insulted. For now he breathed the smell of paraffin and singed dust. A bird or an animal scrabbled on the roof. He was about to fall asleep when she said: I'm a fool. A fool, yes, he thought, for thinking that I was capable of behaving like a normal, healthy male – but that did not seem to be what she meant. What must you think of me, she said, springing it on you, as if— She hit herself in the forehead with the heel of her hand. Bloody fool! He sat up and told her not to be silly, and as the light of the storm lantern burned lower they cheered one another up, agreeing that it was nice here, after all. She turned her back to him and laced herself into his arms so that her hair tickled his nose, and they slept.

When he woke the lantern was dead and the dawn gloom ash-blue. He touched her shoulder. It must be time for them to get back to the house. Surely they had not been meant to stay here all night. Sarah stirred and mumbled but did not wake. His muscles ached in unfamiliar places, and his sore head was a distraction from the first twinges of regret. Then she turned over to face him, and her eyes opened, and this time they found that there were no difficulties at all.

That morning came back now as, with tiny, exact movements, Sarah guided him. His arm was twisted and he could feel twinges of cramp beginning in his hand, but there was no stopping and no breaking the rhythm they had found, because she was breathing steadily as the rope beat on the flagpole, pushing her head against his so that their faces touched and their breathing mingled, their heads touching as if it should be the easiest thing for the walls of the skull to dissolve and their heads merge so that they could sink together into a single memory of that morning, remembering how it had been full daylight by the time they stole out of the Shingle House and back down the hill, how they had met Mary in the kitchen and she had given them a look that said she did not for a second believe Sarah's story that they had been out for an early morning walk, and how Arthur had not minded in the slightest, because he was exalted, aching, lost in the lustre of the world, thinking of the wood pigeon that had perched outside the window making its throaty noises throughout and of the small triangular stain that had been uncovered on the sheet as they climbed out of the makeshift bed up there in the house among the trees, and now Sarah lifted her head away from him and turned her face to the sky, and he could not have pulled his hand free if he had wanted to, because it was held with the strength of a giant's hand, Sarah holding herself quite still, and although the pain was getting worse he didn't mind, because the pain didn't matter and he would have it go on and on while above him her head showed dark against a bright gap in the clouds.

He was woken by specks of rain on his face. The sky had clouded over. They had dozed lying back on the blanket, his cheek at her hip, the leaves stirring above them. Now Sarah was sitting up to fuss with her dress. He wiped his hands on the grass. The rug was damp from the ground, and his clothes were itchy and moist; there was a blot of mud on the knee of his trousers. They began to clear up the remains of the picnic. She bent to retrieve the fallen lemonade bottle. He rolled up the rug and they stood facing one another across the flattened grass.

Once they had packed up, they walked on through the park. Sarah looked at her wristwatch.

'What now?' she said. 'You choose. Couple of hours till you're due at the clinic.'

She was a sworn supporter of his work with Venn. She never asked much about it, but she admired it as a serious form of self-improvement and would never hear of him missing a session. She took his arm and shook it gently, trying to dislodge a response.

'What about the pictures?' she said. '*The Thirty-Nine Steps* is still playing.'

Arthur nodded. It would be nice to see that film again.

They had gone last week, and in the scene where the two fugitives undressed in a hotel room while handcuffed to one another, Sarah had laid her hand on his knee. They had laced their fingers together.

She nudged him with her shoulder. 'If you like, we could sit at the back.'

He tried to smile, but there was no putting it off any longer. If he'd told her at the school gates he would now be beyond reproach.

'Actually,' he said, 'do you know, I ought to be getting along.'

He did not look at her.

'Oh,' she said, after a pause.

'I'm supposed to be meeting Louis.'

Sarah let go of his arm.

'Righto,' she said. She nodded, businesslike. 'Jolly good.' She cast around as if to make sure that she hadn't dropped anything. 'I'll leave you to it, then.'

'No, no,' Arthur said. He had phrased it wrong. 'I said we'd have the whole afternoon to ourselves, but he turned up this morning and wanted to meet, and I couldn't . . .'

She was walking over to the river, and Arthur heard the wheedling note in his voice as he followed, telling her that heaven knew he didn't *want* to be running off, certainly not when we've just—

'Just what?'

'I mean,' he said, 'I know it's bad form . . .'

She had turned from the parapet.

'Why bad form?'

'Well, one doesn't like to—'

He stopped, not knowing how it was that they were now standing on a bleak footpath having a quarrel. His feet felt greasy in his shoes. He wished he were in the washroom at the Calvary, scrubbing himself with a cold flannel.

She watched him.

'I'll leave you to it,' she said. 'I ought to be getting home.'

She walked away, hugging herself into her new coat.

When she had gone he turned and headed towards the Albert Bridge. Sometimes it was as if Sarah and Louis conspired to put him in an impossible position. Was it any wonder he'd hesitated to mention that Louis wanted to see him? She took offence whenever he spoke Louis's name, and Louis was just as bad. After the time in Dorset, Arthur had confided what had happened, hoping for a word of approval at least, but Louis was incapable of giving one, much less of admitting that he had been mistaken and that Sarah was not the dull prude he had made out. Instead he'd listened in pained silence, as if these developments only confirmed his suspicions and all he could do now was bite his tongue. And now here Arthur was on his way to answer Louis's summons. He had no desire to do so. He didn't know why he'd chosen to let Sarah down rather than disobey. The two of them were as bad as one another: why they couldn't be reasonable was beyond him. He crossed the river and began to walk along the Embankment.

Arthur had not seen Louis by choice since the beginning of the summer, when they had met for lunch in a Lyons tea room. Louis ordered a cup of tea and a packet of assorted biscuits. He arranged the biscuits in a row on his plate and began to slide them around. When Arthur said something about Walker, he looked up in surprise.

Didn't I tell you? I'll not be seeing him any more.

Arthur was dumbfounded, as much by Louis's offhand manner as by the news itself.

Which to eat first, which next, which next, and which last, Louis said. Usually the ginger is reserved until the end, of course, but there are arguments to be made for the petit beurre and even for the digestive.

What are you talking about? Arthur said. Why?

Louis broke a biscuit in half and dipped it in his tea.

I've got what I need now, he said. No reason to keep seeing him.

He swigged his tea, then tipped back on his chair to catch the attention of a waitress. My darling, he said, so sorry to be such a nuisance but might I beg the favour of having this filled with hot?

Arthur watched him smirking at the girl. It was remarkable. Had it not occurred to Louis that suddenly breaking off contact might have an effect on Walker? Did he not understand its significance for a patient who had never had an ordinary friendship? Was he unaware that Arthur had gone out on a limb to arrange it, and that Arthur was the one responsible if Walker reacted badly now?

He stared at Louis, wanting to ask these questions. Then he gave up. Louis would do what he would do, and there was no use in arguing. Arthur just hadn't imagined that the man's selfishness could extend this far. As he boarded a bus back to the hospital, he told himself that they would not be seeing one another again.

The whole of July passed without communication, and life was simpler for it, but in the second week of August they ran into one another on Malet Street. Louis looked more like himself, younger, fitter and better fed. He told Arthur that the book was going well, that he was doing nothing but writing. It was unprecedented. Every day he rose at noon and walked to Bloomsbury to see Venn, then went back to his digs and wrote until dawn. That was all. It was an ecstasy of unprocrastination. The analysis was making progress, too, and there hadn't been a whisper of his old complaint for weeks. They parted civilly and carried on in their opposite directions. Not the worst way to end things, Arthur had thought, feeling pleasantly melancholy as he walked on.

Daylight seeped through the panes of the Cross Keys, falling across the shoulders of two or three old chaps brooding over their newspapers at the bar, and across Louis where he sat at a table under a stained-glass panel. In the gloom the light touched his pint of stout, the top of his stick propped beside him and the brown paper packet undone on the table. A typescript had been opened into two stacks, the thinner face up and the thicker face down. Louis turned a sheet from one stack to the other.

Arthur sat down.

'Is that—?'

Louis nodded.

'Is it—?'

Louis nodded. 'After this pint I'm away to send it to Gryphon.' He closed his eyes and inhaled deeply.

'And then?'

'Lie a while amid the effluvia,' Louis said. 'Wait for Cope to send it back, I suppose, with a covering note disclaiming all his previous expressions of interest and begging me henceforth to seek employment in one of the analphabetic professions. But there'll be time for all that.'

He grimaced at the typescript in front of him. Then he

turned it into a single pile, squared it up and laid it in the brown paper. The top sheet was blank except for the word *Jott* in the centre.

'This was what you had to tell me?' Arthur said.

'Partly. Also that I'm going to tell Venn I've had enough.'

There was no reason to carry on with the analysis, he explained, because the work had been done. He really thought his physical complaints had given up the ghost. Venn's theory was that the migraine with its associated somatic miseries was a symptom of repressed hostility towards certain persons in his family: one in particular.

'Apparently,' he said, 'I suffer from unresolved ambivalence, which means that I can't bear consciously to acknowledge my feelings of hatred for my beloved mother. So I've repressed those feelings all my life, and these last years they've been coming out as headaches and the rest of it.'

Arthur didn't doubt that this was correct. He had assumed as much back in Dublin when he first proposed that Louis's symptoms were psychogenic. This was the silliness of the whole business: here they were, still groping towards the answer that he could have supplied years ago. But of course guessing at reasons in the abstract was no use. Avoid premature interpretations, Venn always said. There's nothing more futile than telling a truth that the patient is not yet in a position to hear.

'Once I had an attack in the middle of a session,' Louis was saying. 'Venn was delighted. Said it demonstrated the transference at work. I was experiencing antagonism towards him, he said, and since I couldn't acknowledge it consciously what with him being a figure of transferred parental authority, on came the headache. After that I kept feeling I ought to produce more of them to please him.'

He folded the brown paper around the typescript.

'I have another theory myself.'

He thought the attacks were caused by his long failure to write, he explained. He began to tie up the string. They were the symptoms of the story that wanted to be written, so that as the words finally came the pain faded away. It wasn't that he disagreed with Venn, he said: he liked that theory too, and saw no need to choose.

'Well,' Arthur said. He patted the table top and pushed back his chair. 'If that's all.'

'What are you drinking?' Louis said. He gestured towards the bar. 'Come on.'

'I'd best be getting over to the Malet.'

He stood up to leave. He had taken two steps towards the door when he stopped and turned back.

'Walker sends his regards,' he said.

Louis finished tying the string, then sat back and folded his arms, considering the statement. Arthur waited, determined not to give way. If he was ridiculous so be it.

'I could have gone on visiting,' Louis said at last. 'But it would have been because I owed it to him. He wouldn't have forgiven me for that.'

He rummaged in his jacket pocket and brought out a carpenter's pencil. He pushed his spectacles up his forehead. When Arthur left him he was writing the address on the package, scoring thick marks into the brown paper.

Towards the end of April Louis had brought a sheaf of type-written pages to the Calvary, pulling them out of his satchel and slipping them into Arthur's hand as they were parting at the gate. Arthur had been presented with dog-eared, smudged, rubber-banded typescripts often enough by now to know when Louis wanted a reader for something he had written. At least this was a slim one, no more than thirty or forty pages. It's a fragment, Louis said. Work in progress found wanting and ruthlessly excised. You might have a use for it, seeing as it's no good to me. Arthur was puzzled enough to take the pages up to his room and thumb through the sheaf at once. The thing was a single block of prose, unbroken into paragraphs, he saw with misgiving; but he turned back to the first page and began to read.

When I was a boy my mother knew my secrets, ran the first sentence.

At night I lay awake in the dark in my small bed and although she was in another part of the house she knew that I was not asleep. I knew that she knew this because she told me. She told me such things often. You came from my body and so I know everything about you. I know what you think and what you feel. I feel your every breath and the beating of your heart in my own body. You can never lie to me. This was what she said. My mother knew my secrets and I knew hers.

On the evidence of the first few lines, Louis had given up the barnacled prose of *Sham Abraham* in favour of a style that was a little stilted but straightforward enough. He would be able to say honestly that it was an improvement. Not that Louis had seemed to be looking for a response: if this was a cancelled fragment, already eliminated from Louis's book, Arthur wasn't sure what he was supposed to be doing with it. He read on. The unbroken column of text was written from the point of view of a young man, in the manner of a confessional autobiography or even the sort of monologue one might address to an analyst. The narrator lived in a world strangely stripped of proper names: he had no name of his own, and neither did his family, nor the town in which he grew up alone with his parents in a large old house from whose upper windows he could see the spire of a cathedral. The father was a remote figure, seen going to work, returning from work and retreating into his study, and only occasionally stepping forward to administer a lesson, as when the boy had spent a morning making a family of dolls with pipe cleaner bodies, cut-out paper clothing and bottle caps for heads. He showed them to the father, who pulled them apart and threw them away, telling the child that it was time to grow up. But it was the mother who dominated his thoughts, because if the father was an absence then she was his inverse, an overwhelming presence. As well as convincing the boy that she possessed a magical knowledge of his thoughts and feelings, so that he grew up in the belief that he had no privacy she could not penetrate, she taught him that her emotions were at his mercy, so that when he found her weeping in the kitchen, as he often did, he knew it was because of some betrayal that he must have committed in his mind. Just as she knew every thought that passed through his head, so he was responsible for every feeling that wrung her heart. Louis had written a portrait of a severely neurotic woman who, prompted by ungovernable emotional needs, had turned her relationship with her son into one of complete mutual dependence. When the narrator was sent away to school he described his departure in the same flat tone he had used from the start.

She gave a coin to the man who had carried my luggage. She plucked a thread from the sleeve of my new overcoat. She did not touch my hand. She did not observe my face. I climbed into the carriage and seated myself by the window. She stood on the platform and I saw that she was impatient to be gone. I waved but she did not notice. The engine moved and she turned to depart.

Like everything in the young man's world, the school at which he arrived was nameless. It was a shadowy place where halls and playing fields were dim and empty, portraits of benefactors lined long corridors and boys in top hats and tailcoats moved along stone cloisters in the middle distance, always too far away for their voices to be heard. To the young man it was an uncanny imitation of a school, where the ancient stone buildings were stage flats and masters and boys went about their routines like black-clad automata with no glint of life in their eyes. In spite of this, he seemed to settle in well, doing all that was required of him and acquitting himself respectably in his lessons and games. *As an automaton I was exemplary,* he said. *I took my place among the dead figures in motion.* The young man's first months of school passed with no hints of friendship with other boys, nor even any notion that they were individuals with whom one might conceivably become friends. He was alone in a society of puppets.

For some reason to which the young man was not privy,

he could not go home when the term ended, so he remained at the school, which was deserted except for a skeleton staff and a handful of other boys with nowhere else to go. As he wandered the empty buildings and their wintry grounds his isolation seemed complete, and yet this was not so, because he was becoming aware, gradually and dimly at first, of a surprising fact. He had discovered that another place existed nearby. He had not known about it before, but now that it had come to his awareness its fascination grew on him by the hour and he set to finding out as much about it as he could. Its name was Lissen. The young man devoted much puzzlement to the question of what kind of place it was. Like the school, it was a cluster of old stone buildings set in parkland. It was inhabited by a large number of young people, mostly female, and for a time the young man speculated that the place was simply a girls' school, the counterpart of his own. But he knew this could not be the answer. For one thing, there were boys there too, though they were unrecognisable creatures, living freely as they did among the budding women rather than stewing their youths away in a fug of unrelieved maleness. *I also suspected that some at Lissen could not be described as either female or male.* And although there were older figures, mistresses and matrons among the young, it was obvious that Lissen was not essentially concerned with education, or not in any sense that the young man's schoolmasters would recognise. Even the climate there was different. While the young man waited out a season of lead-grey skies and damp draughty rooms, winter in Lissen was vivid. Crisp sunlight released the colours of the stone walls and set deep regular shadows in place behind the pillars of the colonnades. Gouts of steam burst from the mouths of the girls skating on the lake. They

115

chased one another across lawns alight with frost and disappeared among the trees. The young man thought about Lissen all the time. He wondered whether they knew about him there, and whether they would welcome him if he came. Sometimes a knowing flicker in the faces of the girls hinted at an answer that he could not think about for fear of feeling an excitement he could not bear. *In the rich darkness they murmured together.* It was not clear quite where he believed the place was to be found, or what kind of existence he attributed to it. Sometimes it seemed only a fantasy, a private story to dream over and embellish at will, but at other times he felt Lissen was an actual place, lying just over the horizon so that he might reach it if he knew the way. Occasionally he became convinced that it lay closer still: it was somehow hidden in the same volume of space that his own school occupied, so that if he could penetrate the surface of the ordinary world, peeling it away like a strip of wallpaper, the light would pour over him and he could step through. But he did not know how, so through that winter holiday and into the spring term he stayed as he was, an obedient automaton performing its tasks and dreaming of the bright world where he had never been. At the end of the school year he went back to his parents. Lissen was more distant when he was at home. *The image had retreated from me and yet I cherished it still*, the narrator said. *Inside myself I turned always towards the fleck of sunken brightness. My mother did not know this. It was mine alone.* The young man had learned long ago to present an unreal self to the unreal world around him, and this he continued to do, so that as years went by he remained the good son that he had always been. He went to school each term and was a model pupil, then returned each holiday to his mother, who remained intent on penetrating

116

every corner of his heart, and his father, whose health had deteriorated so that he seldom stirred from a cane armchair in the study. None of it could touch him, because his real self was sealed inside where no one had ever been. In there, where he was safe, he could gaze forever into the brimming light.

The years went by without touching him, and soon it was time to go up to university. He had won a scholarship, and, since what happened in the outer world made no difference to him, he went where he was expected to go. *It was best always to consent to the wishes of the dead world regarding the disposal of my body.* The city was not named. The young man spent his first days there in a light trance: he walked along streets lined with secretive old buildings, under long walls of yellow stone with high leaded windows, glimpsing inaccessible gardens through iron gates. He saw terraces of red and yellow houses vanishing away down side streets, and a river that flowed under stone bridges and through trailing vegetation. It was a brisk autumn, and as he drifted around in the sunlight, ignored by the undergraduates and townspeople, it came to him that he was on the brink of a discovery. At length he found himself in the quadrangle of his own college, a stone box filled with evening sun. A slant pyramid of apricot shadow stood in one corner of the quad. The light glowed in every blade of grass in the lawn, flashed from the pane of a window half open overhead, and revealed the weave of the black straw hat worn by a young woman stepping discreetly from one of the staircases. As he stood there he realised what it was that he had discovered. The fantasy of Lissen had faded over the years, but he had never lost sight of it entirely, and now it told him what he needed to know. The light that filled the quadrangle was the same light that had overwhelmed him through that winter holiday. The voices that murmured in Lissen were the same voices that called along these narrow streets. In some way that the young man could not fathom, the place of his adolescent imaginings and the new city in which he had arrived were one and the same. Seen in this new form, the old images were somewhat altered, the elements of Lissen appearing in new attitudes and configurations of sunlight and shadow, stone and water, eyes and voices. But the essence was the same, and this meant that all his certainties were wrong. The outer world was not dead after all, because the glory that lived in his dream of Lissen was alive here too, present all around him. He did not try to guess why the world had practised this deceit, but he knew that an all-consuming task now lay ahead. Two pigeons watched him from a housetop: he saw that they were staring out of reality as eyes stare from a head, and saw too the affinity of this sign with the small upper windows that held thumbnails of sky, with the transitory spaces among the leaves of trees and with the sliding of two omnibuses past one another in the High Street. All took part in a common symbolism. The edges of something vast and singular were showing, and he must act lest he miss his chance. He could not guess how it should be that the universe was one single, enormous message, coming from a single origin, moving towards a single end and turning in its entirety on a single pivot which was himself, but he could not delay to ponder. He set to work to read the message, to hear the sentence that the world was whispering for him. Light in leaves, shadow on stone, the glances of eyes and sounds of voices were his to grasp. When the mood took him he spoke to his fellow human beings about his discoveries, gifting them the tiny particles of the truth that could be put into ordinary language, and he saw the wonder dawn in their faces. His motives were not selfish. He could not yet say what form his offering to the world would take, though even now, with the first step barely made on the journey, he foresaw that it would amount to a new way of being for every soul in creation. For now he was content to watch for the signs and follow where they led. Of particular promise was one of the women's colleges. Its location, hidden at the end of a leafy avenue in a quiet district at the edge of a parkland, and its outward appearance, with a demure white campanile rising behind a front wall of dark-red brick, placed it in an unusually precise relation with the angles and atmospheres of Lissen and made it likely that much might be revealed here. The young man took to spending hours near the front of the college, loitering under the trees where he could study the significance of light and shade passing across the brick and of the figures that passed in and out. Sometimes they glanced at him, and one day, as he stood watching for the signs, a figure in a black straw hat walked along the pavement. She lifted the brim enough to catch his eye, and smiled. You're going to get yourself into trouble, young man, she said, and stepped through the gate. He reeled away from the scene, turning the words she had spoken back and forth, examining them from every side, trying to establish their nature as warning, as clue, as promise of revelation. *My researches were advancing more quickly than I had anticipated.* Eventually, sitting on a bench beside the canal with morning dew forming on his coat, he decided that returning to that gate was out of the question. His enquiries there had been answered, and he must seek elsewhere for the next sign or syllable, which would be the last. *The meaning of things was at hand.* He wandered and watched, haunting the places that he felt as most propitious, and his patience was rewarded when he saw her step from an alley on the High Street. He went to meet her. As she drew close, he noticed that her hat was of felt, not straw, and that her clothes, her gait and her face were not as they had been, and he almost faltered; but he held firm, guessing that here was a final test of his resolve. Now that the time had come, he saw the form the revelation would take. He and she would come face to face, and they would speak to one another. *Each would speak words that were true.* He stepped in front of the woman and opened his mouth, but the universe did not reveal itself. Instead the words died in his throat. She gave him a doubtful look and hurried on her way, and, as surely as a mirror that has been falling all these years must hit the ground at last, the world shattered. Light splintered, space collapsed, time broke. The young man was devoured alive by something evil and mindless. He was torn to pieces cell by cell and his dust scattered across a dark ocean to sink slowly in depths that had no meaning and no end.

After an infinity of darkness he found himself lying in a bed of nettles beside a footpath. He had lost his shoes, his socks and his shirt, and he was wearing a coat that he had never seen before. The spires of the city marked the distance. Close but out of sight, a river ran smooth and fast. None of these things mattered, because the world was dead. Birds rustled in the bushes, the river gurgled in its eddies and the far-off city grumbled, but he was in the ashes of a universe that had ended. He walked through meadow and woodland, ignoring the brambles that caught at his legs, slowly making sense of what he had learned. The sun set and rose as he walked, then set and rose again. It was obvious now that the world had been destroyed by a parasite, a mindless, invisible, virulent organism

120

that entered the human body, ate away from the inside until the victim was hollow, and then animated the shell of what it had consumed, so that what gestured and spoke like a person and went through all the motions of a life was in fact a dead puppet. The parasite had long since infected every human being in existence, so that for countless generations no one had truly been alive. All the centuries of human struggle had been a mechanical pageant enacted by nobody, on nobody, for nobody. *A purposeless churning.* For a time the young man puzzled over why he had been singled out as the witness. *What aspect of insentient creation had troubled itself to demiurgy on my account.* There was no mistaking the fact that he was the only survivor, and as he walked and the sun rose and set, the explanation came to him. The parasite was transmitted not by physical contagion or airborne germs, but in words. Whenever one person used words to communicate with another, the infection was passed on. Thus his survival. He had spent his life keeping his real self sealed up where no words could break through, but now there was a crack in the shell and he would never again be quite safe from the horrors that he had tasted, the mindless evil and the meaningless abyss. To risk it again was unthinkable. Walking beside the river now, he came to a footbridge and paused halfway across. The water ran strong below, the core of the river drawing itself forward like a great liquid rope, and he saw how much safer he would be if he were submerged: water filling every opening in his body so that no words could find their way in. *Ears, eyes, mouth, lungs and entrails, all stopped.* That it would mean the end of him was of no importance so long as he could escape the plague that had annihilated the world. The young man climbed the parapet.

The typewritten pages had ended there. Turning over the last sheet, Arthur had pushed back his chair and sat up, easing his spine. It was night outside, and the room was dark except for the disc of light from the desk lamp. The fictitious young man certainly resembled Walker on the surface: the background, the family circumstances, the education and the attempted suicide matched what was known of his history. Perhaps the inner life was Walker's also. It could be that Louis had somehow extracted a history from the patient and had set it faithfully down, mapping the path that had brought him to his leap from the bridge and in due course to the Calvary. On the other hand, perhaps Louis had made it up.

Arthur thought of that night's reading as he left Louis in the Cross Keys. There was time to walk to the Malet, so he set off away from the river. For a few minutes after finishing the typescript, he'd felt that Louis had given him the key that would unlock the analysis: perhaps, equipped with this insight into Walker's psychosis, he would be able to make contact at last. But almost at once he had realised his mistake. Even if Louis's story did bear some resemblance to the patient's inner life, there was no use in it, because the story allowed no possibility of help or improvement. It was so taken up with seeing things from the sick young man's point of view that it refused to admit there was anything wrong with him. Taking things on Walker's terms was all very admirable, but the fact remained that the man was ill, and he would be better off if he were well. Could even Louis think otherwise?

A middle-aged woman walking a West Highland terrier gave him a look. He'd been arguing with himself under his breath. He grinned in what he hoped was a reassuring way, and walked on. If Louis was right, then everyone was stymied.

Arthur had tried his best, checking every day to make sure that he was thinking of his patient as a person and not merely a set of symptoms or a problem to be solved, remembering that whatever Walker's delusions might be, they seemed real to him. But Louis was asking him to accept that there was truly nothing to choose between those delusions and reality.

He'd once had a glimpse of what it might be like. One night in Dublin, twenty years old and hung over, he had fallen asleep in his college room in the early evening. He woke up just before midnight, but it was as if he had slipped on the step between the dream and the waking world, so that he scrambled out of bed not knowing where he was, not knowing his name, only knowing that it was an emergency and he must take action at once. All around him a disaster was in progress, but he didn't know what the danger was or what to do about it. He was surrounded by a jumble of forms, bodies in space without meaning. He had forgotten the words for the electric lamp burning above, for the darkness beyond the glass and for his own hammering heart muscle. He stood paralysed in the middle of the room for an unmeasurable length of time – perhaps half a minute – and then the meaning flowed back. The nameless forms became a chair, a desk, the wall, the bed. Front Square was calm outside the window. There was no disaster. He made a cup of tea and was himself again, but he had not forgotten the moments of terror. It was the closest he'd come to visiting the place where Walker lived.

And that wasn't enough, he thought. He crossed Shaftesbury Avenue. It was plain by now that he would never really know how Walker saw the world. He would always be a tyrant in a white coat. No wonder Walker preferred Louis's company, Louis who liked him all the better for his madness. Other people tell us about ourselves, and we all want someone who will tell us the story we'd like to believe in.

It was the same with Sarah. He only wanted her to try and see things from his point of view. He didn't know why she took such exception to Louis. He didn't understand why she had quarrelled and gone off in a sulk this afternoon, or why she had looked so disappointed as she turned away. Worse than disappointed, she had looked like someone concealing physical pain, as if she were hurt by any suggestion that Arthur's oldest friendship still had a claim on him.

He couldn't understand it, he thought, walking up Gower Street. He turned into Malet Place, where once he had seen her waiting at the foot of the clinic's steps. She had turned towards him as he hurried forward to meet her, and as they walked away from the Malet into green twilight there was no question of understanding or misunderstanding, because in that moment there had been no doubts at all: he had seen the choice he had to make and had known that it was no choice, because his doubts were gone, cast off like Louis and all the other burdens of his past, which he could shed, now, for her.

Remembering that evening, he climbed the steps to the clinic. But when the office door opened and Venn came out, bowing, holding his hat in anticipation of the usual walk, Arthur could only murmur an apology. He turned and ran back out into the street, and did not stop until he was at Sarah's door.

THREE

Sarah muttered to herself and threw off the blankets. The bed-springs jangled as she swung her feet to the floor. Arthur roused himself enough to see her sitting on the edge of the mattress, her head bowed and her hands pressed to her abdomen. After a minute she breathed out carefully. She edged around the end of the bedstead, ducking under the slope of the ceiling, feeling her way in the half-light. She paused to steady herself on the doorframe as she left the room.

Arthur heard the creak of the lavatory door. He reached over his side of the bed, found his wristwatch on the floor and peered at the face. He could doze another twenty minutes. He lay down again, pulling the covers to his chin to keep out the cold air, and listened. She was taking a long time.

They had got used to disappointment, which had come punctually for the first six months of trying, and they had not let it trouble them unduly, telling themselves that if not this month then perhaps the next, that they could afford to be patient and that it was too soon to start worrying. Then Sarah missed her usual date. A day passed, and then another. By the time she was a week late they were padding secretively around the flat, saying little and never referring to the possibility directly. They had come up with a brilliant notion that would be lost if they tried to put it into words too soon. Arthur caught himself imagining that the crucial events were taking place not inside her body, right here in front of him, but in some other space that was vast and dark and impossibly distant, as if heavenly bodies were rolling to conjunction in another solar system. More time passed and they held their tongues, but by the time she was fully two weeks late they were catching one another's eyes, all but allowing themselves to admit what they were thinking. Without saying it aloud, they had agreed that disappointments were done with. So that now, if her taking so long in the lavatory meant that they had got it wrong and it was to be disappointment after all, it would be a disappointment of a different kind.

He heard the scrape of the chain, the rattle of the mechanism, the gurgle and cascade, the knocking of the pipes and the final belch of air. Water ran, and there was silence as she passed through the small, jumbled room that served as their parlour and kitchen. He lifted the covers and she climbed back in beside him. The bed tinkled and shifted on its joints. The tarnished brass frame had been in residence when they took the flat, and filled the room almost entirely. It must have been built in here.

She turned her back to Arthur and shouldered her way into the warmth. He moved a hand to her stomach. In reply, the chilly soles of her feet pressed on his insteps.

She sighed and settled, and her breathing grew heavy, but he lay awake. They were still safe, then. It was still true. Everything that had happened in the past was a funnel narrowing to this space of heartbeats in which the two of them lay together in a warm bed in a cold room, in the dark of dawn, holding one another and knowing what the future was to be. For this, Sarah had sat beside him in the front seat of the soft-topped, racing-green Austin 7 Tourer that he had hired to drive to Dorset for the wedding. A white silk scarf patterned with strawberries had been knotted around her throat, its ends flying in the wind with the ends of her hair, and he had worn a pair of thin leather gloves bought especially for the occasion. Motoring down from London had seemed like a lark, as if they had been playing at getting married in style.

On that journey Louis had been crammed in the back seat of the car, his knees sticking up around his ears, his arms folded and his chin buried in the lapels of his overcoat. Each time Arthur caught sight of him in the rear-view mirror he looked a little more miserable. His head wobbled with the jolting of the suspension. When they arrived in the village they dropped Sarah off at her father's house, then drove on to the hotel. Louis brightened up a little at the sight of the place, with its cobwebbed attic windows and its exterior plaster eaten away by sea air, and speculated aloud on whether there was a word in English for precisely this mixture of the dingy and the sinister. Arthur had imagined that they would spend the evening together: he was hazy on the duties of the best man but he had been picturing a night of heartfelt whiskies in the hotel bar, with fond recollections of the past and then the future envisioned, Louis telling him that he was now a proper man who was stepping forward into the prime of his life and that this was right and good and worthy of affirmation. In the event, after Arthur had put his suitcase in his room and hung up his suit for tomorrow, the best man was nowhere to be found and the groom had an early night. In the morning Arthur took up a position at the church entrance, fiddling with his buttonhole, while Louis mooched off around the back with his hands in the trouser pockets of his old black suit. When the bridal party came into view, Arthur went to fetch him from where he was kicking his heels and smoking a cigarette among the headstones.

After the ceremony Arthur and Sarah stood outside the church and greeted the guests as they filed past. Sarah, dressed in a dark-blue dress and a coat with a fur collar, stood at his side, smiling and nodding at unidentified friends and relations, accepting congratulations and waggish advice. Arthur did his best to follow her example, as if they were an official couple performing some civic role. Perhaps this is what it means to be married, he thought; perhaps everything is settled now as far as she's concerned. But then, as the last of the guests moved away, Sarah brushed her knuckles against his and caught his eye.

Hello.

A couple of stragglers came out of the church, and Sarah threw herself into their arms. You remember Cicely, don't you, she said, and this is Edith. Arthur shook hands with a young woman whose high forehead crinkled sardonically when he asked whether she had met Sarah through the Women's Health and Beauty Association as well. No, she said, with a wry emphasis that he did not understand. Not exactly, she added, as she moved on.

In the hotel bar Arthur sipped a glass of mild while Sarah spoke to her friends with large gestures and whoops of assent. Louis set to work winning the favour of the elderly female guests. He moved around the room, a firm masculine figure, straightening his back so that he looked inches taller and grinning his most wolfish grin. His eyes gleamed grey behind the steel-rimmed spectacles. He leaned down to Sarah's tiniest aunt to share a confidence, his lips at her ear, then reared up again as she laughed and touched his arm. Minutes later he was telling a story to three well-upholstered cousins-once-removed of Sarah's, who were hanging on his words, delighted. Sarah's sister stood a little way off, immobile in the stiff black silk of her bridesmaid's dress, wearing the expression of one who knows that the entire scene has been devised for her mortification. Arthur's parents were in conference with the vicar. The beer had a silty texture. Someone tapped his elbow and Edith was beside him, knocking her glass against his.

I hope, she said, that you're going to make it up to her. Arthur began to smile, guessing that a joke was to follow, but Edith was straight-faced. You're aware of the marriage bar, she said. Today is the end of her teaching career. I trust it'll be worth it. Across the room Louis had an audience of aunts and great-aunts in fits of giggles.

Later, on his way to the gents, Arthur encountered Cicely coming out of the billiard room at the end of the corridor. She slipped past, threading a strand of hair behind her ear. Arthur was about to go into the lavatory when Louis, too, emerged from the billiard room. He coughed into his fist and gave Arthur a reassuring best-man-is-on-top-of-things nod as he returned to the reception.

The dinner was well-done beef, boiled potatoes and a heavy Yorkshire pudding, with red wine that tasted exactly like the beer and shared its sourness also with the rhubarb pie and the coffee. Sarah's father got to his feet. When the room was silent, he blew through his nostrils a few times and opened his speech, to general laughter, with a couple of obscure threats against Arthur's person. No father wants his daughter to marry an Irishman, he went on, but it could have been worse. This one's always had peculiar notions. I wouldn't have been surprised if she'd gone for a gypsy or a Chinaman. So when you look at it that way, a Paddy isn't too bad. Satisfied with this, he sat down, and Arthur got up, wondering whether Mr Beamish had spoken off the cuff or learned his text by heart, and impressed either way with the ease of his delivery.

Arthur had toiled for a long time over his own speech. For weeks he had been struggling to write down what he had to say about the occasion, covering sheet after sheet with reflections on what it all meant, but finding that when he crossed out whatever sounded false or nonsensical he was left with nothing but platitudes. It meant a great deal to have family and friends gathered here today; he felt that he was the luckiest man in the world; he would always do his best for Sarah. These statements sounded like the flattest clichés, but the trouble was that they were true. When he had clutched his brow, chewed his pen and strained his moral and imaginative fibres to articulate the truth of what he saw and felt and knew about their approaching marriage, this was what he had come up with, and so he stood in the hotel dining room mouthing the banal phrases, hoping that their meaning would come through. Louis listened gravely, his right hand resting by his coffee cup, his middle finger tapping on the tablecloth now and then as it did when he wanted a smoke. He gave no speech himself.

And then all that remained was to slip out as some of the guests began to leave and others settled themselves in the hotel's saloon. The sun was sinking as they walked to the car, followed by Louis, who was carrying their suitcases in a

132

good-natured parody of flunkeydom. You'll be all right then, Arthur said. Never worry, Louis said. Once you're in the clear I'll make my own escape. He hefted the cases into the boot and slammed the lid. Ceres' blessing so is on you, he told them, and was framed in the rear-view mirror, against the red sky above the cove, as the car crawled out of the village. Thank God for that, Sarah said. And perhaps this was the purpose of a wedding, Arthur thought, if not of the entire institution of marriage: to make possible the moment in which the bride and groom can flee from all that grotesque rigmarole into what they now understand is their life together.

They drove along lanes between high hedges, Arthur at the wheel and Sarah reading a map. It was dark by the time they reached the guest house they had booked. They collected their key, signed the register and carried their bags upstairs to a room in which the wooden bedstead, the old-fashioned wash-stand and the murky mezzotint on the wall were more remarkable than any furniture they had ever seen, and the air itself was charged with promise, as if the future had an odour of mothballs and musty bed-sheets. They had made it: they were on the run. Too excited to settle, they walked out to explore the unknown town. They followed the sound of music to a pub where three old men were playing fiddle, banjo and tin whistle while others sang and stamped their feet. It did not look the kind of place to take kindly to outsiders, but the men recognised Arthur and Sarah for the happy fugitives they were, and made them welcome. When Arthur confirmed that they were just married, a bottle was produced from under the bar, and he had never tasted spirit like it, so sweet and salty, as potent as the sea. Sarah asked for a song she loved from long ago and the men knew it well, and sang. It was very late by the time they walked into the night, hearing waves breaking in the darkness and holding one another so that they did not stumble until they fell into their room, calling themselves husband and wife and undressing one another as if to do so were a strange new transgression. They passed out at dawn, curled together in the bed, his lips to her nape, just as they lay curled, now, under the sloping roof of their cold attic room.

Sarah was sound asleep again, so he eased himself out of bed, gathered up his clothes and went into the other room where he could get ready without disturbing her. The early weeks were exhausting, he knew, with the hidden changes taking place, and she had to sleep as much as she could. He washed himself standing up in the bathtub while the kettle boiled, and dressed while the tea drew. As he finished tying his shoelaces she came out of the bedroom, put her arms on his shoulders and leaned against him, swollen-eyed and tousled, with warmth coming off her through the cotton night-dress. She was carrying herself carefully, as if already the balance of her body was beginning to shift. Taking care not to tread on her bare feet, he smoothed the cotton and asked how she was. He would have to start rationing himself. He'd madden her if he spent the next nine months demanding to know how she was feeling all the time.

She straightened up, placing her hands on her abdomen.

'It aches,' she said. 'But in a good way.'

She lowered herself to one of the kitchen chairs, and winced.

'Things are happening.' She breathed in deeply. 'Getting started.'

Arthur put on his overcoat, then hitched the knees of his trousers and squatted beside her.

'Don't do anything, will you? I mean, try and rest.'

134

'I promise.' She chuckled. 'I think I'll tell Cicely tonight. And Edith.'

'Tell them,' he said. 'You're not still going?'

'I'm not suddenly made of glass.'

'Right, no.' He hesitated. 'You're going to tell them?'

'I don't see why I shouldn't.'

She slid her fingers into his hair and smiled down at him. He saw that she did not mind what he said. He could be as solicitous as he liked and it would not disturb her calm, because now she had resolved all doubts. She was holding the future inside herself. Her fingers worked deeper into his hair. They gripped and drew him to his feet.

'It's time you got to work.'

After a four-day honeymoon along the coast, Arthur and Sarah had driven back to London and moved into the bedsitter in Pimlico where they would live for the first six months of their marriage. There was a deal table, an armchair upholstered in bilious orange and two single beds. The one-bar heater was too feeble to warm the room, and the window, which lacked a curtain, gave a view across weed-choked yards to a canal. A miniature sink was plumbed into one corner of the room, but the bathroom and dank lavatory were at the other end of a corridor, shared with other tenants. The kitchen was shared too, a tiny room at the back of the house equipped with a portable electric ring for cooking. In the months they spent there they never saw anyone beside themselves, though they often heard doors slamming, and occasionally found the cistern refilling in the lavatory or discovered a smell of scorched grease in the kitchen. In their room they pushed the beds together, but the springs were so bad that when they lay down they fell into two separate troughs of sagging mattress. On the first night they clasped hands across the join and looked up at the maps of mildew on the ceiling. All in all it was unimprovable as a setting for the start of married life.

Arthur had just started at the Bradshaw and the days were long, but each evening, coming back late, he was revived by the thrill of descending the three steps to the battered front door and letting himself into a house as ugly and anonymous as all the other houses on the street. He would press the timer switch and climb the stairs to the room, where he would exclaim over the small transformations that Sarah had brought about during the day. At the end of his first week in the job, he came home to find that she had bought two pieces of checked cotton, pinning one across the window as a curtain and spreading the other on the table. The night being warm, she had opened the window so that the fabric bellied and sank in the flow of air. A pair of stockings was drip-drying over the sink. She made him sit down at the table, on which she had arranged two jam jars, one containing a candle stub and the other a bunch of wild flowers she had gathered along the canal. She poured red wine into the crystal goblets that had been a wedding present from a distant but generous relation. The wine was cheap and vinegary and the second sip was twice as delicious as the first. They ate fried potatoes covered with spicy tomato ketchup from a tall glass bottle with Chinese writing on the label. Sarah moved around him, barefoot in her blue satin dressing-gown, clearing the plates to the floor and opening a paper carton that contained an exotic sweet: a dense slab made of thin layers of pastry and chopped pistachio nuts soaked in honey. It's called baklava, she said. It's my

136

favourite, he said. Let's have baklava every day. As she refilled their goblets and the unfriendly grumble of Pimlico sounded close and continuous outside the window, Arthur thought that he could live like this forever.

Sarah did not seem to agree, in spite of all that she had done to make the room into a spick-and-span nest for a pair of married lovers. He couldn't see why she was in such a hurry to move, but he couldn't deny that the place she chose was suitable. Wesley Street was a placid avenue of tall red-brick terraces with a horse chestnut tree on the corner. Spiked capsules rolled underfoot. The flat was four flights up an oblong stairwell with a worn wood banister. Sarah could hardly wait to show him the small, clean flat with the slotlike kitchen tucked at one end and the immovable brass bedstead filling the bedroom. She had reached an arrangement for them to rent an extra room on the ground floor of the building: this was to be Arthur's consulting room, where he could see the private patients that Venn wanted him to start taking on for analysis. The room was in a bit of a state at the moment, she said, but she had persuaded the landlord to let her fix it up. It would give her something useful to do.

It was a relief that she could occupy her time. In the first weeks in the new flat, he sometimes imagined a tap on his elbow and Edith asking: how would you like it, if *she* swanned off every morning to do her oh so important work in the great wide world, and left *you* here alone to get the dinner in and do the laundry and scrub out the bathtub? But Sarah had a talent for finding worthwhile activities. She painted the flat. She was expert at tracking down cheap, decent, second-hand furniture and pictures, and within weeks had equipped the flat with a set of four bentwood bistro chairs, a sideboard, a dining table, a boxy cane armchair and a two-seater sofa, slightly threadbare but still rather grand-looking, with deep-buttoned bottle-green upholstery. She went zealously to her Health and Beauty Association classes and played tennis with Cicely twice a week, on top of which Edith had persuaded both Sarah and Cicely to take up self-defence. One ought to know how to subdue an aggressor, Edith said, and so they were going to a ladies' ju-jitsu class in East Putney. At Arthur's request, one night Sarah put on the special cotton pyjamas she had acquired for the purpose: she gave a twirl, then demonstrated how she could pin his arm behind his back, sweep his legs from underneath him and hold him face down on their new rug in such a way that he couldn't get up. He strained and heaved until she relented and let him turn over. She settled herself more comfortably and leant down to him with a forgiving look in her eyes.

The following Saturday morning she was in the bedroom putting up her hair when the bell rang. Arthur went down to open the door and Cicely and Edith walked into the hall. They were draped in gold-and-green sashes. Sarah came down, glamorous in a tweed skirt suit and pearl necklace and her own sash, and accepted the money tin that Edith handed her. They were going to spend the day collecting on Oxford Street, because the Women's Liberation League was having a fund-raising push. He watched from the window as the three women walked down the street and turned the corner. He had not completely grasped what went on at the meetings that Sarah had been going to on Thursday evenings – it had, in fact, taken him some time to realise that the Liberation League was an entirely different enterprise from the Health and Beauty

Association – but it always gave him a proud, possessive feeling to see her setting out with her WLL badge on her lapel, and he liked to stay up until she arrived home, late and excited, a wife who was not content with conventional domesticity but who cultivated interests of her own. At any rate, it showed how much Louis knew.

Now Arthur descended the stairs, running his hand along the smooth-worn wood. At the bottom he glanced back at the flat, four flights above. Since moving in, he had had dreams in which the stairwell was much larger and curled up into itself like the interior of a nautilus shell, the hand-polished banister spiralling away to vanish at an impossible height.

He stepped on to Wesley Street, pulled the street door shut behind him and set off towards the tram stop. These days he enjoyed the bustle of it, joining the thickening crowds as the city went to its day's work. To pass through it was to be ignored, shouldered, scowled at, treated as obstacle and inconvenience, and yet he had come to like it, because by taking the city's knocks you earned your right to be part of its great flow. You proved yourself its equal. For many of his patients a commute like this would be intolerable: they would feel themselves dissolving. Even a year ago, Arthur would have felt something similar himself – but then, looking back, the Calvary had been a period of strange confinement, as if he himself had been ill and was only now clear of his convalescence.

It was thanks to Sarah that he was not still working there. If not for her, he would have accepted the extension to his contract and would be there right now, trapped in the drudgery they wanted him for, growing ever less likely to move on. He should find a way to tell her that she had done all this and that he was grateful, but really there was no need, because she knew. This morning, as they woke, the shape of things had been clear to see. The funnel of the past curled and narrowed into the present: a shape both geometric and natural. This, he thought, was the shape she had made. A stairwell, a spiral shell, a space inside her where the future could lodge and grow.

The Bradshaw Hospital stood in Denmark Hill, ideally situated near the railway station and the tram line. The Calvary was a hospital that turned in on itself behind its walls and its woodland, but the Bradshaw was not like that. It was on sociable terms with the surrounding city, so that Arthur could hop down from his tram, walk part way along the hospital's compact neoclassical front, trot up a short flight of steps and push through the revolving door to enter the foyer.

And yet once you were inside the Bradshaw it was no less a self-contained world than the Calvary. In this world the air was dry and warm, the acoustics were muffled, the floor was lined with tough linoleum and the walls protected by indestructible mushroom-coloured paint. He passed the library, the dispensary and the path lab, and stopped in at the Hospital Secretary's office to collect the notes for the morning round. As he gathered the files he nodded a greeting to the secretary herself, Mrs Kempe, who granted him a glance over her half-moon spectacles. Mrs Kempe was an ironclad woman in late middle age who bore the titanic weight of the hospital's daily business on her shoulders and therefore hated above all to have her time wasted. Arthur liked to think that he had earned a niche in her administrator's heart by recognising this from the beginning and never impinging on her with any but the most essential of requests, stated as concisely as possible.

He left the office. In this world the corridors, which smelled of rubber and disinfectant, were flooded at all times with strong artificial light. The doors were heavy and metal-plated, their hinges covered by thick black rubber strips and their windows reinforced with wire mesh. At each corridor junction a bank of signposts gave you your bearings.

Arthur crossed the sealed bridge connecting the central building with the female ward block. On the other bridge, another white-coated figure was crossing to the male block. The figure was indistinct behind the smoked glass, but it looked like Jacobs. The female block, like the male, contained three wards, each with twenty-four beds, arranged over three storeys with the most serious cases on the ground floor and the mildest disorders on the top. Arthur climbed a flight of stairs and let himself into the ward, which was not locked. The main wards of the Bradshaw were never locked, because hospital policy was against certification. No patient was to be treated against his or her will. This principle could only go so far in practice, and a small separate block in the hospital gardens did house a locked ward for those needing high supervision, but even there patients were not mechanically restrained. With a sufficient ratio of attendants to patients we can dispense with such inhumane methods, Hassel had told Arthur at the interview for the job.

The interview had been Arthur's first encounter with the Medical Superintendent of the Bradshaw. Ernest Hassel carried himself with an air of preoccupation and a forward stoop that looked like the result of a collapsed vertebra, as if his responsibilities had imprinted themselves on his body.

His manner was confidential as he explained that the Bradshaw was conceived and run as a hospital that would prevent admissions to asylums by intervening in mental illness in its early, curable stages. We are interested in *acute recoverable cases*, Hassel said several times, his eyes bulging under the long tufts of his eyebrows. Arthur began to assure him that this was the attitude at the Calvary as well, until he realised Hassel wanted him to agree that the two institutions were entirely unalike, the Calvary belonging to psychiatry's past while the Bradshaw embodied the future. The size, organisation and ethos of the Bradshaw, Hassel said, were such as to avoid the dehumanising effects on both patients and healers of the routines of large asylums and even middling-scale sanatoria. Here there was no stasis, no hardening of habit and no institutionalisation. Patients passed continually through the hospital, always in dynamic process towards health, benefiting from the interested attention of physicians and students who benefited in turn, never forget, from their encounters with the patients. It was a place for discussion and enquiry, with patients and physicians working together for the greater knowledge, deeper understanding and more humane and efficacious treatment of mental disease. Hassel wrung his hands as if he cared greatly for Arthur's good opinion of the Bradshaw's philosophy.

The top female ward currently housed eighteen women, varying in age from sixteen to fifty-nine years and recovering from conditions including neurasthenia, obsessionalism, anxiety, general neurosis, manic-depressive psychosis and hysteria. They were on the top ward because they were doing well, and all could hope to leave the hospital soon: this kind of round was largely a matter of monitoring progress and deciding who looked ready to be discharged. He checked the notes. Mrs Morley might get home today if all was as it should be. He nodded to the charge nurse and began the round.

At the Calvary a single ward round had been enough to leave him drained for the rest of the day. It was embarrassing to think of how poorly he had done that work and how much worry it had cost him – remarkable, too, that he had managed it without causing any serious disasters, considering how small a clue he'd had of what he was supposed to be doing. But he could forgive his former self all that, because nowadays a round held no fears. He could circulate through the ward feeling brisk and friendly, wishing good morning to the nurses, stopping long enough with each patient to hear anything that she needed to tell him. Some were eager to assure him that all the news was good, while others merely tolerated the inter-ruption. To Arthur it made no difference: he spoke gently and firmly, listened closely and sympathetically, was sceptical yet benign. Playing the authority figure still didn't come naturally, but he fancied that this worked to his advantage. With the usual sensitivity of a psychiatric ward's population, the women knew that he got no satisfaction from striding around the place dispensing judgments. He did it for their benefit, not to assuage private insecurity or gratify professional libido or make himself feel generally important. They sensed this and responded well. As he made his circuit the ward settled into a placid mood that reminded him a little of postnatal wards he had known.

One young woman scowled as he approached, so he took the time to sit down and speak to her about how she had been getting on. She snorted and rolled her eyes, but Arthur did not mind. It was a question of tone, and after a minute's exchange, hardly more than pleasantries on his part and monosyllables on hers, she bowed her head, accepting that she was not allowed to give up on the work of getting better. He wished her good morning and continued along the ward. If only he'd been half so competent back in the Calvary days; but it had all been necessary, he now understood. Making the mistakes there had meant he could get it right here. Some things must end so that others can begin. So too with Louis. That friendship had reached its natural end on the day he married Sarah. Soon afterwards Louis had set off for a stint of European travel, not saying precisely where he intended to go, or why he was going: he had made arrangements that would take him as far as Hamburg, but after that nothing was certain except that he intended to be away for a long time. And the fact was that what Louis did was no longer Arthur's business. Arthur went to Victoria to see him off, but it was a formality. They stood side by side on the platform, and at length Louis mentioned that he was ending his analysis, against Venn's advice. He's disappointed in me. Just when I was on the point of becoming the *uomo universale*, here I am chucking it all in. Arthur only nodded.

He waited until the end of the round to speak to Mrs Morley. She was sitting in a pine armchair at the far end of the day room, holding a paperback open on her lap, but her eyes had barely left Arthur since he had come on the ward. As he walked towards her, she shut the book and drove her thumbnail into its spine hard enough to slit the binding. She had the look of a woman convalescing from a hard physical illness. Her hair was tied tightly back, the skin of her face fragile. She had been admitted with an acute psychotic episode the day after giving birth to her first child, and had been in the Bradshaw for six weeks now.

Arthur drew a stool up beside her and turned a page in his notes.

'Let's see, now,' he said. 'All well today?'

Her hands kneaded the paperback in her lap.

'You've been making excellent progress,' Arthur said. 'I should say it's high time to think about going home. How do you feel about that idea?'

She was twisting the book as if she meant to tear it in half. It was an orange-covered Penguin, face down so that Arthur couldn't see the title. In fact she had known for several days now that her time in the hospital was coming to an end, and some anxiety over this was to be expected. It wasn't unusual for a patient, however keen she might be to leave, to shrink at the last moment from the prospect of going back to life in the world.

The book slipped off Mrs Morley's lap and she pressed a hand to her chest. Her face was damp. She was in danger of hyperventilation, Arthur suspected. If he liked, he could tell her that she was not yet ready to leave the hospital, and she might be grateful if he did. But in the end it would not do her any good. She hadn't seen the baby since the birth. On an instinct he touched her forearm, and after a minute her breathing began to ease, matching itself to his own, slow and steady, regulated from the depth of his expertise.

'It's daunting,' he said. 'But you'll have help.'

He would have liked to say much more. He wanted to congratulate her and be congratulated in turn. He had a curious urge to tell her his news. As it happens, we have our own on the way! But, after all, none of this needed to be said.

Shared humanity, cause for optimism, the ordinary decency of the world into which she was now to return: all of this could be conveyed with the touch of a hand.

'I'll see you in the outpatient clinic.'

She was chewing her lower lip. She drew a shuddering breath, and nodded.

'Good,' he said. 'You'll be discharged this afternoon. The nurses will make the arrangements.'

He clapped a hand to his knee to mark the end of the interview.

'Well. Good luck.'

That was all, but as he stood up a generous smile broke across her face, as if she had guessed what he really wanted to say.

'Leave some for me,' said Jacobs, appearing beside him. They helped themselves to the last two servings of shepherd's pie. They had come in late to lunch and the canteen was almost empty. As they sat down, Hassel, who had been eating alone at one of the other tables, was getting to his feet, dabbing at his mouth and then at his brow with a paper napkin. He saluted them with a circular motion of the napkin before limping out of the canteen, taking with him the many responsibilities that were locked into his anatomy.

While they ate, Jacobs talked about his latest disagreements with the higher authorities of the Bradshaw. He had asked for permission to carry out insulin coma therapy with a patient on the locked ward, but Hassel had refused outright.

'He used the word *barbaric*,' Jacobs said. 'The hospital can't open itself to such practices, apparently.'

It was beyond a joke, he said. The therapy was clearly indicated – the patient had been admitted with a mild depressive episode but had then taken a violent turn for the worse – but Hassel wouldn't hear of it. Jacobs paused to steer a forkful of mashed potato, mince and peas carefully into his mouth. His hair was receding, with springy curls around the back of his head giving way to the front half of a bald pate. His face was boyish, small-featured and bright-eyed, and he grinned readily, but below the neck he carried himself like someone older than he was. All his movements were slow, as though he had learned to compensate for natural clumsiness, and he walked in a scholarly shuffle that did not match the general pace of the hospital. He was always being overtaken in the corridors. Altogether, Arthur thought, you might take Jacobs for a placid individual, wrapped up in his thoughts: but then you noticed the gleam when he found himself at odds with some aspect of hospital policy or practice.

Jacobs chewed and swallowed, his elbows on the table.

'I won't leave it at that,' he said. 'I don't hold out much hope of changing the old boy's mind, but we can't go making it easy for him.'

Jacobs had the rhetorical habit of assuming that in these matters Arthur's sympathies matched his own. They had struck up a rapport during Arthur's first weeks in the job, when, chatting as they turned over newspapers in the doctors' mess or loitered in the corridor by the secretarial offices, Arthur realised that here it was possible to think of psychiatry as an optimistic endeavour. When you spoke to Ben Jacobs you felt that medical science was on the cusp of curing the major mental illnesses, that schizophrenia and manic-depressive psychosis must be on the point of crumbling before the march

147

of progress. Jacobs never seemed to doubt that this was the purpose of their work. Not that the Bradshaw was perfect, he told Arthur: the problem was the old guard. Hassel and the other senior physicians were timid caretakers, and their much repeated ethos of early intervention in acute recoverable cases was a fudge. Hassel's vision of a hospital that respects the persons of its patients and treats no one who does not wish to be treated might be admirable in theory, Jacobs said, but in practice it means an institution that's frightened to make any kind of medical intervention at all. We have the tools, if only we had the nerve to use them. We no longer need to rely on cold baths and basketry. Cardiazol shock, ECT, prefrontal leucotomy, intravenous barbiturates: these are among the treatments that Hassel likes to pretend don't exist, supposedly due to ethical scruples but in fact because he has no interest in helping seriously ill patients. To do so would jeopardise the system. The Bradshaw is supposed to be the state of the art, but how do we go about creating that appearance? Why, we're selective. We choose our bets. It's neat. We admit the easy cases, the ones who are halfway to getting better of their own accord. We discharge them quickly and tick the box saying *cured*, so that we get a brisk turnover and a success rate that looks good when Hassel goes to his masters to beg for funds. And meanwhile, Jacobs asked, what becomes of the people who most need our help?

'I can tell you what'll happen to my man in the locked ward,' he said now. 'We'll do nothing for him, he'll sink, and the Bradshaw will find that it's no longer equipped to accommodate him. He'll be shunted off to Cranfield Park or worse. Within a month he'll be a chronic case and ten to one he'll never see the light of day again.'

Alongside his work at the Bradshaw, Jacobs held a post as medical officer at Cranfield Park Lunatic Asylum, a pauper hospital in a suburb in the north of the city. It was a hopeless place, Jacobs had told Arthur when it first came up in their conversations. But he sounded almost affectionate when he complained that going through the gate at Cranfield Park was like stepping back twenty years. Far too large, desperately understaffed and outmoded in its facilities, the asylum was not equipped to offer its patients any meaningful form of treatment, and did not pretend to try: in effect it was a prison for those who had committed the double crime of being poor and sick. There was no excuse for the existence of such a place in the modern era, Jacobs said, but that was why it was necessary to pitch in. Nothing short of radical reform of the entire infrastructure of care for mental illness throughout the country would really solve these problems, but in the meantime he would do what he could for the patients that the current system had abandoned. Arthur, impressed by Jacobs's conviction, had managed to restrain himself from saying that he really ought to do something of the kind himself. He knew he should, but he couldn't imagine where he would find the time.

'Absolutely,' Arthur said now, shaking his head at the stupidity of the authorities. It was easy to agree with Jacobs, not only because he assumed your agreement but because he was right. He was in the habit of being right. Everything that he thought and said and did was consistent because it was founded on the bedrock of his moral intelligence. He wasn't a prig about it, didn't flaunt his virtue or bully you into submission, but he spoke from his conviction and expected that you would speak from yours, and so it was easy to agree with him. And yet. 'On the other hand, though,' Arthur said. Because

149

while Jacobs meant no harm with his enthusiasm, simply to agree was to bow your head and make yourself a timid junior, overwhelmed by another will – and what use was that to anyone? Jacobs didn't want a colleague who shared all his opinions. That had been part of the unfamiliar pleasure of those first talks in which they had discovered that they were basically in sympathy but also that they differed in their particular concerns and commitments, and that this was all to the good. They could respect one another even where they held different views about what was most important.

'Just don't be hasty,' Arthur said.

Jacobs, chewing, tipped his head to show that he saw the value of Arthur's counsel, though he couldn't accept it. They finished their food, each his own person: Jacobs who could not compromise or retreat and would stake everything on a fight for the interests of a single patient; Arthur who was perhaps more flexible, perhaps more circumspect, perhaps a necessary counterbalance; Jacobs who saw the new physical therapies as the key to progress; Arthur who had his doubts and was more committed to psychological methods; Dr Bourne and Dr Jacobs who respected one another's positions. When they talked, it became clear that these were the people they were. Arthur, like Jacobs, was a serious man who under-stood the complexities of things, who chose his ground and stood on it. They were equals.

Arthur had Jacobs to thank, too, for his ongoing relations with William Walker. In the final weeks at the Calvary, knowing he'd soon be leaving to take up the Bradshaw post and resigning himself to the fact that there would be no break-through with Walker, Arthur began to bring his chessboard to the sessions, and they spent their last couple of weeks in a silence more companionable than before. Walker won most of the games, but Arthur didn't mind. Later, when he told Jacobs about his work with Walker, the story took on a new shape: a Jacobs-like shape, with Arthur as a doctor who was firm in his commitment to psychoanalytic therapy and had, accordingly, struggled and won out over a sluggish, reactionary hospital management to put his methods into action for the good of his patient. And perhaps, he felt, telling the story, that really was how it had been; perhaps it had only seemed at the time that he was dismayed and uncertain. When Jacobs asked how Walker was doing now, Arthur admitted that his move to the Bradshaw had disrupted the analysis, and added that it would really have been best not to break off so suddenly. Jacobs had nodded, bright-eyed, never doubting that Arthur would do what he judged to be right, and by the end of the day Arthur had arranged with the Calvary that he would come for a weekly session with Walker. It had been going on ever since, and he was due there this afternoon, but it wasn't too bad. An hour of uncomfortable silence a week was a fair price to ease his conscience.

'Right,' said Jacobs, straightening his arm to shoot his wrist-watch free of the cuff. 'Must dash.'

Arthur got up too, and they carried their trays to the counter. Lunchtime candour was finished, and as they left the canteen Arthur could feel Jacobs shrugging on his formal medical bearing, checking its straps and pockets. He was doing the same himself. But before they parted in the corridor Jacobs looked at him guessingly.

'You're in good form today, aren't you?'

For a moment Arthur was tempted to tell the news – but he was circumspect. He would tell soon enough, but not yet.

He raised a hand to wish Jacobs a successful afternoon. There would be plenty of time.

On his way home Arthur made a diversion to Portobello Market. It took him some time to find the shop: they had been once, months ago, but he had forgotten how far it was along the road. Then he recognised the arrangement of furniture and bric-a-brac behind the dust-caked window – a rag doll and a clarinet on a chaise longue – and went in. The bell jangled.

The street's afternoon light was held in the glass of picture frames, cabinet fronts, chandeliers and ornaments. The shopkeeper was perched on a high stool among the stock, his spectacles glinting. Likely it's been sold, Arthur told himself, peering around; but the chair was there, half hidden behind a three-panelled screen printed with an oriental design.

As he picked a way through the jumble, his hand rested on the canopy of a crib, a handsome object of glossy blond wood. It moved on its rockers. A lucky discovery, an invitation to change his mind in favour of something more suitable? But he had not come here to furnish a nursery. The impracticality of the chair was the point. It was a high-backed armchair made from hard black oak, with scrolled armrests, spiralled legs and a headrest carved with the characters ANNO 1660. When they had come in here before, Sarah had gone straight to it and sat down possessively. He had learned that chairs, tables, bureaus and cabinets had meanings for her that were opaque to him. He tried to persuade her that they should buy it, but she refused: it was too big and heavy and dark, there was nowhere to put it in the flat, and it was too expensive anyway. Now he would bring it home in defiance of all these sensible arguments. It would stay with them forever and whenever they caught sight of it they would remember that he had given it to her today.

Under the shopkeeper's eye, Arthur made a brief show of checking over the chair for whatever it was that one checked for: sturdy joints, he supposed, and general soundness. He felt the grain of the wood, fingered a notch in the headrest and finally signalled to the shopkeeper, who grumbled to himself as he clambered down from his stool. Having taken Arthur's money he disappeared into a back room, indifferent to what the chair's new owner did with it next. Arthur set a collection of brass fire irons clattering on their stand as he hauled the chair out of the shop. Once he was in the street he put the awkward thing down. He found that he could embrace it from behind with his arms under the armrests, his hands clasped and the seat sticking out in front. Craning to see where he was going, he lugged the chair towards the bus stop, covering the last twenty yards at a crabbed run as the number sixteen pulled in.

The conductor looked dubious as Arthur tried to catch his breath. Then the man stepped down, amused, and helped him hoist the chair up the step.

'Didn't think this one through, didya,' he said, and Arthur gave the self-deprecating chuckle that he was supposed to give.

'Present for the wife,' he said.

The conductor winked. 'Say no more.'

He stood at the rear, holding on to the chair as the bus halted, lurched forward, halted again. Several young men in black uniforms were standing on a street corner, one speaking through a loudhailer while the others held formation behind him, holding their pickets like soldiers presenting arms. Each placard bore the emblem of a lightning bolt in red, white and blue. One of the men eyeballed him through the glass. The bus lurched again, and he thought of a night when he had come home from the Bradshaw later than he'd intended – he always came home later than intended – to find her still at work on the office room. The renovation was coming on well. To begin with the room had looked to be beyond recovery, its walls blistered with damp and marked by several blotches of mould the size and approximate shape of human beings. Loops of cobweb trailed from the ceiling and the carpet squelched when you stepped on it. A staved-in wardrobe leaned beside a pair of eviscerated armchairs. Sarah had set to cleaning and mending, getting the furniture removed and the window replaced, then tearing out the carpet and scrubbing the filthy floorboards until they were bright. That night Arthur came home to find her standing in the clean, empty space she had created. She was leaning on the mop, but she was resting her head on her hands and when she looked up at him her face was streaked and swollen. He took the mop from her and stepped into its place, a prop to lean on. Her face blotted his shirt. She let him try to comfort her, and after a few minutes they sat down on the floor beside the paint pots. Arthur rested his head on the wall, noticing for the first time the intricate ceiling rose. The light fitting had been repaired and the room was lit by a naked bulb that picked out a lunar map across the ceiling's plasterwork.

Nothing had happened, she told him. It was just this room. Arthur, perplexed, said that the room was looking wonderful, that she had transformed it. I know, she said. They were quiet for a while, and then she told him that she had once been to a public meeting of the Blackshirts. Don't think the worse of me, she said. She gave a small laugh, her shoulder hitching against him. It was four or five years ago, when no one knew much about them. She had heard talk of the burly, vigorous, handlebar-moustached leader in his black silk fencing shirt: he offered a new vision in place of the tired old politics of the out-of-touch traditional parties, and he alone had a plan to lead the country out of the economic mire. There was a meeting at the municipal hall. Women were welcome in the new movement – all female members were to be trained in first aid and self-defence, she had read in a leaflet – but, as it turned out, the crowd was overwhelmingly male. The hall was packed with men standing four-square, their feet planted wide, their arms folded and chins raised towards the stage, each taking up all the space to which his bulk entitled him. They did not move to let her through. The man on the stage was not the burly leader but a scrawny fellow with oiled black hair and a pencil moustache. He exuded sweaty energy and, crowded as the hall was, spoke as if he were addressing an even larger audience. Judging by how he waved his arms, he had practised his speech with a great amphitheatre in mind. He talked about economic crisis, about the need for firm planning and decisive action, and Sarah thought he sounded convincing enough, like someone who was at least willing to be realistic about the difficulties the country was facing. The crowd seemed only mildly stirred by the argument. Then the man began to talk about the ghettoes of Europe evacuating their waste into Britain, and declaring that it was only when a solution to this abuse of our liberties was found that the nation would get back on its feet. The crowd shifted and grew more attentive. The answer, the man said, was to set up a network of compounds around the country, to which all Jews would be compulsorily removed: these comfortable, modern habitations would enable the Jews, together with other groups such as sexual inverts and the mentally deficient, to be kept under the necessary degree of observation and control, and to be put to productive work. At this point Sarah stopped hearing the speech, because she had realised how much the man on stage reminded her of her father. Some of the listeners were jeering at the speaker and others were applauding combatively as Sarah walked out of the hall to find fresh air.

As they sat on the floor of the empty room, breathing the bright stink of the paint, she spoke about her father. Her father was frightened of many things but of communists and Jews above all. He had done his best to teach his daughters to fear as he did, haranguing them, when the mood took him, about those hateful species that were plotting all the time to drain the blood from honest Englishmen. He had especially wanted Mary to understand him and would often go down on one knee in front of her and hold her by the ears, staring into her face, as he instructed her in what the world was like. Sarah had been peripheral to these lessons. He would cut sidelong glances at her as if she could not be expected to understand, or, she sometimes thought, as if he knew that she understood all too well and was too deceitful to admit it. She was the communist and Jew of the family. She had a vivid picture of her father kneeling to Mary, giving his lesson, nodding over at her for illustration. Like our Sarah here. She thought the image must date from when she was ten years old, shortly after her mother died, but she couldn't remember clearly. She fumbled in her sleeve, blew her nose and looked around the empty room. I don't know why I've done this, she said. I don't know what it's all in aid of.

Arthur cautioned himself that the last thing she wanted was for him to start telling her the reasons she had for happiness. Then he did it anyway. He praised the many worthwhile things she found to do, from furnishing the flat with such economy and flair to taking an interest in the liberation of women. She got up to pick at a fleck of paint on the new windowpane. She gazed through her reflection into the dark, as, gingerly, not quite knowing why he brought it up, he reminded her of conversations they had had in past months: conversations about how life was exceptionally busy just now and it only made sense to let things settle down before they thought of taking on further responsibilities, about how it would be wise for him to put all his energies into establishing himself profes-sionally for the next few years at least. He even spoke about how unjust it was that women should be made to feel that the only fulfilment they could hope for lay in the sphere of home and family, and how important it was to hold out against that tyranny in one's own life. These were doctrines she had taught him. But Sarah did not turn around, and by the time he finished speaking he knew they had made a decision.

He manhandled the chair off the bus and began to lumber it along the pavement, his shins knocking against the crossbar. At the corner of Wesley Street he paused to work the stiffness out of his arms. He sat down in the chair.

He crossed his legs, twitched the crease of his trousers and looked up the street, picking out the window of the flat at the top of the building. Above him the branches of the horse chestnut tree were bare. A very small alteration to the usual point of view. He steepled his fingers. He wished that she would come along and find him like this, being playful and eccentric. He knew what Louis would think of the way they had made the decision to try for a child. Often enough when they were students Louis had railed against the compromises that ordinary life imposed, and had shuddered in particular at the power of women – those beings who could demand your life of you at a stroke, and do so without a qualm, by some mysterious entitlement that made you the villain if you refused. And so, he muttered in Arthur's mind, that night was your chance to show some backbone. You might have insisted on your freedom, refused to be dragged into someone else's mundane idea of a life. It was an argument Louis would never make out loud, not nowadays; but he didn't need to make it out loud.

Still, he'd been given his answer the next time they'd seen him. After he had set off for Germany there had been no word for months, but one afternoon Arthur ran into Myles MacDonagh on the platform of Kennington tube station and learned that Louis sounded well enough: his postcards complained of poverty, lethargy and his failure to write or to want to, but he was still working his way across the cities of Germany and through their galleries and art collections. Sponging up old pictures at a fierce rate, Myles said. Myself, I'd have reached the point of saturation long ago. Arthur had not had any postcards of his own, but at length a card arrived at the flat with a reproduction of a Poussin Venus on the front, and on the back Louis's scrawl announcing that he would shortly be in London on his way through to Dublin. A fortnight later he came to dinner at Wesley Street. July had brought light evenings in which they could open the windows to the warm air rising from the streets, as if they were in another climate and this were another stop on Louis's foreign itinerary. He was only going home for a brief visit, he said, probably a week, no more than two, after which he would be back to the trenches. So you're on leave from the front, Sarah said, and Louis's lip twisted. The *Wanderjahr* has its rigours, he said. Some chaps simply fall to pieces, don't you know. Arthur said he was sure Mrs Molyneux would be glad to see him in Dalkey, and Louis agreed that his return was bound to induce agitations of some description in the maternal breast. Kinder to stay away, maybe, he mused, but I can't afford to get too free of the old scenes. Where could I find new misery to compare? In the past that sort of remark would have annoyed them, but now, as Sarah passed Arthur a bottle to open, they agreed without a word that this evening they would be indulgent. Arthur bent over the corkscrew, conscious of Sarah switching here and there behind him in her cotton print dress, blue with yellow buttercups, as she checked on the chicken and washed the greens. Louis was restless, moving from the sofa to a seat at the table and then springing up to study the bookcase. He examined the window sash and the dado rail, touched the mantelpiece and peered into the bathroom, as if he were noting the features of an interesting little chapel on which he had stumbled in a Mitteleuropean backstreet. Frowning with concentration, he accepted a glass of hock without taking his eyes from the gouache-on-cardboard of a beach by stormy moonlight that Sarah had found on a market stall the other week. Arthur set the table and after a short time Louis came and took his seat of his own accord. They encouraged him to tell them his adventures. While Arthur carved, Louis rattled off names of places they had never been, Lübeck, Lüneburg,

Riddagshausen, Wolfenbüttel, Halberstadt, Leipzig, Dresden, Munich, Erfurt, Potsdam. Sarah and Arthur conferred in glances across the table. Living in this flat, working hard, pledging their futures to one another, was an adventure more intrepid than any European holiday, but this was a secret for the two of them, and Louis could not be expected to understand. Instead Sarah coaxed him into recounting the comic misfortunes of an Irishman abroad, from how on his first night in Hamburg a shop-clerk had accused him of stealing a packet of razor blades – a wrong that had gone unrighted and was now graven forever in the tables of injustice – to how in Quedlinburg a policeman had fined him a Reichsmark for walking down the wrong alley, or perhaps the right alley in the wrong direction, or possibly in the right direction but with an inadmissible eccentricity of gait. At the time his German hadn't been equal to the nuances of his crimes. Sarah asked what Berlin was like. They were impressed by the deep-sounding things he could say about painters like Fabritius, Rembrandt, Vermeer, Dürer, Giorgione, Antonello da Messina, Gaunt, Munch, Van Gogh and a score of others whose names they didn't recognise. He talked about the artists he had met in cafés and studios, and about how all the galleries in Germany had been ordered to purge themselves of decadent modern art. The best pictures were being locked in cellars, sold or destroyed, and the artists, superb in their indignation to a woman and man, could do nothing. Louis pushed his plate an inch further away, sat back and sipped his wine, a traveller returned from a more perilous world.

It was only once the plates had been cleared and Arthur was pouring from the second bottle that Louis told them *Jott* was to be published. Arthur and Sarah sat up straight. Louis studied the contents of his glass. Cope at Gryphon had only been and gone for it. Not quite swallowed it whole, to be sure – edits were required, assorted surgeries minor and major, delicate sensibilities of the reading public – but there was every reason to expect that the blighter would be safely interred between cloth covers by this time next year. When they had made sure Louis was quite serious, they toasted him, then toasted the wisdom of the publisher and the future that now arrayed itself. It had got dark while they were talking, but soft July air was still rolling through the open window. The bright little flat was enfolded by a night rich with summer smells and hidden lights. Louis looked nonchalant and said he'd just be glad to have its claws out of him at last, but they saw the smile that he was doing his best to conceal. Tidying up after he had gone, they agreed that they were very pleased for him, that with luck a measure of success would do him good and help him to feel happier in himself. They agreed that they wished him well.

Arthur carried the chair up the steps of the building and propped it with his hip while he fumbled with his keys. In the hallway he stopped to rest his arms and cordially cursed it for an unwieldy brute. He looked up the stairwell, then changed his mind, unlocked the consulting room and dragged the chair inside. To surprise her with it later would be better than crashing into the flat red-faced and sweating. The chair went into the corner behind his desk, beside the bookshelves. He sat down in the armchair meant for patients and let his breathing slow.

But what would they be like now, the two of them? He was on his way up to a flat in which a change had already taken place. The wife expecting him was a new person whom he had barely begun to know, and the husband climbing to meet her, mounting the stairs two and three at a time and helping himself up with a hand on the banister, was a new person as well. She would be asleep now. This past week he had been coming home in the afternoon to find her deeply unconscious, vigorously asleep, sometimes in bed and sometimes on the sofa under a blanket made of interlocking woollen rings, brown, green and blue. He would find his way around as if the flat were new to him, wondering where to hang up his coat and having to search for the tea caddy in the kitchen. Breaths of air would pass from room to room of their own accord, accompanied by dry warmth and a faint smell like bread baking. The kettle would boil and he would hush its noise, lifting it before it could whistle, although there was no real danger of waking her. He would sit for a while, doing nothing except drinking his tea, which was unlike him; but as long as she slept, it was all right, because no time passed and nothing could happen. He had already come to look forward to this as a special little interval in the day.

He reached the top landing and searched for his key, which in the struggle with the chair he'd put back in the wrong place, it turned out, right jacket pocket instead of left front of his trousers. As he let himself in, he realised that this afternoon the flat was empty. Light from the window fell blindly on the wool blanket, which lay crumpled on the sofa. The air was dead in the room. A small object that he couldn't identify lay on the sill, and the mirror gleamed guiltily above the mantelpiece, as if he had come home by mistake to the flat's false twin. Unable to think where she might have gone, he looked first in the bedroom and then the bathroom, but no one was there.

The kitchen tap was dripping and he tightened it, noticing as he did so that Sarah was sitting at the table. He hadn't seen her but she had been there since he came in. She was leaning forward a little with her hands on the table top. A few sheets of paper lay in front of her, some Liberation League things by the look of it, but she was not reading or writing, only gazing at the documents. She didn't seem to have noticed him, and Arthur had a brief horror that they might stay like this, unable to make their presence known to one another, for minutes, hours or days. Then she looked up and gave him a strange smile.

'Are you all right?' he asked. 'Nothing wrong?'

It was curious that he should ask the question in that way, when he really had no wish to be disingenuous. It was as if his words were loaded with a treachery that only sprang free when they were spoken. It was obvious what had happened. She got up, still smiling, and filled the kettle at the sink. She struck a match but stopped before lighting the gas, holding herself in an awkward, hobbled attitude and placing three fingertips at a point on her lower back, two inches to the right of her spine.

'It's rather an uncomfortable one this time, actually.' She was keeping her back to him. 'No point moaning. It never lasts long.'

She lit the ring and rinsed out the teapot while Arthur stood helplessly behind, hands ready as if she might toss a piece of crockery over her shoulder. He couldn't think of anything useful to say. He had forgotten the unhappiness of these past months. As the layers of disappointment had settled, he had begun to think that if it went on for much longer they would not be able to carry the weight. He had forgotten, too, about her way of being disappointed, her insistence that nothing was the matter and there was no sense in being upset. When he tried to comfort her, he managed to get a few words out before she changed the subject impatiently or found that there was something she needed to do in the other room. And he had forgotten the fear, easily dismissed at first but returning stronger each time, that they weren't just being unlucky – that there was some flaw in his body or hers, or in the way they fitted together, that barred them from the future they had chosen.

'Drink up,' she said. 'You're going to be late.'

He accepted the tea. It was stupid for her to soldier on. He wanted to say that he was concerned for her well-being both physically and emotionally, and that he was going to telephone the Calvary and cancel Walker, but as Sarah sipped her own tea she was studying the papers on the table, running her finger down a column, her face stern and absorbed. He drank, rinsed his cup and checked his watch. He moved towards her, hesitated, stopped, nodded and left the flat. As he started down the stairs he saw it again, the smile she had given him: the eyes deep in the sockets, the tendons showing in the neck, the lips drawn apart, the brittle teeth exposed.

The treatment room was windowless and bright, lit by caged bulbs whose reflections ran in the white-tiled walls. Walker was lying on a table, held by straps across his chest and thighs. The wet pack made his body childlike. The tight canvas wrapping that covered him from neck to feet gave him the look of something preserved by ancient burial practices, an embalmed body whose head, by some witchcraft, was still alive.

164

The face was barely recognisable. Crepe bandages wrapped his head in three bands, holding dressings in place. His right eye gazed at the ceiling, but the left was buried in a mass of purple inflammation. The bruising spread all the way down his cheek and across his nose, which had been smashed out of shape. His mouth was a bulging wound. His nostrils flared and narrowed under the bandage.

On his way into Sinfield House Arthur had been intercepted by Nurse Parry, who had explained that Mr Walker was having a bad day, and was in a wet pack in Treatment Room Four. Shortly after the duty nurse had reminded him that he'd be seeing Dr Bourne this afternoon, he had run into the latrines and begun to beat his head against a radiator. He got in a few good cracks before we reached him, Parry said. Broke off the tap. He was calm enough now, though, and awake. Four hours in the pack should see him right.

The surface of the table was a shallow basin with a drain in one corner. Patients were often wet-packed to subdue recalcitrant moods, but Arthur had never known it to be necessary with Walker. He drew his chair a little closer and bent forward. Walker's good eye found him, but there was no change in the broken face under the bandages. The chest strap tightened and eased. A minute went by before the lips parted, the tongue quivered, and Walker spoke.

'Practice, dear boy,' he said. 'Practice.'

He was trying for his usual insouciance, but he sounded as if his mouth were wadded with gauze. His eye strayed back to the ceiling.

Arthur sat back. Do everything you can to avoid making interpretations, Venn often said. If you give in to the temptation to say what things mean, you'll only slow things down, because the patient is the one with the answers and he must uncover them for himself. Easy to say, but no help when it came to Walker. Obviously Arthur was in the bad books, but he'd known that ever since the move to the Bradshaw. He knew a patient like Walker must feel a great deal of anxious dependence on his sessions, and that, for all his inaccessibility, he was sensitive to any sign that he was being treated as unimportant in his analyst's life. He'd known this, but it had not occurred to him that Walker might be capable of taking such a brutal revenge. The man was mad, but who would have guessed that he could be so unreasonable? There was a complacency in the way the swathed head lay on the table, Arthur saw now: it was the head of someone who had made his point. You are at my beck and call, and don't you forget it.

A queer wheezing noise was coming from inside the bandages. It must be what careless laughter sounded like through a broken mouth. It grew heavier until Walker was panting down his nose and trying to writhe under the straps. His body flexed but he could not move. It was a marvel, the instinct by which Walker had chosen today to do this, as if his malign perceptiveness extended the length and breadth of Arthur's life. Well, let the man feel the consequences of his actions. That was sanity: cause and effect. If you harm yourself out of sheer vindictiveness, then you're going to find yourself sedated and restrained. If he chose to go to such lengths to make his point, so be it.

Walker stopped struggling. Arthur uncrossed his legs and recrossed them, repenting. He didn't want Walker to suffer. He knew the conversation he'd have about this with Venn. They'd conclude that whatever guilt and anger he might feel was finally beside the point, because Walker's behaviour

166

could only be understood as an expression of an inner turmoil out of all proportion with external events. Not to be taken personally.

Which was all very well, but it wasn't as if Venn was so infallibly wise. Sometimes when they set out from the Malet they would not follow the usual circuit that brought them in due course back to the clinic, but instead would press north and west through Chalk Farm and Belsize Park to arrive by the end of their allotted hour at Venn's home. He lived in a Georgian terrace on a tranquil street that ran into Hampstead Heath at the far end. The glossy black front door and the lion's-head knocker demonstrated that he was a more solid and grown-up person than Arthur could hope to be. They would finish the session with a brandy in the small basement sitting room that Venn said was his domain alone, with the house quiet above them. There was never any sign of the family, and on one of those nights Venn had admitted that the house was empty these days because his wife had gone to stay with her family in Torquay. Difficulties had been fermenting in the marriage for a long time. He puffed out his cheeks, opened his hand and let it fall on the arm of his chair. I am the difficulty, he said. She's right to have gone. She is safe by the seaside. Our son is at school in Yorkshire. Meanwhile I work here to solve the difficulty that is myself. He spoke for a while about the latest professional quarrel in which he had become embroiled. I'm tired of it, he said. I've been thinking of giving up my career. He chuckled. I'd like to be a potter, I think, or a merchant seaman. No, no, I won't do it, he said, as Arthur began to protest. But doesn't it ever strike you as unbearable? To live in a world where everything means something else. He drained his brandy and got up. Come and let me show you this. They climbed the stairs to the top of the house, into a room dominated by a large table whose surface was filled with an elaborate model town. Its construction was still under way, Arthur could see: the only other piece of furniture in the room was a workbench along one wall, neatly crowded with pieces of balsawood and stiff white card, small paint pots and fine brushes, matchsticks, model lamp posts and garden fences, little model people as tall as the first joint of his thumb, scalpels and tubes of glue. I spend a great deal of my time up here, Venn said. He leaned over the model and drew Arthur's attention to its features. Here's the seafront, he said, and here's the town hall; see the clock tower? The girl is wheeling her bicycle up the slope. This dog got his bone from the butcher. The bandstand was tricky. Next I have to finish the school: it goes here, you see, across from the barber's shop. Arthur, not knowing what to say, had leaned in beside him and made appreciative noises. Later he would wonder why he had felt such a prim, squeamish need to leave the room as quickly as possible. He had walked home that night suspecting that he had failed some test and might never be invited back, and feeling that if this were so he would be relieved.

Really what Walker needed was kindness, Arthur thought, looking down at the bandaged head and the childlike mummified body. He needed a physician who would be unfazed by the worst he could do, who would tolerate all his evasions and hostilities and wait patiently for him to move beyond them. Seen rightly this wobble was an opportunity for progress, because at least what had happened was a palpable psychodynamic event between them, and that was a step towards communication. Perhaps Walker had done more than he knew to help them both.

The small body stiffened and pushed against the straps again, then stopped and lay motionless except for the hitching of the chest. The eye was open. A blood vessel had broken in the white. Perhaps he had a cramp. Perhaps he didn't understand why he couldn't move. Arthur leaned closer.

'Do you know where you are, Mr Walker?'

The open eye stared up at the bulbs, not blinking.

'You're having a bad day,' Arthur said. 'Try to rest.'

He looked at his watch. Patients were wet-packed for a minimum of four hours. They could be left in for longer if they needed it, but they must not be released early. This ensured that the benefit of the cooling and constriction was felt. Walker had been in for less than an hour. He looked like a doll, a bundle of canvas and bandage, less than life-sized. A spot of blood was seeping through the bandage near his temple.

'Let's sit for a while,' Arthur said. 'We don't need to talk.'

That was the right tone. Simple and generous. Perhaps it was all very simple: he was Walker's friend and companion, and the mere fact that he was here, sitting with him through a trying episode, was proof enough that the events of the day had brought them closer together. He wanted to say more, because he hadn't yet got across what he felt – this forgiving warmth that was welling up in him, this readiness to make amends. We don't need to talk, he wanted to say, but I will listen. What I can do to help you, I will do. He thought of a fortified town in an endless desert. It was his dream of last night. He had been the father of a small child, the only protector of a vulnerable creature who trusted and depended on him absolutely. A horde of barbarians had been sweeping across the plain towards them, he remembered: the barbarians were monsters, torturers, fanatics, and although they were distant as yet, they would certainly overwhelm the town and deal most cruelly with those inside. There was no possibility of resistance or escape, only the remaining span of life before the horrors arrived. Nothing else happened. The mood was a kind of stunned fatalism, but there was an exultancy, too, as the Arthur of the dream stood with his dream child on the wall of their desert town, looking at the horizon and wondering what to do with the time they had left.

Walker's eye stared up at the lights. His chest laboured under the straps. Arthur said nothing, holding that simple, generous feeling in both hands, taking care not to spill a drop. They had done it, then. Soon he would go back to Wesley Street to find Sarah suffering, transfixed by disappointment, and it would be awful. But however much they might wish it were otherwise, he now saw, there was something of value in what had happened. Not for Arthur or Sarah, indeed, but for William Walker; that was the strangeness of it. Arthur's eyes prickled. Walker's self-assault had been not an act of aggression but an expression of sympathy. If his weird sensitivities had moved him to make a martyr of himself, today of all days, it was his curious way of showing that he cared, and of showing, in turn, how mysteriously one heart's unhappiness could weigh for the good of another. Arthur fancied that three hours from now, when the nurses released Walker from his pack, the patient who rose from the table would be subtly changed, because now there was no denying that they were fellow human beings.

Walker pushed against the straps as if undergoing some form of involuntary spasm. He was panting, quick and shallow. The canvas-wrapped body fought the restraint for half a minute, then collapsed.

'Actually,' Walker said. His voice was raw, barely audible. 'One thing you can do.'

Arthur was startled despite himself. It hadn't occurred to him that the change could happen so fast. But if now was the time, he thought, so be it. The day's disasters had brought them together, and Walker was finally ready to begin.

'Tell me,' Arthur said.

He leaned closer, to make sure he caught the words. Walker's eye found him.

'Please let me out.'

One evening towards the end of the summer, Sarah had decided they must go on an expedition. It was late and Arthur would rather have left it till another day, but she led him on to an eastbound tube that took them through Euston Square and Farringdon and onwards into districts that he had never thought of visiting, through Aldgate and Whitechapel to Mile End, into streets where small, broken-down terraces were interspersed with lodging houses and a park that ran its railings darkly beside them for a stretch. They passed beer shops and dance halls, and as the streets grew busier he began to see shop signs in unfamiliar characters – Cyrillic, he thought, and Chinese – and to smell pungent dockland smells. Don't worry, Sarah said, it's not all opium dens and murders. Actually they cleared the slums a few years ago, and I believe it's all quite nice now. And indeed the street they turned into next was broad and clean, with most of the windows shuttered at street level, dim lights glowing behind curtains above and a few grocer's shops and tobacconists, none of their signs in English, scattered among the houses. Two sailors with neat dark beards passed near enough for Arthur to catch Slavic accents. An English woman put her head around a door and called in foreign syllables to an Asiatic-looking child, who ran promptly across to her, almost colliding with Sarah's legs. They were being left alone. Space opened around them as they walked, and all heads were in the act of turning away. Sarah led him into a restaurant that he would later remember as a vast, low room filled with Chinese people drinking tea. She chose a table and they sat, Arthur trying to guess whether their being here was a mortal insult or merely an irrelevance to the patrons and proprietors. He was about to suggest slinking away when a middle-aged man in shirtsleeves appeared and, without a word, placed a pot of green tea on the table. They sipped from cups like egg cups, finding the tea bitter, and were conscious of attracting no attention from their neighbours, four men playing mah-jong and a young couple dining on unidentifiable pale objects.

In Arthur's memory, that night had fixed itself as an unlikely figment, a vitrine tableau. It was an emblem of something in Sarah that was mysterious to him, and its atmosphere was in the kitchen, now, as he came home to find her making supper with violent efficiency. She diced an onion with hard strokes of the chopping knife, grated a lump of cheese down to the knuckle, slopped oil to snarl on the hot pan, snatched the lid from the boiling pot and tore around the rim of a can with the iron tooth of the opener. She broke two eggs into a bowl, then turned and knocked one of the wine glasses into the sink, where it rang but did not break.

She set the glass back on the draining board, saying nothing, but by this time Arthur could not contain himself and asked if she wouldn't let him do the rest, because she should be sitting down. Was she in pain? She shook her head and beat the eggs. But it's no good to pretend, he thought, and when she had clapped the plates on the table and they were sitting across from one another he began to suggest that they ought to discuss what had happened. Sarah paused with her first forkful halfway to her mouth. She put the fork back on the plate. Nothing's happened, she said, so there's nothing to discuss. She pushed her chair away from the table and pressed a fist to her abdomen, then got up and tipped her plateful into the rubbish. I'm going to be late, she said. Arthur didn't immediately understand what she meant. It was self-evident that this evening they must stay here together and take care of one another. Be tender and sad.

'Look here,' he said. 'I won't hear of it.'

A minute later she was walking fast down Wesley Street. He locked the street door and skidded along the pavement, catching up with her at the corner. Specks of sleet flowed past. Above, a cyst of light was draining from the cloud cover.

'At least put your coat on,' he said, offering it.

At the tube station he followed her down to the Northern Line. As the train began to move he didn't try to say anything. He only watched the tunnel walls go past, soot-larded and pipe-veined. After they changed at Leicester Square her stance softened and she let the jogging of the carriage turn her towards him and nudge her shoulder into his. But she was facing the image in the glass and her expression was too distant to read.

Sarah's chapter of the Women's Liberation League met in a church hall in Earl's Court. A timetable for the week was pinned on the noticeboard in the entrance, listing the meeting along with choir practices, bridge nights and a talk by a local antiquarian. Cicely and Edith were just arriving: when they saw Arthur they turned to one another, then to Sarah.

'Well, we're always saying we must do more to educate them,' Edith said.

In the hall thirty or thirty-five women were pushing trestle tables against the walls and arranging ladder-back chairs into an inward-facing ring. Most of the women seemed to be around Sarah's age, though some were older. One or two heads turned Arthur's way, but they turned away again without interest or surprise.

He sat down next to Sarah. Cicely and Edith took seats some way around the circle. When everyone was ready the meeting began. He listened, trying to gather clues to what they were talking about: within a few minutes he heard the names of a dozen leagues, unions, associations, councils and committees, all of them dedicated to campaigning for the betterment of spinsters, widows, married women, unmarried women, women teachers, women civil servants, office-working women, working-class women, retired women, young mothers in unfortunate circumstances and women in general, and none of them in agreement about how exactly that betterment was to be defined or achieved.

'The debate flushed them out,' a tall young woman was saying. 'Cooper, for instance.'

'Oh, yes, he was very clear in his position,' Edith said. 'We *deserve* less than men because our work is naturally less valuable. It's really quite simple, you see, ladies.'

As they talked, Arthur gathered that a parliamentary vote of some importance had just taken place. The women were going over the story with outrage and satisfaction, in much the way that he could remember Donard boys post-morteming cricket friendlies in which stout play had been set against unfair odds, poor conditions or a biased umpire. For several years, it seemed, a campaign had been under way for equal pay for women in the civil service, on the principle that reform in that profession would open the way elsewhere. But how was the case to be made, with the economy as it was and the national mood still cautious and fearful? This had been the question for the women of the NAWCS and the CWCS who were to address MPs on the issue at a House of Commons meeting. If they allowed equal pay to be labelled a women's issue it would be dismissed, and so the thrust of their speech went in the opposite direction: equal pay for women was a means of reducing male unemployment, they argued, because if the civil service were forced to pay women an equal wage, women would no longer be hired in preference to men because they were cheaper.

'Thank goodness someone was thinking of the men for once!' called a voice on the far side of the circle. Sarah and Cicely laughed across at one another.

'But of course the honourable members were delighted,' Edith said. 'The speech tickled their tummies so thoroughly they ordered the text to be printed and distributed to the House.'

'They do enjoy the sight of a woman putting their interests ahead of her own,' someone said.

The story of the equal pay campaign had a sting in its tail. Arthur listened and pieced it together. When the vote had come, dozens of usually obedient MPs had defied the whips, and the outcome had been victory for the campaigners. Triumph of the democratic process. The principle of equality

175

between the sexes recognised by the elected representatives of the people of the United Kingdom. Humiliation for the government. Quite satisfactory. But did the Prime Minister accept the will of the House? Good heavens no. He insisted that the vote be taken again, and this time as a vote of confidence – with the result that just enough MPs, unwilling to see the government resign, caved in. It had been blackmail pure and simple, and thus the spectre of equal pay for women in the civil service was dispelled.

The discussion moved on to other matters. One of the older women raised the case of a local barmaid who had been raped by a customer, and had then made the mistake of going to a police station, where after reporting the assault she had been raped again by two officers. The mood of the meeting quickened, and other reports followed. A fourteen year old was on trial for attempted murder after giving birth in a park and abandoning the baby in the bushes. A well-known music hall promoter used his position openly to impose himself on girls hoping to make a living on the stage. A woman had been committed to an insane asylum on the strength of her husband's testimony, for what he termed her difficult behaviour. A woman had died giving birth to her fifth child in four years. Arthur listened, losing track as one voice gave way to another and story followed story of women denied education, employment, dignity and safety, women ridiculed for demanding justice, women murdered by their husbands, their fathers, their brothers and their neighbours. As they spoke, he felt attention turning towards him. He wasn't naïve, he knew that incidents like these took place, but when they were recounted in this way, piling one on top of another, the catalogue of atrocities became hard to take seriously. There was something hysterical about it. In truth, he was a little shocked by the women's readiness to dwell on such unpleasant matters, and as he grew aware of attention bearing down on him, invisible but insistent, he wondered whether he should say something, not for his own sake but for the good of the meeting, because the mood was becoming feverish and it was surely counterproductive for these women to approach their cause in such a confrontational spirit. It would be helpful for them to bear in mind that most men were in fact decent and reasonable and all in favour of the betterment of the female lot, and that if the women of the WLL were prepared to listen to the male point of view they would come to see that Arthur, at least, was on their side and that this deserved some credit. It was no good, though. He knew that if he were to say anything here, if he were to shake his head or move in his seat or make a response of any kind, it would prove his guilt, and so he sat, penitent, until the discussion ended and the next part of the meeting began.

Chairs were being moved around, trestle tables were being pulled away from the walls and stacks of letter paper were being distributed. Sarah led Arthur to one of the tables, where Cicely was setting out three portable Underwoods. Edith had produced three glasses from somewhere. She pulled out a hip flask and poured generously. Then she waggled the flask at Arthur. 'Cheap gin or nothing,' she said. 'Fetch yourself a glass from the kitchen.' She pointed to the end of the hall, where a door stood ajar. When he came back in to receive his drink, the typewriters were clattering. Cicely wound a finished page out of her machine and marked off a name on a list. Then she steered Arthur to the other end of the table and sat him down in front of two stacks of paper. She showed him how to fold them down the middle and put them together to make a pamphlet.

'Neatly,' said Edith.

The cheap, blurred print consisted mostly of reports on meetings, talks, debates and rallies around the country, as far as he could see. He began a stack of assembled copies on the corner of the table, noticing that Sarah, Cicely and Edith were able to type steadily and carry on a conversation at the same time. The talk had circled back to the subject of the equal pay campaign. Sarah drained her glass and said that it was beautiful, what they did, in its way. The economy, the worry about jobs, the talk about silly girls clinging to office chairs that belonged by rights to the men: the campaigners judged it impeccably, and they used the backlash against women's jobs to win a vote for equal pay.

'Ju-jitsu,' she said. 'You use your opponent's weight against him.'

Arthur watched her stick down an envelope, add it to the pile and wind a fresh sheet on to the roller. An involuntary memory came of Walker begging to be released from the pack and himself sitting speechless, unable to respond. Plenty more of those in store, no doubt. He tasted his gin, which had a vaporous stink like surgical spirit. He couldn't remember ever having been given neat gin before. With its taste in his mouth his thoughts loosened, and he found that he was no longer following the conversation. He heard Cicely say: 'Yes, but surely we have to be practical.' He had only slipped for a few seconds, but he had lost track. He applied himself to getting the folds in his news-sheets just right, and heard Edith say: 'As far as persuasion goes, I can't see what's wrong with a swift knee in the goolies.' He nodded as if he knew exactly what she meant. He heard Sarah say: 'They don't know the value of symbols.' He wondered what Louis would make of this. Probably have them all eating out of his hand by now. Bad habit to be thinking of Louis all the time. When Louis had passed through London for the second time in the summer, on his way back to Germany after his visit home, he had refused Arthur's invitation to dinner but had agreed to call in at the Bradshaw and take an afternoon stroll around the district: an occasion for masculine confidences, Arthur felt, for catching up between old friends who saw less of one another these days, but who, given the chance to be private together, could still draw on the old times and talk and listen as ever – and he was glad of the opportunity, because it had been an eventful year all told. He wanted to let Louis know what a welter of incident and emotion he had undergone lately, but he had hardly begun to put it into words when he realised that Louis was bored. He changed the subject to Louis's travels, but Louis was monosyllabic on this too. They soon fell silent, and parted quickly, and as he walked back to the Bradshaw he was relieved to be alone.

Edith poured more gin into her glass. The typewriters had stopped now and the women were leaning back in their seats, their work done. Arthur straightened his pile.

'He won the vote,' Sarah said. 'But everyone knows he lost the argument.'

Cicely nodded, and they began to explore the notion that the whole incident could be seen as an analogy for relations between the sexes in private life.

'The woman gets what she wants by making sure the man believes he's getting what *he* wants,' said Cicely. 'She wins because he thinks he's winning.'

Edith snorted. 'So that's how it's done.'

'The art of persuasion, yes.'

'Keeping the poor darlings happy.'

'Can't be doing with it, myself,' said Edith.

She glanced at Arthur.

'Our trouble is, we're late,' she said. 'We live in the aftermath of a heroic time. Arrests by the thousands, speakers clubbed by policemen, demonstrators in chains, hunger protests. Back then, women knew what was at stake. The new lot have no understanding of what their mothers were fighting for. Don't you think, young man?'

It took Arthur a moment to realise who she was addressing, but all three women had turned their eyes on him and were waiting for his reply. Three coolly interested faces, and of the three Sarah's was the least familiar. What a strange being, balanced so finely on her chair, leaning back with her legs crossed at the knee and the point of one elbow on the table, one hand dangling her heavy glass in which the dregs ran around in an endless quick circle; what a strange being, with pale brown eyes, a strand of brown hair curling by her neck and a heart full of hidden things that no one could guess. But they were waiting for his reply, and the same faint smile had formed on all three faces. The women had straightened in their chairs as if they were readying themselves for a concerted physical feat, and Arthur wondered whether he would be a match for all three if they were to attack him bodily. Obviously not. He imagined them surrounding him, six strong hands tearing at his clothes. He had opened his mouth to answer the question some time ago, he noticed. Now he shut it again. The three smiles softened, and the women turned back to one another and resumed their conversation. He adjusted the top pamphlet on his stack. He was light-headed with the desire for revenge. Did they think they could get away with it, luring him here and then making him sit like a lump while they flaunted their grace and cleverness? He would say something, an utterance so laceratingly witty that their heads would snap back with shock and laughter and they would look at him anew, astonished to find their whole view of things so transformed.

He said nothing. He was too tired. They were talking as vigorously as ever, but he no longer tried to listen. He only sat, leaning on the table, letting the talk continue and the time pass, until his head dropped as if a string had slipped and the room slid sideways.

'Oh, look,' Sarah said. 'Someone's had enough.'

As they walked into Earl's Court she took his arm, gathering it in to herself. She growled at the cold and rubbed briskly at his coat sleeve. An impression brushed past from years ago, a student night in Dublin when he had stayed out so late that as he walked along the quays his breath streamed into air blued by the dawn and a few stars hardened in the heights of a dirt-streaked sky. As strong as gin in the mouth and gone in a breath, he thought. It wasn't so very late now – there was the tube station, spilling light from its open throat – but he couldn't shake his disorientation. He felt as if he had woken up too quickly. He blinked and yawned, not looking where he was going but trusting Sarah to guide him across the road, down the steps and into the confusion of clattering gates, howling tunnels, carriage doors closing and opening and closing, time slipping its cogs, corridors in which dead faces hallucinated themselves, tiled shafts where darkness flickered behind the lights. He swayed and jolted with the impacts of travel and kept hold of her hand until they were back in the cold air. His stomach was sore. She'd make him something to eat when they got home, she promised. They were nearly there now. He nodded, noticing how fast the tiny specks of sleet fell and how they vanished at the instant they touched the pavement. He stood on the step with his hands in his pockets while she unlocked the door, then followed her into the hall. But as he put his foot on the stair he faltered. The sense of something buckling made him think that the banister had given way under his hand, but it was only his face that was crumpling out of shape, only an imaginary structure inside his chest that was collapsing. He saw himself standing on the wall of a desert town with his hand in the hand of the child of his dream, and he now remembered how as they stood there he had tried, with the groundless urgency of dreams, to express a paradox that had revealed itself to him. Fathering a child is selfish, he had explained, but what you gain is unselfishness. When he had woken in the small hours he had tried to hang on to this thought so that he could tell Sarah, but it had slipped away, and he had lain for a while in the dark, wondering why, really, they wanted to do it. Perhaps because it was the kind of thing that human beings did. He remembered the sensation, in the dream, of the child withdrawing its hand from his own. He leaned on the stairs in front of him and tried to contain the hitching noises that wanted to come out.

Sarah was half a flight up, but she heard, and hurried back down.

'I know,' she said. 'I know.'

His eyes were hot. She turned him around and helped him

to sit on the stairs. She sat beside him and wiped his face with the palm of her hand. She had opened her coat and he could feel her warmth. She put her arms around his neck. He put his arms around her waist.

'There,' she said. 'I'll take you home.'

FOUR

Each morning as soon as he got up Arthur stripped his blankets and folded them away, then dismantled his bed, rolling the metal struts in the canvas to make a bundle that he could put out of sight in the corner. He punched the cushion into shape and repositioned it on the armchair. Patients mustn't guess that the consulting room was a campsite. Last night he had draped his brown suit over the headrest of the black oak chair, concealing ANNO 1660. The chair had been wedged in the corner for six months.

He was in the habit of rising early these days. It meant he could steal up to the flat to wash himself, eat something and be off to the hospital before she was awake. He kept a stash of clean underthings in the desk drawer down here, so that he didn't need to get into the bedroom and root through the wardrobe, but even so the mornings had become a farce of dressing, undressing and redressing. Now he climbed the four flights from the consulting room to the flat with his shoes unlaced and shirt unbuttoned. All was quiet in the flat: the bedroom door was closed.

He hung the suit jacket on a chair and took off his shirt, which was badly creased. He put up the ironing board, lit the gas in the kitchen and set the iron on the hob. The bedroom door remained shut. While the iron was heating he locked himself in the bathroom and washed standing up in the bath. The water was cold. He rubbed the soap in the hollow of his chest to work up a handful of lather, then scrubbed himself with a flannel, catching the stale odour of his lap. Shrivelled and rubbery this morning as for many mornings past. He tried to soap away the smell. Pits, pads and parts, they had been taught at Donard, the code of basic hygiene that he still recited inwardly every time he washed. But sometimes soap and water seemed to lack their ordinary virtue. He chased the suds down his shins and into the plughole, knowing he'd be noticing the staleness all day long. He towelled himself and brushed his teeth.

He could not bring his face into focus. Sleeping in the consulting room encouraged a headache, a drop of poison behind each eyeball. He pressed a finger and thumb to his lids, then pulled one eye wide. Crimson canthus, rheumy membrane, floaters reeling. He sat down on the lavatory. His bowels were heavy, the mass toxic. If he could rid himself of that the poison might drain from his skull, but nothing was moving.

When he came out of the bathroom in his trousers, vest and stockinged feet, Sarah was ironing his shirt. She wore the flannel pyjamas she had bought him for Christmas in Pimlico. She had opened the window. March had been wintry and April was cold so far.

'There's no need,' he said. He moved towards her, then stopped. 'Please, you shouldn't.'

She finished the shirt with two neat strokes, then hung it on the chair and disappeared into the bedroom. The hot cotton cooled as he fastened the buttons. She had left the bedroom door ajar, and he hesitated, wondering what that meant. An invitation to say something, to call out some easy pleasantry while she dressed? He couldn't leave now without seeming rude. She had complicated matters needlessly by doing his ironing. He owed her something for it but there was no telling whether she would prefer polite conversation or a quick departure. He compromised by putting the kettle on. It was simple enough to fake a domestic scene, after all, spooning tea leaves into the pot and pouring the water. She came back, dressed now. She lit the grill and cut two slices from the loaf.

A few minutes later she was sitting at the table and sipping her tea while he stood in the doorframe, holding a side plate to catch the toast crumbs. A motor car passed in the street below, merging with the general drone. You could imagine that a few well-chosen words might change the situation. Simple words that a husband would say to his wife at breakfast: if you could find them and say them right, everything would lock back into place and they would be themselves again. There were no such words. In recent months he had become aware of a seam in his life, a flaw that ran back through Trinity and school to the place in childhood where he had first failed to get to grips with the world in some way he still could not explain. Foolish to think that things had changed with marriage: to imagine that inside himself he wasn't the same creature he had always been, culpably innocent, sealed like an egg, too soft and stupid for the transactions that took place between real men and women. He had done her a great wrong. Perhaps he had only done it because she was the first woman to take an interest. How could he prove otherwise, even to himself? It couldn't have happened to Louis, heart-scarred Louis, wise to the world. No wonder he had scowled at their wedding.

And now he was hovering in the doorframe while she sat

over her teacup like a woman who was beginning to suspect that she wasn't alone in the flat. Lately he had been trying to guess what would happen when they found the courage to make an end. He'd go back to the life he'd been trained for, he supposed: move into single doctors' accommodation at the Bradshaw and henceforth keep his mind on his work. It would probably be the making of a distinguished career. But what would Sarah do? He pictured her going back in disgrace to her father's house, never to leave again, which was ridiculous, because nowadays failed marriage wasn't the end of the world, not even for the woman, and surely she would be better off in the end if she were free. But then perhaps this was one of the ways in which the world looked different to her and he would always fail to understand. Perhaps she truly would prefer to carry on like this forever.

He put the last corner of his toast into his mouth. He wasn't hungry. He had allowed weeks and months to go past and he still didn't know what she wanted. He ought to sit down and insist that they discuss their situation and reach an agreement. It would be unpleasant, but if they did it now the worst would be over by the time he left for work. They could start planning their respective futures. The toast was dry in his throat, and he drank tea to stop himself from coughing. Sarah got up, went into the bathroom and locked the door behind her.

He washed up the breakfast things. The light hurt his eyes. He could hear no noise from the bathroom. He let himself out of the flat and started down the stairs.

Arthur had begun private practice by taking two or three referrals from Venn, who had too many patients already. One was Evelyn Burden, forty-one years of age, unmarried, a school music teacher. She had presented for treatment with a persistent feeling that she wanted to cry and, as she put it, go on crying forever. Venn had seen her for a preliminary interview, and had formed some ideas about the nature of her difficulties, but naturally, he had said, it would be for Arthur to take his own line.

One of Miss Burden's merits as a patient was that she made herself responsible for easing the small social awkwardnesses that were inevitable in the opening minutes of a session. Now, as she arrived, she managed the journey from street door to consulting room by chattering about how she had been trying to observe her own thoughts in the way that Arthur had advised, and how it had been really very interesting and had brought up a lot that she would like to talk about, making much play meanwhile with her hat, shawl, mackintosh, umbrella, handkerchief and handbag, so that by the time she was arranged in the low armchair with her accoutrements suitably disposed around her, and Arthur, having closed the door, had taken his seat opposite, it seemed that they were already past the shallows and into the analytical work, Miss Burden saying that she had found herself brooding again for some reason or other on a small incident that had happened months ago and had passed out of her mind for a while but yesterday had come back to her as vividly as ever, which she thought might be significant and in need of investigation. Miss Burden was an enthusiastic student of the principles of analysis – perhaps too enthusiastic, it had occurred to Arthur, but there was no denying she seemed keen to make the most of her treatment. She was always ready to cooperate by going over stories of her childhood or of the trivial events of her day, following trains of association, reporting marginal thoughts, involuntary images and physical sensations, telling her dreams and daydreams. She gave every sign of being willing to do the work.

Now she paused to dab at the end of her nose with her handkerchief. She was a gaunt woman with large, moist-looking eyes and long dry hair that hung in curtains on either side of her face, giving her a girlish look in spite of the grey threads among the brown. Where her face was visible it was raw and reddened. She had had the same cold for the four months Arthur had been seeing her. She rolled the handkerchief up in her hands and pushed it into her sleeve, where it made a large bulge, one corner trailing free.

The small incident that had come again to her mind was that of Edward at the recital. Of course Arthur knew the story but, yes, she said, if he liked she would talk through its events again, telling them as they now came to her. Edward had been one of her pupils, an excellent pianist, one of the most promising students she'd had in some time and a pleasant, polite boy with it, rather on the quiet side. She had discovered that he had a special affinity for Chopin, who as Arthur knew was her own very favourite, and they had been working on the Nocturne in E flat major, which he played so sensitively that it made her proud, the notes falling like raindrops under his fingers. They decided that he would perform it at the school's end-of-year recital. But (Miss Burden said, remembering anew) it was awful, he had been so nervous. He'd never shown any nerves before, but his hands fumbled with the sheet music, and when he sat down at the instrument he didn't draw the stool up properly, so that he played the entire piece sitting too far out and at an angle to the keyboard. He played mechanically, as if she had failed to teach him the first thing about how to understand a piece, and then he actually stumbled and stopped. He went back, stopped again and limped his way to the end in disarray. Teachers, parents and pupils must have been asking themselves how she could have put the boy up to play a piece that was so far beyond his abilities. If only he hadn't sat down askew like that. Shortly afterwards Edward had decided to leave school and get a job, the specifics of which she didn't know, because when a pupil left her she could never bring herself to find out anything about where he was going. But she remembered the hall growing dark with mortification, and the faces of the women as they observed her defeat. Those puzzled, intelligent faces. Of course she knew she could not change any of this, would never be able to undo the humiliation of that day, and she had no illusions on the point, she said, speaking briskly and brightly as she always did. But what frightened her was the pain. The recital was only one of a thousand incidents – just the one that had happened to rise to the surface of her mind this time, lifted by who knew what current – but it made her want never to stop crying, and it frightened her that she could be hurt so much and be helpless to prevent it. The memory had come to her in the afternoon, halfway through a class, and she had stopped dead in the middle of a sentence up at the blackboard, not knowing how to carry on.

He shifted in his seat, frowning with attentiveness, and said something about wondering why it was that the incident had caused such strongly negative feelings in her. He hesitated, not wanting to say too much, but Miss Burden was nodding emphatically before he had finished speaking. Yes, he was so right, of course. He'd hit the nail on the head, as usual. She gave him a quick smile of gratitude and admiration. Because, yes, it was another example of what they'd talked about before, her habit of investing too much of herself in the achievements of her boys and feeling that their successes belonged to her, as if they were living for her sake rather than their own. It was an example of her inability to put herself in the other person's shoes, she said. When she thought of the recital she ought to be thinking about what it was like for Edward himself, because it must have been worse for him than for her, mustn't it, and he must have had his own reasons for not pulling up his stool properly, deep-rooted reasons that made it necessary for him to let her down in public, but she hadn't thought about that, she had only thought about the wrong to herself, and it was obvious, now that Arthur had pointed it out, that it was her selfishness at work again, that she was only complaining of a blow to her narcissism. She flashed him another smile. Thank goodness. That cleared that up.

The trouble was, she said, that it was so hard to find a way out of this terrible selfishness of hers, because even when she saw, as Arthur's wisdom had enabled her to see, that she was innately flawed by her inability to place herself in another person's shoes, what concerned her wasn't really that she seemed incapable of knowing or caring how that other person felt, but the other side of the problem, which was that no one could ever know or care what *she* felt or what *she* was like, and so she was still being selfish, and that was why the people who she called her friends could sense that something was missing in her, so that they were frightened and kept their distance; and who could blame them when she could behave so callously, taking any chance she was given to load her misery on to them with no consideration for what they might

194

already be having to cope with, as in the case of Judy: poor Judy, kind Judy, her only true friend on the school staff, who that summer had been having problems with her stomach and was in constant pain, and yet was strong enough to notice Miss Burden's unhappiness and had cared enough about it to invite her to come and stay, which Miss Burden did for weeks, and in so doing cast *herself* as the sick person so that poor kind Judy ended up tending to her. Judy had listened to Miss Burden's complaints for hours on end, smiling sympathetically through the stabbing pains. That had been the summer before Miss Burden came to the Malet Clinic for help, and subsequently her work with Arthur had enabled her to see that she had quite deliberately been seeking to hurt Judy, really to torture her, unconsciously motivated by a jealous hatred of her friend's capacity for disinterested love of others. That had certainly been a helpful thing to discover about oneself. But still, deep inside, she didn't care, because she couldn't, which was peculiar, because she knew that she was not actually incapable of humane concern. On the contrary, she was often overwhelmed by her sympathy for the sufferings of all the unhappy and downtrodden people of the world. Sometimes when she was alone she felt a physical ache in the region of her heart for all those who were the powerless victims of tyranny. Women, for example. She felt occasionally that she was a bottomless well of love for all women, those weak, frightened creatures, born slaves. It was only when it came to particular people like poor Judy that she could not manage to care. I know that when I sit here and talk about it, I talk in this brisk sort of cheerful way, she said, as if I'm making a scientific study and this is all of purely objective interest, but that's just my way of speaking so that I can manage to speak at all, so that I can sit here calmly and say these things and you can sit over there and listen and nod cleverly as if you understand me just as you're doing now, instead of saying it the true way, which would be not to say it at all but just to sit here and cry without stopping, which I can't do, because it would be a dreadful waste of time and money. But I *am* crying, always, except that I don't let the tears come: I cry invisibly, which is ridiculous, but it's all the more ridiculous to be sitting here telling you about it in my brisk cheerful way. I wonder why I'm bothering, because if I were fifteen or sixteen years old, say, it would be worth trying to clear up the mess, but when it's gone this far what, really, is the point? Which sounds rather hostile towards you, Doctor, and now that I think of it perhaps I am feeling rather hostile. I think I have an idea that you haven't been listening to me very carefully today, or that you don't especially want to hear what I have to say. Sitting here I've been thinking about how the books say that a good analyst has to be happy and secure in himself, because if he's not, if he's anxious and insecure, then he'll be afraid of the anxieties of his patients and will try to avoid having to hear about them, maybe by saying empty easy things instead of actually listening. Perhaps I shouldn't say this, perhaps it's against the rules. But it doesn't matter what I say, does it? We both realise that talking on and on like this is my way of avoiding what I really need to talk about, and that when I do my reading-up on analysis it's not because I want to make better progress but so I can spout the jargon at you and sound clever and avoid having to really think about things. Talking like this never gets us anywhere, because however much we say and analyse and understand, the real problems stay just out of reach, because as soon as you put something into words it stops being real and the reality moves on. I don't know what I mean by the reality. I keep looking around this room and thinking about how you have a life of your own, and how much more you must care for your own life than for mine, which is only natural, of course, but it makes me angry to think of it, because the truth is that I want you to exist solely for my benefit, which is unforgivable, isn't it? Quite monstrous. But it's strange how I can feel that but then also feel as if I'm completely at your mercy, sometimes, as if you're God or Fate, passing these cruel judgments on me. Do you know, you're the only man I've spoken more than three words to this week? And now I ought to stop talking because the time is nearly up and I expect you feel that you need to say something to remind me that you're in charge and draw the session to a nice sensible conclusion. It's all right, I'll just gather myself up now, because I know it's time. I know it's not generally considered a good thing for the patient to bring the session to an end, because it betrays her need for control or her anxiety about dependence on the analyst, but I'm afraid I can't help it: I do prefer to notice for myself when the time is over. Right, is that everything? Umbrella, bag? I think so. Same time next time, then. I can find my way out, yes. Thank you, Doctor, I'm terribly grateful, I don't know what I'd do, a thousand thanks, yes, thank you, thanks.

Lambert was standing at the far end of the Hospital Secretary's office, passing the time of the morning with Mrs Kempe. Lambert, a tall, narrow-shouldered JHO with blond hair cut close around his bald patch, had only been at the Bradshaw for a couple of months, but Mrs Kempe didn't seem to mind him standing with his hands in his trouser pockets, bouncing the fronts of his thighs against her desk. He was saying nothing of importance but he was in no hurry to move on. Her spectacles hung from their chain, resting on her bosom.

Neither looked at Arthur. As he was collecting together the files for his ward round, a nurse arrived and glanced around the room before walking over to Lambert and showing him a slip of paper.

'Just a signature,' she said, as he scanned it.

'Any old signature?' he said. 'Elsie, I'm hurt. I thought you wanted *me*.'

Clicking his tongue, curving his eyebrow, Lambert picked up a pen from Mrs Kempe's desk and signed with a flourish. He handed back the slip to the nurse, who turned and walked straight past Arthur. She smiled and rolled her eyes as Lambert called after her:

'How are you going to make it up to me?'

Arthur bent to his files. If a doctor's signature was all the nurse had wanted, she could have asked either of them, and hadn't she been closer to Arthur as she came into the room, and wasn't he more senior than Lambert, and hadn't Lambert been absorbed in his chatter while Arthur had been standing here available to be asked? And yet she had walked by as if it were assumed that even his signature on a form was not quite to be trusted. Perhaps this was one of those incidents that pierces deeper than you know at first, so that afterwards as the minutes go by you gasp and grit your teeth and then gasp again as you realise that here is going to be another memory that will never stop mattering, a lesion that doesn't heal. No, not that bad, probably not one of those. But of course one thought leads to another. All the times you've made an idiot

198

of yourself are linked together like stops on the map of the Underground, so that you can ride around for as long as you please, starting off at one of your quiet little outlying mistakes and travelling inwards by one route or another to connect yet again with the terminal humiliations – and so now you start remembering the worse ones, the unforgivable ones, like the incident in April when one of the patients on the locked ward had accosted him on his round and asked when she was getting out. Joan was far from ready to leave the ward, being of an aggressive and unpredictable bent even on her best days, but she never got tired of insisting that she needed to go right away, and the nurses spent a good deal of time telling her that she wasn't yet well enough but that she was making good progress, that she must put it out of her mind and concentrate on getting better. Given firmly, this kind of answer usually satisfied her, and she would shake her hair moodily and stamp away. This time, though, Arthur was caught off balance by the question, so that instead of answering her from the textbook he found himself mumbling something to the effect that he wasn't sure, that he didn't have time to discuss it now but he'd see about it tomorrow. Retreating from her glare, he hurried on with the round. The following day two of the nurses told him that Joan had been banging about the ward triumphantly because, she said, the doctor had told her that she was getting out today. The nurses were deadpan. It wasn't for them to decide what to do about it: theirs only to mop up afterwards. Arthur found Joan and began to explain that she should not expect to leave for some time yet and that the wisest course for now was not to think about it too much. He had stepped away from her and was moving on with the round when one of the other patients laughed. It was a brief bitter laugh, no doubt a response to some purely internal stimulus – she was a thin young woman, always passive and sunk in thought – but it was unfortunately timed, and Joan attacked her, striking her head against the doorframe before knocking her down. The young woman made no sound as Joan grabbed her hair and slammed her head against the floor. Three nurses pulled Joan off her victim and got her face down, one holding each of her arms and one kneeling on her legs. A fourth nurse injected a sedative. Arthur, feeling that his presence could only complicate matters further, left the ward. He cleared off sharpish, the nurses would be saying. He made it back to the main building and into the gents on the ground floor before he stopped and let out the breath he had been holding, leaning on the sink as a severe headache sprang fully formed into the front of his skull.

That incident had lodged in him. Walking down a crowded street many days later he had been struck again by what had happened, and had stopped in the middle of the pavement, unable to see in front of him or hear the noise of the traffic, until he felt a sharp tap on the back of his head and he turned as a voice said Wake up, wee man! He was pushed bodily aside, out of the road, by a man whose grubby collarless shirt was open to show a triangle of raw skin. Arthur watched the man walk away, carrying a long-handled shovel, chipping its blade against the cobblestones, moving with an easy pace. Arthur wanted to catch up with him and commit the terrible act of violence which alone would soothe his heart; but the man vanished into the crowd. Arthur could not breathe. Blood pounded in the place where his skull met his spine at such a pressure that he thought something might burst. He could taste pennies between his back teeth. He tried to fix the man's features in his mind so that should they ever meet again he would be ready to take his revenge. He moved out of the thoroughfare, reminding himself to keep things in proportion. He wasn't a madman, needing to shriek and flail at every passing insult. He was sane, hopelessly sane, obliged always to be civilised and careful, to rise above the affront, to remain unimpeachable and remember what he had to lose. The world could do as it liked with him and he must not complain.

He left the Hospital Secretary's office with the files tucked under his arm. He walked slowly, stooping to favour a cramp. It seemed denser now, the toxic stuff coagulating. On his way to the ward he stopped in at the post room. His pigeon hole contained a telephone message slip from the reception desk, filled out in the usual hard-to-decipher scrawl.

FROM: Miles Mc Donnach
TIME: 8.40 a.m.
MESSAGE: Louis Mollyneu taken ill last night. Admitted to Dublin Baggot St Hospital condition grave.

Some of Arthur's clearest memories of Donard were those not of any event in particular but of the empty periods when the timetable set you loose to fend for yourself. Often at those times he had simply wandered around the school. When he had to pass through corridors and common rooms where other boys were loitering, he would try to look as if he were on his way somewhere – the trick was to seem preoccupied but not too much so – but better was to find himself alone, so that he could pace along the dormitory corridor or around the back cloister unobserved, slowing almost to a stop if it felt safe enough and setting off again when he sensed movement nearby. He would always be disappearing from one part of the school to another, never quite present where he was.

Now he moved through the Bradshaw in that mood. He was due on the ward, but halfway across the covered bridge he stopped and looked down into the hospital's grey gardens. He yawned until his jaw clicked, then doubled back into the main building, where he walked along corridors and laboured up and down stairwells for a while. The message called for him to spring into immediate and decisive action, he supposed, and fly to the aid of his stricken friend. He was holding the slip of paper in his hand. Myles had not left a phone number. Even at Trinity he had sometimes wandered like this in the spare hours between lectures and demonstrations, feeling it was safer to disappear and haunt the campus and the nearby streets than to let anyone suspect that he didn't know what to do with himself for a free period. There had been a kind of excitement in it, as if he were the first person to notice that schedules, timetables and appointments, all those requirements to be in a certain place at a certain time to do a certain thing, were not the steel pillars of the universe, as he had been taught: they were not real, and you could walk away from them any time you chose.

Back in January he had wandered around the Bradshaw's corridors for a while, after Jacobs told him that William Walker had been moved from the Calvary to Cranfield Park. Jacobs had been examining new admissions to the asylum and had recognised the patient by name and from Arthur's description. He was on the reception ward now, Jacobs said, under reasonably close supervision, but pressure on beds was high and he would be moved to one of the general wards within a day or two. Arthur thanked him for passing on the news. There must be some mistake, he thought, wandering the corridors. He'd heard nothing of Walker since the incident of the wet pack had convinced him that the charade of analysis was doing more harm than good. In the end he telephoned the Calvary, imagining that he might speak to a secretary or an archivist who might look up the file and clarify what had happened to Walker in the four months since, but instead the operator put him straight through to the Physician-Superintendent. Discomfited, Arthur explained his former connection with the Calvary and with Walker in particular. There was a silence, as if the line had failed; then the Fletcher-Foxe drawl. Ah, yes, our Mr Walker, of course. Terribly good of you to ask after him. Yes, no longer with us. It became impossible for him to stay. A question of funds, you see. No, no idea, none of our business, naturally. Some change in family circumstances, I believe, death or bankruptcy or whatnot, none of our concern. Strictest confidence of course. It became evident that the Calvary was not the place for someone in his condition. We are, as you know, an institution for the *curably* insane. At Cranfield Park he can be cared for much more in accordance with his needs. Very much for the best all round, yes. And now, Doctor, if you'll excuse me. Arthur put down the telephone and told himself it was none of his concern. Walker was a former patient for whom he was no longer responsible, and he really didn't see what Jacobs expected him to do about it. It wasn't Arthur's fault that Walker had been ejected from the place where he might have hoped to see out his days, and funnelled into the grim throwback of an asylum that Jacobs had often described. He pictured

Walker on the brink of a dark, cavernous space filled with cries and vague struggle.

Now he slipped into the gents. If he could ease the weight he would know what to do next. He locked himself into a stall and sat with his head low. Nothing moved. The sides of the stall were tiled in dark green, the door painted pale green. Someone had used a sharp instrument to score three parallel lines into the paint. He sat for a long time, listening to the gurgles of the plumbing. Eventually he gave up. Coming out of the stall he caught sight of himself in the mirror above the sinks, his face pouched with green shadows. He held his hands under a trickle of water and gazed into the glass. It was difficult to recognise the face as his own. The hair was thin and colourless and the shape of the skull was apparent. He leaned closer and the face leaned towards him. The pores of the nose were plugged with black stuff. Under each eye was a grey dent, as if someone had pinched the skin until it bruised. The eyes themselves were unreadable. The longer he stared into them the harder they stared back, incredulous and hostile. He began to feel that it might not be safe to look away. Then he caught a movement in the gloom behind the face in the mirror: someone had been at the urinal and was now turning, fastening his fly.

It was Jacobs. Arthur moved his fingers in the water, then lowered his face and lifted the cold water to his eyes. He had only been standing at the mirror: it was hardly a crime to rest in here for a minute or two. Jacobs was washing his hands methodically, rubbing soap between his palms and then working through a series of hygienic gestures, palm to palm, thumb to palm, fingers interlaced, fingers interlocked. He rinsed off the lather and glanced at Arthur as he dried his hands. His shoulders were slumped as usual, the jacket rumpled and the hair untidy, but the eyes were bright with concern.

'Do you mind my asking,' he said. 'Are you quite all right?'

Louis had been walking alone down Henry Street shortly after eleven o'clock at night when he had fallen down unconscious. This was the testimony of several witnesses. There had been no accident or assault, no obvious cause for the collapse. He had shown no signs of intoxication. The convulsion had been spontaneous. He had been taken to Baggot Street and so far had not woken up. At present there was nothing more to tell.

Myles MacDonagh poured coffee into a china teacup and passed it to Arthur, who sipped the bitter fluid and felt his insides clench. He had come straight to Chelsea from the Bradshaw. Myles set the pot down in a clear spot on his desk, which was strewn with the materials of his work: stacks of cheap school exercise books, a typewriter, a two-volume French dictionary, a *Modern English Usage* in a faded mint-green dust jacket, and, piled in disorder, dozens of assorted typescripts and manuscripts. There was something forlorn about the mass of papers, all of which were marked up with arcane squiggles in red ink. They could have been mistaken for the obsessional work of a patient, the productions of a psychosis that for their creator held the most awful revelations when in reality they meant nothing at all. He looked around the room. Myles's books, half of which were brand new and the other half ruined with use, were in the process of colonising the flat, spilling from the home-made shelves to form banks and towers that reached halfway up the walls.

'They rang this morning,' Myles was saying. 'I'd been working all night.'

Arthur nodded. He didn't care much about any of it. In the lavatory at the Bradshaw he had felt what a relief it would be to confess everything to Jacobs: that he had been losing his grip for months now, doing his job incompetently, living under false pretences, and that now he was hiding in the jakes because he didn't know where else to go. It would be a relief to throw away the pretence that they were colleagues and equals, to admit that he was sick and beg to be told what to do. Instead he'd assured Jacobs that he was perfectly well, just a little disconcerted by bad news he had received about an old friend in Dublin. Jacobs had insisted he must go to his friend right away, and had volunteered to cover his responsibilities at the hospital. As they clasped hands Arthur had noticed that in the centre of himself he didn't care. In that tranquil place he was not troubled in the slightest by the news that Louis was ill, nor by his failure with Sarah or his incompetence at work or anything else that had happened, good or bad. He acted out the appropriate responses and that was all. He had hurried across town to knock on Myles's door not from any overwhelming need to learn what had happened to Louis, but because it seemed to be what he was expected to do.

The tips of Myles's fingers were stained yellow. He was explaining that the call had come from some member of the Baggot Street staff, who had found his telephone number on a card in Louis's pocket. Myles, in turn, had rung Wesley Street and then the Bradshaw. One point of Myles's button-down collar had come loose and curled up on itself, and his woollen tie was a hard knot. He had shown no surprise when Arthur

206

had turned up on his doorstep, and had brought him straight up to the sitting room where, now, he began to shuffle through the papers on his desk. A cardboard suitcase lay open on the sofa with a few items of clothing inside.

'I tried to catch the day mail,' Myles said. 'I went to Euston as soon as I got the message, ran halfway there, but I missed it.'

He sat down at his desk and rested his head on the heels of his hands. He glanced at his wristwatch.

'Nine hours and fifteen minutes till the night mail goes.'

He dropped a sheaf of papers back on the desk, sprang up and began to pace, pushing back his fringe, checking his wristwatch again.

Five minutes later Arthur was heading in the general direction of the King's Road. The coffee jogged in his stomach. It had done nothing to loosen the congestion lower down, which seemed to have hardened into a handful of stones. He could follow Myles's example, catch the night mail and be at Louis's bedside in Baggot Street by this time tomorrow, haggard with love. Perhaps that was the only conscionable course of action. What did *convulsion* mean? Louis lying in the gutter with burnt matchsticks and cigarette butts swirling past his face as he shuddered with some mysterious form of grand mal, the symptom of a long-incubated neurological disorder, some organic malignancy that had been growing in his brain for years if not decades, causing migraine, depression and altered personality. A disorder that might have been discovered at a much earlier stage if he had not had the bad luck at a crucial juncture to put his trust in a callow doctor who happened to be in thrall to psychological medicine and all too ready to misdiagnose a genuine physical illness as a neurotic complaint.

If he was going to Dublin he ought to tell Sarah first. He ought to race back to the flat, explain the situation, pack a bag and set off right away. Twenty yards ahead a queue of passengers was shuffling aboard the number thirty-four. He could catch it and be home in half an hour. But he walked on past the stop. The bus overtook him a minute later, and he lost sight of it as it turned into Sloane Square. He kept walking. Not that he knew whether Sarah was at home: he didn't ask her where she went or how she occupied her time.

That day in December, they had believed for a few hours that they were going to have the child they had imagined. The following morning they came around slowly, curled together in the bed. They greeted one another with slight movements, still more than half asleep, their heads still sunken in the pillows. She rolled over to face him so that they could lock hands in the last of their sleep. Her eyes opened, and as they began the day, moving around one another in considerate silence – his hand steadying her elbow as they dressed in the narrow space between the bed and the wardrobe, her fingers on his wrist as she passed his cup of tea – it seemed that they had found the way through. They would live in this sad closeness for as long as they needed to. They would be brave, they would be kind, and what would happen would happen, but if they were to be childless it would bring them together, not break them apart, because they knew one another better today. We know now, he thought, as he kissed her goodbye and set off across town for his day's work at the Bradshaw, that it's up to us to make our own kind of future. And after all, Sarah did not believe in placing all her hopes there. Arthur was relieved that over the weeks and months that followed she became more seriously involved with the Women's Liberation League.

208

She threw herself into a campaign for equal representation of the sexes on juries, and into the debates that, she said, were going on vigorously within the organisation about the need for parity of moral standards for men and women (Arthur, nodding, wondered what this meant). She attended meetings, wrote letters, raised funds and recruited new members. Before long the League was paying her for a day's paperwork in an Earl's Court office each week.

One Saturday morning she left the flat early, dressed up and wearing her green-and-gold sash, carrying a tin of cakes that she had baked to be sold at the fundraising fair the League was holding in Hyde Park. It was a major event in the calendar, she said, with forty stalls, a merry-go-round, a tombola, a raffle, a brass band and a stage where distinguished women would be giving talks all day: all her friends would be there. But when he got home that evening she was lying across the sofa in the near dark with her face buried in her arms. She seemed to be asleep, though when he touched her shoulder she sat up at once. She had left the fair halfway through because she was sick of looking at the young mothers. Everywhere I turn, women and their bloody children, she said. Arthur put on the lights so that the pale evening glow turned to darkness outside the window. Then he sat on the edge of the sofa and tried to reason her into a better mood. She didn't argue with him, only laid her head back down on her arms and closed her eyes. Her face was peaceful.

He cut across a corner of the park, then began to walk along Wigmore Street. He was circling back towards the flat more by default than intention. He was an intruder there. Sarah didn't want him in the place because she was fully occupied with nursing her sadness. She nourished it and tended to its needs, clutching it so close to herself that although Arthur knew it was there, and even that it partly belonged to him, he never really caught a glimpse of it. Instead he left for work early and got back late.

All of this was valuable material for the training analysis. On the day that he set up the camp-bed in his consulting room for the first time, he told Venn what he had done with a certain pride: here at last were some difficulties to speak of, and perhaps they would make him a real and serious man. It was hard to think what to say about them, though, and Arthur found himself wondering aloud whether their failure to conceive – they had been trying, by then, for a year and a half – might not have a psychosomatic basis. Might it not be a manifestation of some hidden reluctance in himself or Sarah or both of them, a symptom of their inability to give themselves to one another heart and soul? In retrospect, that speculation had been the death of the analysis. It had been such a stupid thing to say that he couldn't forgive Venn for pretending it deserved consideration, absorbing the suggestion in thoughtful silence and finally asking: do you believe that this is the reason? As Arthur walked away from the clinic that night, the whole flimsy construction fell apart and he saw that Venn was a limited man who cultivated his psychoanalytical mystique to seem impressive but had no better idea than his patients of how to live. His tricks were cheap, and once you had learned them he was at your mercy, yours to manipulate and fool. At their next session Arthur proposed suspending the training analysis for a short while because, he said, the unexpectedly turbulent state of his private life made it impossible for him to give their work the attention it deserved. Venn had agreed that analysis was best undertaken during settled periods, and that, although breaking off partway through was strongly contraindicated as a rule, he was willing to endorse a temporary suspension under the circumstances. Arthur had known he would agree. It was the only way the man could salve his pride and avoid acknowledging that the analysis was over for good.

He stopped under the horse chestnut tree at the corner of Wesley Street. Their window was closed. She might or might not be inside. Odd to have come all the way home on foot, today of all days, when there was no time to spare: he ought to be tending to his patients, he ought to be flying to the bedside of his stricken friend, he ought to be talking things out once and for all with his wife. It appeared that he had walked all this way simply in order to put off deciding what to do next. He turned and carried on along Marylebone Street.

He walked beside Regent's Park, through Camden Town and into Kentish Town. Soon he had been walking for two hours. No one knew where he was. If he fell down a manhole no one would know what had become of him. He crossed Tufnell Park and pressed on into Upper Holloway. It was the kind of long, aimless stroll that he had not taken since his student days. He was in Archway. His feet ached. A cramp went through his abdomen. The steady walking pace was kneading his clutch of stones into something ever more immovable. He looked at his watch: it was a little more than three hours since he had left the Bradshaw. He was curious about where he was heading, but he preferred not to think on it too deeply. He only watched the streets go past as he walked through Crouch End and into Muswell Hill, not paying attention to his route, hardly thinking of anything at all, unaware of any possible destination until the very moment that he passed through a point-arched iron gateway and into a broad, straight avenue lined with elms and leading to the massive frontage of a building, too large to take in all at once, with a bell tower rising above a central block and to left and right two long wings that housed the wards. He had walked the length of this avenue many times, but not since the spring, and where before the trees had swayed and rustled they had now been pollarded to clubs. The avenue led to the front of Cranfield Park Lunatic Asylum.

The door closed behind him, the locks turned and Arthur was left to his own devices on General Ward One. The porter who had brought him from the front hall had shown no interest in determining who he was. At the nurses' station a male nurse ground out a butt in a heaping ashtray. He gave Arthur a long look, then put his lips to the pack to draw out a fresh cigarette.

The patients wore asylum uniforms. All the figures he could see as he looked down the ward's main room, male or female, sitting or lying on the benches, leaning against the walls or wandering in the central space, had a clownish aspect thanks to their outfits of grubby white drill trousers and loose fustian jacket. The cheap, heavy boots were manufactured in a workshop somewhere in the asylum itself: they came without laces and were always too big, so that all the patients dragged their feet when they walked. The uniforms also officially included cloth caps and neckerchiefs, he knew, but few patients wore these. Perhaps they chose not to for some reason of local custom, or perhaps they tended to get lost. On Arthur's first visit, Jacobs had railed against the rules on patients' dress. How would we feel, he asked, if when we came into a hospital for treatment we had our clothes confiscated and – having done nothing wrong – were forced to put on a prison uniform? It has no conceivable purpose except to humiliate people, and it's poorly thought out as well. For one thing they aren't issued with rain cloaks, which means they get soaked through in the airing courts. Everyone has a cold all the time and we're always dealing with cases of TB and pneumonia. It was deplorable, Arthur agreed, but he couldn't help feeling reassured by the uniforms. They meant that when he went to leave the ward the nurse would not look at him without recognition and tell him to sit down and wait for his medicine like everyone else.

On that visit they had walked the length of this room together while Jacobs counted off the asylum's faults. Cranfield Park housed just over thirty-five hundred patients, he explained, and as a part-time medical officer he had four hundred people under his immediate care. He was a dogsbody: every minute on duty he was doing clerical work, filling out forms and returns, keeping up case books, reading letters written by patients and letters received for them, admitting new patients, doing morning, afternoon and evening rounds, visiting the farm, the workshops and the laundry, writing prescriptions, carrying out minor surgical procedures and answering emergency calls. Oh, it's what we're here for, Jacobs said. It all has to be done, but don't imagine we have time on the side to practise psychiatric medicine. The asylum isn't built for it. When I started here, I asked where I could speak with patients in private, and they looked at me as if I was mad. Why should a doctor need to see a patient alone? We don't treat them as individual cases, we just feed them and drug them. When they damage each other we patch them up and when they hang themselves we cut them down.

To Arthur's left a short corridor opened off the ward. It was lined with three doors, each with a bolt on the outside. The first door was open to a vacant room: inside, a thin coconut-matting bed on the floor, a rubber chamberpot, a high shuttered window and the residue of a stench suppressed with disinfectant. The other two rooms were bolted shut and the bolts padlocked. The occupant of one of them was groaning: a drawn-out noise of boredom or horror with no particular cause. Arthur put his eye to the spyhole, but only saw darkness. The other room was silent, but as he listened something struck the door from the inside. He imagined the inmate pressed against the door, testing its solidity with a blow of the hand or head. No one should be confined like this, Jacobs had said when they stood in this corridor last January, but I've ordered it myself on many occasions. There's no alternative. A violent patient needs close supervision from a dedicated nurse, but we don't have the staff for that, and so the most troublesome cases are put in these solitary cells where they sink all the faster. We're supposed to call them single rooms. I once went to the Medical Superintendent about a patient who had been in a cell for three weeks straight, and he patted my shoulder and told me not to worry. He said that when he was medical officer he'd kept patients there for six months at a stretch and that no one had come to any harm.

The main space of the ward was a long, broad room, eighty feet by forty, according to Jacobs, comfortably large enough for a game of tennis. Three empty fireplaces were protected by steel guards. One side of the ward was lined with windows, their glass toughened with wire mesh, looking down into the grey sinks of the airing courts. Two day rooms opened off the other side of the main space, as did the lavatories and the bathhouse. The dormitories were locked in the daytime. Such were the dimensions of the world occupied by the one hundred

214

and twenty-eight men and women who lived on the ward. Many were immobile on the benches, some sunk in exhaustion or despondency, others fixed in contorted postures and a few rocking or otherwise caught in loops of stereotyped movement. Still others wandered around, each in his or her own manner: timid, louring, haughty, anxious, serene.

Arthur glanced into the first of the day rooms, which contained a billiard table without balls or cues. Beside it, two men were standing eye to eye, both at a loss for words. Then the tension between them broke and one of the men strode off into the ward, muttering under his breath. Arthur would fare poorly as a patient, he knew, because he was not nearly good enough at reading the intricate, unspoken signals that governed the social life of a ward like this: the near invisible insults, bargains and kindnesses that made the difference between peace and violence. On one visit here he had seen the attendants snap a woman's collarbone in the process of breaking up a scuffle, while on the far side of the room two elderly men, one grey-bearded and the other with a handsome, hollow face, bowed their heads together in erudite conversation. A lot of these people are asylum-made lunatics, Jacobs had said. With proper treatment they might have been recoverable, but confinement has made them permanently insane.

No sign of Walker. As he continued down the ward a group of four female patients drifted towards him, a chorus coming to beg a boon or whisper a secret. Before they could explain what they wanted, they were scattered by an attendant who strode through them as if they weren't there. Arthur nodded what he hoped was a brisk doctorly greeting, but the man ignored him and walked on to join his fellow at the nurses' station.

A third attendant was on table duty, sitting with his boots

up on the long deal table top, ankles crossed. He looked sick with boredom. Behind the table, ten patients sat in a row with their backs to the wall. They would be here for the rest of the day, and most seemed resigned to sit inert, although at the far end one woman was whispering darkly to the girl beside her. The girl was twisting her head away but keeping her shoulders rigid, as if she were forbidden to move from the neck down. On other visits Arthur had seen fights break out behind the table. One mealtime a young man who spat in his neighbour's food had been rewarded with the stroke of a ragged thumbnail that opened his cheek from eye to mouth.

The tabled patients were in worse physical condition than those who were free to roam. Most of the faces were blotchy with sores, and over here the rancid smell of the ward was stronger. Arthur held his breath. These patients were one slip away from a single room. Certainly they needed a close eye on them all the time, Jacobs had said, but this was not the way to do it: the behind-the-table system was another unnecessary brutality, caused purely by institutional stupidity and penny-pinching. If the asylum were prepared to pay for as many attendants as it needed, and if the patients were properly classified and divided according to their illnesses rather than being thrown together in a single oversized ward, then there would be no need to treat the sickest among them like this, subjecting them to circumstances in which anyone might go insane for want of anything else to do.

Walker was not behind the table. Arthur turned his attention back to the main room, where nothing was happening. It was one of the intervals at which the coercions of the routine gave way to empty time. And perhaps if the attendants were to leave him locked in here to become just another inmate, he would manage, after all. He did have his schooldays to fall back on. Perhaps those days had taught him what it would be like to live in the ward with its washed-out light, its human statues and its wanderers. You would be harried through the checkpoints of the day – rising, dressing, drugging, eating, washing, airing, resting – but in between you would be abandoned to defend yourself however you could against the devils assigned to your persecution. After his second or third visit to Cranfield Park, Arthur had dreamt that he was in purgatory, a bland, eventless place like a railway station where travellers were waiting, milling around a series of echoing halls where no arrivals or departures were due. He answered a ringing telephone, whereupon a voice told him that for his pride he was damned and without further ado the dream collapsed under his feet, tumbling him into hell, which was General Ward One, although the ward's wood-block floor had become an endless sea of mud in which you could never get purchase with your feet but were always sliding and scrabbling and falling down. In the unchanging twilight under its groined ceiling the nightmare ward extended to infinity, its landscape wet and cold, shell-cratered, hacked up with trenches and barbed wire and studded with ruined structures like churches that had been bombed. Damned souls cowered in these wrecks, hunted by ghoul gangs intent on mutilation and rape, but, sprawling in the mud, Arthur understood that this was not truly the Inferno, because in this hell the punishment was not to be put in your place but to have no rightful place at all. He surfaced from the dream thrilled with discovery, convinced he had achieved an insight into Walker's experience of the world, but moments later, as he came fully awake, he knew he had done nothing of the sort. Perhaps Fletcher-Foxe had been right, though.

Perhaps Cranfield Park was the best place for Walker, because perhaps conditions in the asylum were a fair approximation of the conditions that prevailed in his mind. If you had to be mad perhaps it was a comfort to find your madness made real around you. Nonsense thoughts, Arthur told himself. Fletcher-Foxe doesn't know what's best for him, and neither do you.

He found Walker in the second day room, staring at a big piece of sunlight that lay broken across the wall. The twenty or so patients on the benches were abstracted and motionless, some sitting in ordinary poses like people in a waiting room, others twisted painfully into themselves. In the coarse outfit and loose boots, Walker was like a child dressed in adult clothes. He looked even smaller than in his days of silk pyjamas and peacock dressing-gowns; younger and more frail. He sat with his hands on his knees, palms upward, as if they were objects he had dropped and disregarded.

Arthur sat down on the bench.

He stole a glance at Walker's face. There were the scars from the Calvary – the puckered lines across his nose and around his eye sockets – but there were more recent marks too. A yellow bruise spread from his right temple across his forehead and cheekbone. He had a sore on his cheek and raw fissures at the corners of his mouth. His hair had been cropped to the skull some time ago and had now grown out to fuzz, thick with dry flakes of scalp.

When Arthur had learned that Walker was in Cranfield Park, he had imagined arranging a transfer to the Bradshaw. There they would begin the analysis over again and this time do it right. They would forgive one another for past misunderstandings and Walker, grateful to be rescued, would finally begin to cooperate. But as soon as Arthur laid eyes on Cranfield Park he knew that it could not happen. The asylum's exterior was enough to tell him that no inmate could hope to make the journey from here to a modern hospital. Walker did not seem to notice his visitor. Jacobs gave them an hour together, and Arthur waited out the time for the sake of appearances, but when he left it was with relief, and with no intention of coming back. A week later he was there again, sitting beside the unresponsive Walker as before, not knowing what he expected to accomplish. On the third visit he brought his chess set. He set up the game on the bench between them, presented Walker with black and made an opening move. Walker barely glanced at the board, but after a pause of fifteen minutes or so he moved a black pawn. It took him half an hour to bring Arthur to a tidy checkmate.

Now Arthur folded his hands in his lap. Walker tipped his head first to one side, then to the other, in a mime of someone weighing up a new piece of information.

'You're not playing white today.'

Arthur hesitated. He hadn't prepared himself to talk.

'No,' he said. 'I came here on the spur of the moment, to tell the truth.'

Walker made a noise like a chuckle.

'On the spur of the moment,' he said. 'To tell the truth.'

They were silent for a while. They sat side by side like people resting on a park bench, companions or strangers. Walker was silent but he seemed alert, as if waiting for Arthur to explain why he had come.

Through January and February Arthur had visited Cranfield Park every few days. Jacobs, assuming that he was carrying out a therapeutic experiment, let him get on with it, but of course Jacobs was deceived: Arthur could not have explained why he kept coming to General Ward One, but it was no longer to do with making Walker better. When they paced the ward or sat in the day room with the chessboard on the bench between them, he was free from the humiliations of the Bradshaw and from the silence that was always waiting in Wesley Street. At times he felt that his days and nights were spent waiting for the next chance to go to the asylum. Now and then it did occur to him that by behaving in this way he was betraying every principle of his profession, throwing away all that he had worked for since his schooldays, but when he slipped into Cranfield Park to see Walker his heart beat fast. His nerves were alight with the knowledge that what he was doing could only end in shame and disaster, and he was glad.

Now he said:

'I don't know why I've come.'

They gazed at the wall. The bright lozenge was reaching for the floor. Odd that it should be so difficult to imagine the man's state of mind. They had spent so many hours sitting side by side with these few inches of space between their skulls, but there was still no way to close the gap. In these past months he and Walker had never exchanged more than a few words, but there had been days when he had been sure that at some level, inaccessible even to themselves, they knew one another in a way that was seldom granted to two human beings. Now he had a great desire to speak. He wanted to tell Walker everything that had happened. That in his work he was a failure and a fraud, that he was incapable either of living with his wife or of making a clean break, and that now Louis had been struck down by some malaise calculated to show that Arthur had neglected his duty to his friend. That the only response he could summon to all of this was weariness; that he wished they'd all leave him alone.

On an impulse he got up and stood in front of Walker. Then he dropped to one knee, bringing their faces to a level, and took hold of the upturned hands. The skin caught like emery paper. He hadn't touched Walker's hands before. The impropriety of the conduct was considerable, but he gripped tight. Over his period of visiting Cranfield Park he had become increasingly ashamed of himself, and had often sworn off the asylum as a drunk would swear off the pub or a fornicator the house of ill repute. He had sat on the bench beside Walker rehearsing in his mind what he must say to Sarah as soon as he got home. He must be a man, he told himself. He must explain his position. I made a promise, he would say, and it is my intention to keep it. I wish to make clear that I am determined to fulfil my responsibilities towards you in whatever manner you prefer. I wish to assure you that this does not imply any expectation of access to your person or your private affairs. I recognise that you no longer wish to live as husband and wife and I hope it is understood that I will make no unwelcome advances towards you in that respect. I am merely determined to keep the promise that I have made. Should you wish me to continue as your spouse in name alone, I will cooperate in whatever way you wish for as long as you wish. Should you prefer an end to the marriage I will accept all blame. Often as he turned into Wesley Street, going over these statements in his mind, his eyes prickled at the bitter nobility of it. It was a fine thing to resign one's happiness for duty, to break one's heart before one's word. He would do as she decided. If she wanted rid of him, he knew how these things were supposed to be done, more or less. He'd need an accomplice. Possibly Cicely would be willing, or Edith might actually relish it, or perhaps, strange punishment, Myles could put him in touch with Celia Prentice. Whoever it was, Arthur would have to go with her on the train to Brighton, where they would sit up all night playing cards in a hotel room so that they could be surprised by the chambermaid in the morning and Sarah could petition for divorce as the injured party. Easier to endure a lifetime of false marriage, probably, than to go through with such a charade, but the choice was not his. He would do whatever she wanted. This was what he told himself each time he climbed the stairs to the flat. Usually he found the flat empty or the bedroom door shut, but one night he opened the door to discover Sarah standing behind it with her keys and purse in her hand. She wore a tweed overcoat buttoned to the throat, and her hair was lacquered tight to her head in a style he hadn't seen on her before. She looked older, her face lined, the shadows permanent under her eyes. She hadn't expected to see him here. Knowing this was his chance to explain his position, he tried to remember where to begin. She waited a moment or two, but when nothing transpired she edged past him. He stood in the doorway while her footfall echoed down the stairs and the street door slammed.

Down on both knees now, he gripped Walker's hands. Their faces were inches apart. He let go of the hands and took hold of the head. He touched the face. The skin was soft and flaking as if the dry air of the ward was enough to rub it away. Then he took the whole cranium in his hands, sinking his fingers into the cropped hair. The face wore the expression that was not an expression: the mask of meaningless cunning, rapt attention without an object. Walker no longer seemed to be waiting for anything. Arthur looked into the eyes, a hand's breadth away. The irises were very pale green, the pupils well dilated. The whites were greys and yellows laced with red. Crimson canthus and rheumy membrane. The eyes stared back, steady and empty. Arthur leaned closer. What did they call it when sweethearts kissed by fluttering their eyelashes together? Sarah had averted her eyes as he stood in the doorway to the flat and failed to speak. After she left, he tottered down the stairs and locked himself into the consulting room. Sitting in the black oak chair that he had never carried up to the flat, he found that he had lost his desire to visit Walker in the asylum.

The head felt small in his hands. That old joke: a thousand pounds for Beethoven's skull, five hundred for the skull of Beethoven as a child. He could stare into Walker's eyes like this day in and day out and it would make no difference. He'd been fooling himself, because there was no answering attention there, nothing that would meet his gaze. Sitting in the black oak chair that night he had seen that his visits to Cranfield Park were an embarrassment, a sane man playing at being mad. By turning up on the ward with his chess set under his arm as if he and Walker were old friends, he was making a fool of himself, that went without saying, but he was also making a mockery of his former patient's life. What a presumption it had been.

Letting go of Walker's head, he got up, brushed the knees of his trousers and resumed his place on the bench. And now he had done it again. Coming here today had been another act of self-indulgence, sheer bad taste. He wanted to explain that it wasn't his fault. One definition of madness is that no one is on your side. Sebastian Venn, in conversation. How would it be to cross over? It must be possible, it must happen every day, and really that was why he had been coming here all along, wasn't it, because it would be a relief to confront the real terrors, meeting them face to face instead of bumbling along as if you belonged to normality, stalked by the shadows and doubts you could never quite glimpse behind the surface of things. He would sit here beside Walker until night fell and the nurses came to hound the patients to their meals and medications, and then what could they do if he simply stayed where he was? If they tried to throw him out he would shriek and fight until they had to administer a sedative, at which point his credentials would be established. Before they knew it he'd be kitted out in the clown suit and the oversized boots. All he had to do was follow Walker's example. Lean back and fall.

The piece of light had faded. It wasn't possible, of course. He could no more choose madness than Walker could choose to be sane. He was an imposter and a tourist and he had no place on General Ward One. He leaned forward, propping his head on his hands, resting his elbows on his knees, tired by the events of the day. As he did so his abdomen cramped more sharply than before. Substance shifted. He got up and walked, stiff and quick, out of the day room. Patients turned their heads but he was hobbling past them as fast as he could. The lavatories that opened off the ward were for the use of patients alone, but trying for other facilities was out of the question. He pushed through the doors and into a tiled room where five porcelain bowls were set in a line. The bowls lacked seats and were foully splattered; they had no dividers between them; the stench of blocked pipes and powerful disinfectant stung the throat; at the far end of the room, a few sheets of stiff, translucent lavatory paper hung from a depleted roll. There was no time to waste, but he paused for a moment, filled with a kind of grateful wonder. He was here.

*

224

Near the end of the analysis, Venn had told Arthur a fairy tale in which a knight marries a lovely young woman only to discover in the bridal chamber that she is an enchantress. She offers him a choice: I can be a beautiful but shrewish wife, she says, or I can be ugly and sweet-natured. Whichever you decide is the way I'll stay forever. What answer should the knight give? Arthur had blustered about the relative merits, but Venn had only smiled. Arthur realised that there must be another possibility, a hidden answer that was the right one, but he couldn't think what it might be and Venn was giving nothing away.

He thought of that story now, touching it in passing as you might touch a lamp post on a corner as he turned on to Wesley Street and caught sight of Sarah. Rain was spotting. She was standing at the top of the steps in front of their building, fitting her key to the door. From her stance as she noticed him there was no telling whether she was arriving home or on her way out. She was in her tweed overcoat, but her head was bare and her hair disordered. She slipped her hands into her pockets and watched as Arthur approached.

The pain had gone from behind his eyes and his insides were light, but it was the lightness of exhaustion. He was empty. Travelling back from the asylum without a finished thought in his head, trying and failing to visualise Louis in the gutter and instead remembering Venn in his basement sitting room –Venn smiling at his own mistakes and saying the old boy did get to the heart of the matter, what does a woman want – Arthur had known that before doing anything else he needed to see Sarah. It had been a day's work to come to this, the only conclusion he had so far reached. He didn't know what he was intending to say to her, but it no longer seemed to matter very much.

As he reached the foot of the steps, he saw that she was exhausted too. Beads of rain had caught in her hair. He wondered where she had been. She looked down, four stone steps above him. A small crease appeared between her eyebrows. Her lips were chapped. Her expression was not friendly, but he fluttered his fingers and she took her hands out of her pockets. He placed his foot on the first step and she came down to meet him.

FIVE

Shouts and crashes came from below. Arthur got out of bed and lifted the edge of the blind to Talbot Street, murky in the dawn. Dustmen were emptying bins into a refuse lorry, calling out to one another as they worked. He washed and dressed without turning on the light, then put on his overcoat and picked up the book from the dressing table.

Sarah stirred. He leaned down to her, breathing the warmth behind her ear.

'Don't wake up.'

She dug her head deeper into the pillow.

He left the guest house, turned on to Marlborough Street and walked towards the bridge. A damp chill moved in the air, coiling away towards the river. The sky was brightening as one dome. The book was a stiff oblong in his coat pocket. It was bound in green cloth and wrapped in a cream-coloured dust jacket. One hundred and seventy-five pages long, he had noted when he thumbed through it last night.

Morning traffic had begun. Pedestrians and cyclists passed on O'Connell Bridge, ignorant of one another. Arthur paused halfway across to absorb the river's rank and briny climate. The last time he had been here with leisure to taste the air he had been a student: sometimes in his first year in Dublin he had risen early and slipped out of college to walk to the quays and catch the flavour of the new life, which was never stronger than at this hour of the morning and in this kind of weather, when the day began by releasing raw light into the sky.

He walked along Westmoreland Street and around the front of Trinity. They had agreed to meet back here at four o'clock this afternoon. Until then he would give the day to the book, while Sarah amused herself. Some time alone would do her no harm, she said: they'd hardly been a minute out of one another's company this week. She'd see the sights.

It was true, they had been together almost continually since the evening a week ago when he turned on to Wesley Street and saw her fitting her keys to the door. She had been arriving home after spending most of that day chasing him around the city, searching for him everywhere she could think of, missing him at every turn, getting really anxious about what had become of him. As they climbed the stairs to the flat Arthur cautioned himself not to make too much of her going to these lengths on his account. Of course nothing would be solved by the events of a single day, but if they were very lucky then perhaps the day would be the seed of a long, slow, tentative, gradual process in which they might begin to re-establish communication to the point at which it would be feasible to open discussions of what their future might hold. He thanked her for her considerate behaviour and prepared to leave the flat, but she moved towards him. Unaccustomed to her closeness, he took a step back. Her expression was not friendly. As she took his hand in hers he began to suggest that there was no need for them to do anything that crossed the boundaries of what was appropriate or decent, and that circumspection at this juncture might save them both from what could only make a regrettable situation yet more difficult. As she pulled him on to the sofa he knew that she was mocking him in some way that he didn't understand. By the time they fell off the sofa he was determined to get his own back. Two minutes later he was convinced that the past months of unhappy separation had in actuality been a complicated and mildly perverse form of mutual seduction. Three hours after that, when they woke up in the tarnished brass bed, it was too late for him to catch the night mail from Euston to Holyhead, but this he did not regret. They slept again, his nose to her nape, and in the morning they packed suitcases and caught the day mail from Euston at half past eight. While they were stopped at Crewe he telephoned from the station to inform the Bradshaw that he would be taking a short period of emergency leave. They boarded the steamer at Holyhead shortly after two o'clock. Standing at the rail, watching the water begin to churn below, they could have been on honeymoon, except that no honeymoon could compete for romance with a journey like this, not knowing what scene would be waiting when they reached the other side and hurried to the hospital bed. He put his hand on Sarah's hand and told her he was glad she had come.

He crossed into Grafton Street and walked down to Bewley's. The front of the café projected above the street, a Pharaoh's tomb in glazed tile and varnished wood. Inside was a solid din of voices, crockery, grinders and steam. The place hadn't changed in a decade: the low front windows still screened out the daylight so that the waitresses clipped around among patrons breakfasting in hospitable dusk. He made his way deeper into the café, and found a table under the Harry Clarke windows in the back room. He'd forgotten these windows. He'd have to show them to Sarah. He'd tell her how they had been installed in the last year of his degree, and how that year he had taken to coming into the café to sit in their light. She wanted to know these things.

A waitress in a blue-checked uniform appeared beside him, laughing over her shoulder at something. She drew her notepad from her apron and composed herself to take his order. The café kept getting noisier. Scent of coffee and bacon sizzling. New customers were searching for free tables, and as he thanked her she was already crossing the room, laughing again as she dodged past another young woman, dark where she was golden-haired but wearing an identical uniform. The nurse had been laughing as she stepped around the screen dividing Louis's bed from the rest of the ward, but she had shut her mouth promptly as she met the registrar coming the other way. They found Louis sitting up in bed in a pale blue nightshirt, his spectacles pushed halfway up his forehead. He was chuckling to himself, but he stopped when the registrar ushered Arthur and Sarah past the screen. His smile faded as they sat down. No, he said, I'm fine. I've put you to considerable trouble. Arthur shook his head and Sarah gave a murmur of dissent. But I'm pleased to see you both.

Louis could not explain what had happened. He had been in Dublin for three weeks, drawn back as he periodically was from his continental wandering by penury and fatigue, and by the compulsion to come yet again to his mother to lacerate her with his presence and be lacerated in his turn. It had been worse than usual this time, perhaps because she was an old woman now and seemed to suffer more the older she got. Coming into the last season of her life she had forgiven herself nothing, laid none of her burden down, and home in Dalkey Louis found himself locked into a domestic siege as savage as any he had known. For the first week he was laid up with the flu, which was a mercy, but once he was on his feet the situation became unbearable and he took to leaving the house first thing and staying out until the small hours. He had no memory of the night in question, and knew only by report that the collapse had taken place on Henry Street. He didn't know what he had been doing there. He thought it unlikely that drink had played a part, because he hadn't touched a drop since he got home, and in any case, the witnesses on Henry Street had been in no doubt that the event had been something other than a drunkard's tumble. He had gone down like a felled tree, and by the jerking of his limbs they had taken him for a seizing epileptic. I'm sorry I missed it, Louis said. It would have been an instructive experience, but the first I knew was Nurse Doran smoothing my coverlet. He pulled himself higher in the bed and glanced down the ward. The truth is, I've been perfectly fresh ever since, but your man there won't let me leave. It appears that my case is not without its points of interest.

Louis polished his spectacles on his nightshirt. He was thinner than he had been last summer and his face had fallen into starker lines. He settled back on the pillows, studying his own lean hands. Arthur caught Sarah's eye across the bed, and saw that she agreed: Louis was not feeling as nonchalant about this as he was letting on.

The registrar was at the other end of the ward. He shook Arthur's hand and moved half a step closer, angling his body in the attitude that meant parley with a brother clinician. No, he said, it's hard to say what caused the attack. The doctor's name was Nolan: an Ulsterman, perhaps five years older than Arthur and an inch shorter. He wore a toothbrush moustache.

One possibility is syncope due to cardiac arrhythmia, he said. I've seen it happen. The heart wobbles, the brain starves and you get symptoms of seizure, convulsions. But I understand he has no history of heart problems. No history of epilepsy either, but these things can reveal themselves all of a sudden, can't they? And then again I've known patients to have a single paroxysm that never recurs. Yes, he mentioned the migraines, but that doesn't give us much of a clue. Your guess is as good as mine.

What about a psychosomatic cause, Arthur said. A pseudo-seizure brought on by anxiety. Nolan plucked at his moustache. Anything's possible, I suppose, he said, but I'd rather have an organic explanation. More satisfying, don't you think? He rocked on his heels. Not that we can do much, either way.

I'm concerned, Arthur said. If it's going to happen again.

The moustache bristled. Tell you what, Nolan said. He can stay in a few more days. We'll keep an eye on him, but if he's hale and hearty at the end of the week I'll have to send him about his business.

Nolan clapped his hands together in the sign of a busy man. Right so. Arthur was ready to explain that it was imperative to rule out organic causes for Louis's attack – at the very least those which would indicate that the malady had been latent in the sufferer since his youth, and that the danger might have been spotted years ago by a competent physician with the opportunity to do so – but Nolan was already on his way out. Arthur went back down the ward and stepped around the screen to find Louis and Sarah leaning close, conferring. When they noticed him they sat up.

The waitress brought a pot of tea and was gone before Arthur could thank her. She and the other, the golden-haired and the dark, were managing the room between them. The book lay on the table. The cream paper of the dust jacket was plain except for a hollow green rectangle in the centre of which was printed the word JOTT and, below this, the author's name. Arthur had not started to read it last night. I'll wait till morning and take a run at it, he'd told Sarah. Now he flicked through the pages. The text seemed to be divided into three chapters or sections of roughly equal length, each marked with a numeral but no title. There was no epigraph and no dedication. He turned to the first page.

The first of April and a fine spring morning. A day to make one glad to be alive, if so inclined. This was of no account to Jott, who lay out of the sunshine in his room in a basement on Flood Street. In this room he had lived for almost a year, going forth into the greater world only when absolutely necessary. The days for which he lived were those on which he neither saw the sky nor engaged in social intercourse nor in any other kind. He cherished the hope that today might be such a day. He was in his trunk.

The trunk, built of sturdy oak, was ideally suited to his purposes. It stood at the foot of his bed. It closed on him so snugly that no sunbeam could penetrate. Its dimensions matched those of Jott himself along every axis, provided that he lay on his side in the foetal pose. Either side would do but he preferred the left, perhaps because it placed his heart four and a half inches nearer to sea level. He lay, then, in his trunk, on his left side, naked, with his eyes closed, his spine curled, his limbs folded, his nose to the hinge and his head in alignment with the Crab. To achieve this position was not easy, nor was it easy, the position achieved, to stir from it. Once he was in he was in. The confinement suited him nicely, he was not equipped to imagine a deeper felicity.

Or one only, which was this: as his body lay confined in darkness, his mind to sink into darkness as deep. Left to his own devices he could make the descent in a matter of two or three hours. The sights, sounds, smells, tastes, touches and miscellaneous importunities of the greater world could not trouble him if he were left to his own devices. His thoughts could not trouble him. But without peace and quiet he could not begin. To him that has, more shall be given, thought Jott, but from him that has not shall be taken even that which he has. A pernicious false-hood. All he asked was nothing and yet again he had been denied. For someone was knocking on his door.

That the someone was female was evinced by the asperity of the blows and the precipitancy with which the door was then thrown open. Jott's door had no bolt or lock. It had not had one in the almost a year of his tenancy, a gross defect which nothing but indolence could have kept him from correcting. The intruder was moving about the room, opening and closing the cupboard, drawing back the curtain. Although Jott's room was in the basement it had a small window, the other defect, which commanded a view of a brick wall a foot away. Not satisfied with the curtain, she opened the window, no doubt to let in the fresh air. Even encased as he was Jott could sense the change, the loss of a larger confinement. He despaired now of peace and quiet, but he lay still in his trunk, hoping

236

perhaps that he might yet go undiscovered. In vain. Light broke in on him, the world broke in, and he blinked up at her face.

'*There you are,*' *she said.*

The waitress set a plate in front of Arthur: streaky rashers, sausage, black and white pudding and a pair of egg yolks in a mass of white. He closed the book on his thumb, determined to get it right this time. She was balancing a tray on one hand. She set out a toast rack, a butter knife, a butter dish, a jam spoon, a pot of marmalade and a linen napkin. He waited until everything was in place.

'Thank you very much,' he said.

Her lashes flickered and a smile touched her lips as she straightened the napkin. An acknowledgment if you chose to take it that way. Not if not. She moved between the tables, swinging her hips aside as a customer pushed a chair back. It must be strange to be a waitress working in a busy cafeteria, passing through so many spheres of attention, each to be humoured and pacified and fended off. You'd get to be wise about people in a certain way, to know them from a particular angle. You'd be there to serve them individually but you'd have the advantage of them as a mass. When Louis was in the right mood he'd have every waitress in Bewley's vying to pour his coffee. There was a balance that would never be redressed. On his deathbed he would occupy himself by charming his last nurse, making her giggle and blush.

Arthur spread butter and marmalade and propped the book open with the toast rack. Fifteen hundred copies were due to go on sale on the seventh of May, but this was one that the

237

publishers had sent Louis in advance. He read on. Instead of revealing who had disturbed the protagonist in his hiding place, the narrative stepped backwards in time to sketch his background and personality, which were familiar enough. Jott was another example of Louis's favourite style of character, a shiftless, cynical young man with no obvious redeeming features who was nevertheless understood, on the strength of some indefinable personal magnetism, to deserve the reader's attention. Over two and a half pages Arthur learned that Jott was a Dubliner, *born and raised or the nearest available approximations,* but that for his story proper to begin it had been necessary for him to struggle free of homeland and family – the hypocrisies of his upbringing were dismissed in a sentence – and move to London.

She made a creditable attempt to place her hands on her hips. The woman who had come into Jott's room was described in terms like *billow, blubber, bristle, slack, sag, bloat*: there was no doubting that here was a repellently obese and decrepit lady. Her name was Mrs Prone.

Foremost among her qualities was the scent. This did not announce itself all at once but seeped from her person over the minutes following her arrival. It began with the stench of oil of clove, beneath which would be discerned in due course the secretions of the sudoriferous glands, beneath which would be discerned in due course the tang of an essential decay. Of this tang Agatha Prone was not herself insensible. In her youth on many nights she had gone without sleep to wring her heart over the problem of its origin, but to no avail.

238

As Jott levered himself out of his trunk and she hectored him into his clothes, it became clear that Mrs Prone, a moneyed widow, harboured an unfathomable affection for him. Her desire was for Jott to come and live in her huge empty house, where she would set him up with his own studio and all else that was needful to his vision, because she had got hold of the idea that he was a modern painter of great promise whose art would flourish if only a wealthy patroness could free him from mundane concerns. Mrs Prone knew that Jott was revolted beyond measure by the prospect of becoming a domestic pet, but, a slave to longing, she persisted in her suit. She gave him presents fit for the image whose pupa she supposed him to be: silk ties, stiff shirts, silver shaving things, an ivory-topped cane, a gold watch. She also bought him paints, canvases, brushes and the rest of it. He pawned her gifts and used the money to meet the exorbitant demands of his landlady, a Miss Reeding. Rent paid and the small needs of his body satisfied, Jott habitually disposed of leftover funds by dropping them into the municipal waste bin at the north-eastern corner of Battersea Park, excepting those occasions on which he indulged himself with the purchase of a small bottle of linseed oil to lubricate the hinges of his trunk.

Pressing a set of cufflinks into his hands, Mrs Prone began entreating him to leave this squalor behind and allow her to enfold him in her bosom, but before she had got far another knock came on the door and another woman entered uninvited. This one was the inverse of the first: she was young where Mrs Prone was old, golden where she was grey, slim where she was stout, taut where she was slack, poor where she was rich. The young woman's name was Melissa and the only trait she had in common with Mrs Prone was her helpless devotion to Jott.

She too was determined to tear him away from his chosen mode of life, but the improvements she had in mind were of a different sort. A poor but honest cohabitation, he trotting out to work each morning, she keeping their little flat as neat as a pin, was her model of happiness. She was not equipped to imagine a deeper felicity. Jott gave her no encouragement, but she was a slave to longing and she had staked too much of what she thought of as her virtue to give up now. *'At last I meet the manipulative harridan,' said Melissa, her chin rising in outrage. 'Finally I come face to face with the seducing floozie,' said Mrs Prone, her chins quivering with passion.* Each woman had long known that she had a rival, and each blamed the other for Jott's recalcitrance. The truth of the matter, which had occurred to neither of them, was that he wished both would leave him alone.

Arthur poured a second cup of tea. The stained glass glowed, holding the light inside itself so that the room remained gloomy. The café was less busy now. Most of the breakfasters had left, and the waitresses stood at the counter, watching and talking.

The rest of the first section told of Jott's misadventures after the two women, mortal enemies but of one mind on this point, insisted he must choose between them. Thus hemmed in by Scylla and Charybdis, he first tried to become the diligent provider that Melissa required, putting himself forward for a series of increasingly absurd and humiliating positions, from lavatory attendant at West Brompton tube station to Professor of Philosophy at Trinity College, Dublin, and being laughed out of contention in every case. When he could no longer stand Melissa's scolding he left her and moved into Mrs Prone's house to act the part of the kept artist. A fortnight later, when he could no longer bear that, he returned to the room in which he had begun. There he enjoyed a brief interval of solitude before Miss Reeding told him that the terrace had been condemned and that he would have to make new arrangements. As he was about to climb into his trunk, intending to stay there until the roof came down, Melissa and Mrs Prone arrived together. To Jott's horror they had talked everything through and now appeared to be friends.

'I have been selfish,' said Mrs Prone. 'I see that it is not for an old woman to stand in the way of young love. That is why I intend, without condition, in what modest ways I can, to maintain you happy two in your future together.' Melissa shook her head. 'I have been the selfish one,' she said. 'I realise that I must no longer let my small dreams obstruct the higher cause of Art. That is why I intend, putting jealousy aside, offering what insignificant service I may, to impede your vocation no longer.'

Both were withdrawing their claims, each giving way to the other. Exchanging glances of sisterly sympathy, they told Jott that it only remained for him to decide which of these futures was to be. The women watched as he sat down on his trunk, folded his hands in his lap and sunk into a catatonic stupor. When they saw that he was beyond their reach, they telephoned the men in white coats to come and take him away.

A waitress filled Arthur's teapot with fresh hot water from a jug. The dark girl. She gave him a smile and moved on. The room was almost empty now, and the golden waitress was collecting crockery from the tables. The glow of the windows had threaded itself into her hair. So they were content for him to stay a while. With the early crowd gone, a reflective mood had formed here, deep in the café. He was no longer like the breakfast eaters who bawled their demands over the clatter, filled their stomachs and left. It seemed he was welcome to linger alone with his book under the many-coloured glass. He could feel that he had strayed into a chamber beneath the sea where mermaid sisters strangely generous in their ways entertained the traveller in shifting half-light. It wouldn't feel like that if Sarah were here. If they were here together, they would have found out the waitresses' names instead: they would have chatted about how busy the place was earlier and what was afoot in Dublin today. There would be a less mysterious sense of fellowship in the room. He supposed that some part of himself really preferred to imagine Bewley's waitresses as figures in a stained-glass pane fashioned by a follower of Beardsley than to think of them as women with lives of their own. Being in Dublin with Sarah this week he had noticed the difference. On their way into Trinity they had paused under Front Arch to pass the time of day with the porter, discovering in the course of ten minutes that the man lived in Stoneybatter and had a three-year-old son. In his time as a student it had never occurred to Arthur that such revelations were possible. In Sarah's company the city opened itself in new ways, and this was an aspect of the new state of affairs between them. Because their newborn understanding could not be stated in so many words, it was manifested in how he thought about waitresses, how he looked at the world, how these streets and cafés were the same but not the same as they had been before.

And perhaps that was the nature of it, not to be stated in so many words. He continued along Grafton Street with his hands in his pockets and the book tight under his oxter, then turned into one of the alleyways and cut across to South William Street. He was meandering, stretching his legs, considering where to tackle the next section. A pub, he thought. If he carried on ahead he'd come to O'Neill's. She might be in the National Gallery now: she wanted to look around in there, she'd told him, and she was planning to take a stroll in Stephen's Green as well. They were sharing the day despite not being together, and that too was part of the new state of affairs. It was a matter of knowing what needed to be said and what didn't. When they knew that they were of one mind they could be silent and stronger for it. When they had met Myles MacDonagh in the hospital corridor, he'd been doubtful about going back to London, but they promised him he could leave with a clear conscience because they had decided to stay on until Louis was discharged. They would ring with any news. Myles gripped their hands, accepting the assurance, agreeing that between the three of them they would do their best for their friend.

In O'Neill's he carried a pint of stout to a booth table and seated himself by a window where he could look down at the heads of passers-by on Suffolk Street. The late morning custom was a few solitary men with newspapers and pints. The red-bearded barman stood with his arms folded. No one spoke. You could settle into this masculine atmosphere with relief, or burst out laughing at it. Arthur tasted the stout and turned to his place in the book.

The second section began with Jott's arrival at a psychiatric hospital called the Golgotha. It was obviously modelled on the

Calvary: a passage of rather dutiful description established the setting, from the hospital's location on a private estate in the outskirts of town to the cruciform architecture of the wards to their overheated fug and smell of paraldehyde and bodily waste. Louis seemed to be at pains to show that he was giving an informed portrait of a particular institution. Perhaps he wanted to ensure that no one could accuse him of simply making it up.

Jott's feelings about this environment were not articulated, because the narrative had turned its attention to another character, a doctor called Bell who was in charge of admitting the new patient to the hospital. Dr Bell was an idealistic and ambitious young man, the text explained:

Since earliest youth he had schooled himself in the disciplines, including the biological, the chemical, the physical, the anatomical, the surgical, the psychiatric and the psychotherapeutic, that were necessary to the treatment of mental derangements of every stripe, among them the psychotic, the neurotic, the psychopathic, the neuropathic, the hysteric, the narcissistic, the psychosomatic, the schizoid, the schizotypical, the schizophrenic, the paranoiac, the melancholic, the catatonic, the obsessional, the maniacal, the hydrophobic and the lycanthropic. In his work for sufferers under all these headings he was tireless. In his idle hours, comprehending as he did the value of a rounded character, he exerted his body with a variety of sporting pursuits, such as tennis, golf, cricket, billiards and mountaineering, and exercised his aesthetic and moral faculties through appreciation within reasonable limits of several of the arts, not excluding painting, theatre, architecture, gardening and the light opera. In his yet idler hours he read works of history, science, biography, political philosophy and the poets. A rounded character made for good mental health, and good mental health equipped the physician best to heal his patients. This was the creed of Dr Bell. The passion that ordered his life, setting aside for the moment his devotion to his tender spouse and their two strapping boys, was his natural and unselfish love for each and every patient under his care: his deep apprehension of their agony and his unstinting determination to guide them out of their individual little darknesses and into the glare of the great world. For who, cut off from what was commonly known as reality, would not wish to be hauled back into the farrago by the first possible means?

The day of Jott's arrival at the hospital was memorable for Dr Bell, the text continued. It was one of those days that inspired him afresh to his vocation. He did not hesitate in admitting the prospective patient: Jott had emerged from his stupor to insist that all his actions to date had been reasonable and rational, and such an assertion under the present circumstances could leave no doubt as to the mental condition of the speaker. Jott was led away happily by his new keepers, but the doctor was uneasy. He had seen something in the man that troubled him. Dr Bell was a practised observer of his own feelings towards the sick, knowing that the clinician's responses were a form of diagnostic evidence which it would be foolish to discount, and he was thus aware that his typical inner reflex towards his patients and their infirmities was a sort of violent loathing. *In the privacy of his thoughts he named it the therapeutic hate.* He did not deny to himself that the sight of Jott caused sharper pangs than usual, and, noting this, he resolved to treat this sufferer with even more than his ordinary level of humane concern. Dr Bell could not say what exactly it was about Jott that troubled him so, but he resolved there and then to cure the poor man if it was the last thing he did.

The following pages told the story of Jott's first weeks in the hospital, as Dr Bell subjected him to an advanced regime of interventions. Bell drew on the full array of pharmacological correctives, of course, and also deployed heliotherapy, hydrotherapy, electrotherapy, malarial therapy and dental extraction. He sent the patient for massage under the hands of a burly nurse and for Arts and Crafts beneath the eye of a pitiless instructress. He tried wet packs, dry packs, cold baths, hot baths, shower baths, steam baths, straitjackets, padded gloves, padded rooms, isolation, socialisation, supervision. He prescribed croquet and badminton and dancing class. He shocked the patient with cardiazol and, when that failed to produce an appreciable effect, with triazol. Soon he was at his wits' end. The patient was sinking, falling away from the world and into himself, and all the therapeutic stratagems Bell could muster only made him sink faster. In itself this was not surprising – *indeed it happened at least as often as not, at the Golgotha* – but what was unusual was the effect on the doctor himself. He could not rid himself of the conviction that Jott was somehow getting the better of him. It was a bad time for Dr Bell: the other patients under his care seemed not to fear him as before, the nurses started giving him cheek and he learned one day that the other doctors had been playing tennis without him. Even at home he suspected that Mrs Bell and the two strapping young Bells were forgetting the regard to which he was entitled. He could not say why all of this was down to Jott, but his keen medical instinct told him it was so.

Desperate measures were called for. With all other avenues exhausted, Dr Bell resorted to the talking cure. He attempted to explain the structure of Jott's mind in terms of a grotesque and absurd mythology. Jott, who knew that his mind was structured entirely otherwise, was not discomfited in the least by the mumbo-jumbo, nor by the doctor's fumbling at the catches of his childhood, his dreams, his sexual phantasies and other such fabrications. Eventually Bell came to the point, and told the patient that he would never return to mental health unless he started to cooperate. *Here was an asseveration to which Jott found it worthwhile to reply. 'I am not mad,' he told Bell. 'But through your offices, if fortune smiles, perhaps I shall become so.'*

Bell persisted with the talking cure for a time, interspersing the sessions of chin-stroking with some of the hospital's more drastic physical treatments. He knew that these could only help Jott's cause, but he could not resist them, because they relieved his feelings. Soon a crisis came. Everyone knew he was obsessed. *His reputation was at stake. He was not a combative man but now he could give no quarter.* Brooding through a moonless night, he decided to make a final attempt on Jott. *He abandoned scruple: he was prepared to commit the most abominable acts of medicine if it meant victory.* He considered his alternatives. He might burn away the higher functions of the patient's nervous system, send him into chemical oblivion forever, surgically divide the lobes of his brain. *None of these was enough, none would give satisfaction to Dr Bell.* Finally he made his choice, and when morning came he visited Jott in his pleasant private room.

Dr Bell pleaded for mercy. As one decent man to another,

for the sake of his wife and children, for the salvation of his body and soul, he begged Jott to relent. *'It need not be much,'* he said. *'The smallest gesture would be enough.'* Bell wanted Jott to acknowledge that there was a difference between sanity and madness and that the former was preferable to the latter. *'Only admit it and we are friends. Grant me this much and I will do all I can to make your stay in the Golgotha long and comfortable.'* Jott gazed at the prostrate physician and shook his head. The doctor dragged himself from the room, and within the hour a squad of nurses arrived to inform Jott that he was no longer a patient of the institution. The last paragraph of the section described how his departure was the subject of hospital gossip for a day or two afterwards: there was debate as to whether he had been expelled due to the discovery that he had been incurably insane all along, or whether his treatment in the Golgotha had made him so in the normal fashion, or whether in fact he had been a sane man feigning lunacy for his own reasons. It was an amusing question for the inmates and their keepers, but in practice it made no difference, because in none of those cases was there the prospect of a cure. *And for those whose prognosis was hopeless there was no place at the Golgotha Royal Hospital.*

Arthur visited the gents before leaving the pub. Always make water when you can: another of the mottos they had learned at Donard. That one had been attributed to some English naval hero. His curiosity was exhausted. He didn't much want to think about what Louis meant by the portrait of Dr Bell, and he didn't feel inclined to go on reading the book. Instead he walked the length of Grafton Street and through Stephen's Green on the off-chance that he might catch sight of Sarah. She might have warned him. She had known that the book was a send-up of Arthur and his profession, and she had kept it to herself. He had had no idea that the novel existed as an object until yesterday, when Sarah had handed him this copy, explaining that it had been in her possession for a while. The brown paper parcel had been delivered to her at Wesley Street at the beginning of the month, accompanied by a letter from Louis asking her for a favour. She was to read the book and decide when and how it should be presented to Arthur; she had brought the book to Dublin in her suitcase, and yesterday afternoon she had put it into Arthur's hands. It was due to be published in a week's time, she told him, and he ought to read it before then. She wouldn't say anything about what was inside.

He passed through the Green without sighting her, and crossed to Lower Leeson Street. It was the new feeling between them. There had been a toughness in the way she had given him the book, and an expectation that he would be tough in return. When they had first known one another they were always ready to excuse themselves from what was difficult, always apologising in order to be forgiven for their weaknesses. Not any longer, said the new feeling. On their third day in Dublin, as they were leaving Baggot Street after spending an hour with Louis, Sarah had asked if they shouldn't visit Arthur's parents while they were in Ireland. You're right, I know, he said – but can we leave him? Back along the ward Louis was propped up in bed, reading a copy of *Ghost Stories of Chapelizod* that they had bought for him in Hodges Figgis, looking up now and then to flirt with his nurses. Sarah said no more, leaving it to his judgment, and they caught the train from Tara Street that afternoon, carried along by the action of a conscience that had chosen freely and well.

His parents welcomed them as if they visited all the time.

In fact it was the best part of three years since Arthur had come home, and Sarah had not set foot here before. As they walked through the plain, clean house Arthur found himself explaining how busy things had been, how there was never a chance to get away, how he didn't know where the time had gone. He couldn't seem to stop talking, but if his parents were embarrassed they didn't let it show. His mother laid out cutlery on the scrubbed pine table while his father stirred the pot. The kitchen was the largest and warmest room in the house, and was just as it had always been, the brass kettle standing on the range, the crack in one of the floor tiles as familiar as a face. Sitting on the four sides of the table they linked hands and bowed their heads. His parents' hands were knuckled and stiff, but they gripped with plenty of strength remaining. After the silent grace his mother served the stew with the giant's teaspoon, the spoon that had served every stew of his childhood. Because his parents ate without speaking, Arthur found himself steering the conversation single-handed, bringing up the topics that he knew they would be asking about if they were not so crippled by reticence. Sarah pitched in, taking the cues on the story of Louis, on the news from London, on her impressions of Dublin and Wexford and so forth. She knew what was needed here, understood that it would be cruel to expect the elderly couple to be capable of expressing themselves in any way. Arthur knew their limitations, but coming back home had revealed them all over again: he felt, as if for the first time, how completely his parents were trapped by their virtues of humility, acceptance and silence. He caught Sarah's eye across the table. We who are younger and more free ought to forgive them for being as they are. It must be painful for parents to see their children grown into kinds of liberty that were unthinkable a generation ago. A hurt that they must absorb in bafflement. They sit with their heads low to their plates, and all we can do is try to be kind.

In the morning his parents went out to the Quaker meeting. Arthur went with them, still in the grip of charitable feelings, and Sarah came too, wanting to see it at first hand. She sat for the hour in the meeting house as if she'd been doing it all her life, attending to the silence, not fidgeting. His parents looked small, but not much older than they had always been. No one ministered. The bench was hard. Walking back to the house Arthur was surly and tongue-tied, his patience gone, and they caught the next train back to Dublin.

On the journey Sarah let him talk. Of course he was too old to be getting angry with his parents, but in the meeting house it had been all he could do not to walk out and slam the door behind him. It had suddenly been obvious that his parents were not trapped. Watching them as they sat with bowed heads and peaceful faces, he saw that their mute exist-ence had not been forced on them at all: they had chosen to be as they were. They were perfectly content! Arthur ges-ticulated, bared his teeth and shook his head at the scenery passing the carriage. It takes such a long time to see how your life has been shaped for you, he said. It wasn't as if he didn't know the theory. Analysis teaches that gaps in communication are the places where emotional matter is withheld, bottled up for fear of the pain it would cause, and I grew up in a house-hold composed entirely of gaps in communication. Look at me. He poked himself in the chest. Is it any wonder? A thin-lipped old woman glared from the corner of the compartment and he dropped his voice, but as soon as they reached the guest house he telephoned Sebastian Venn at the Malet and made a confession that he had never made during the training analysis.

When he had told the story of Thomas Bourne's short life, he expounded its significance. A two-year-old child will inevitably experience strong hostile feelings towards his elder brother, he said: is it any wonder, then, that when the brother is carried off by diphtheria the child will learn to believe in the magical effectiveness of his hostility, or that he will fear his own negative feelings and that this fear will root deep in his personality, all the more so in a home where pious resignation is the response to every trial, where voices must never be raised and nothing must ever be mentioned? Is it any wonder that the child will grow into an adult who is anxious and ill at ease and so frightened of his own destructive impulses that he dares not assert himself professionally or personally but spends his life placating everyone he meets? That he has never dared to voice disagreement even with his oldest friend, or that although he takes himself for a rational person he lives his life in terror of magical threats?

Arthur paused and listened to the sound of Venn listening at the other end of the line. You knew about Thomas already, didn't you, he said. Louis told you. Venn admitted that it had come up in their conversations once or twice. But what's interesting is that you mention it now. Your analysis is tidy, I'll admit.

You mean it's *too* tidy, Arthur said.

I don't know, said Venn. What do you think?

Standing in the parlour of the guest house with the instrument to his ear, Arthur allowed himself a smile. I was hoping we could take up the training analysis again, he said. I feel it's time. He listened to Venn's voice in the receiver, then nodded. All right, he said. I'll see you next week.

He came to the end of Lower Leeson Street and paused on the bridge over the canal. He was almost at Baggot Street here. If he turned right and followed the canal for a few hundred yards, he could glower up at the windows of Louis's ward, tear out the pages of the novel, screw them into pellets and fling them at the hospital's red-brick facade. He could go in, sit down at the bedside and patiently explain to Louis the deficiencies of character that had led him to write such mean-spirited and unconvincing twaddle. He walked along the canal, under the branches. Venn would be interested in the book. He had been unable to hide his enthusiasm about resuming the training analysis. Curious that the man who had once been such a canny, grizzled figure now seemed so youthful, so excited that the game was afoot. It would be nice to see him again, and perhaps that was reason enough to go back, even if Arthur still had his doubts about the enterprise, with its simple faith that to put a name to your cage was to make yourself free. There was something in it – some truth to the notion that you could solve every mystery if you dug at the right place in childhood – but that kind of explanation would always be disappointing. He did not doubt that somewhere there existed a deeper and truer kind of secret which analysis would never be able to touch. This stretch of the canal made him feel that a short corridor of countryside had been inserted among the high grey buildings. The watercourse was lined with grassy banks and screened by trees, so that, with Dublin traffic passing a few feet away, you could look along the footpath and see blond reeds, reflected trunks, ripples spreading where a duck had been.

His pace was slowing, and when he came to a bench he sat down. The surface of the canal was still. He held the book in both hands, letting minutes go by. Then he leafed back through what he had read until he came to the passage about Dr Bell's wife. The scene began with the doctor arriving home after a day spent fruitlessly torturing Jott. He was in a state of some dismay, and Amanda Bell's keen animal instincts told her that he needed comfort and understanding:

He longed for the cool hand on his brow, for the touch of soft fingers moved by a soft heart to tell him that it did not matter what trials and hardships the great world might bring because here in the safety of his home, in the bosom of his family, he was adored. That he persisted in wanting such reassurance was wearisome in the extreme, thought Mrs Bell, as was his apparent belief that she was under some obligation to supply it. He did not grasp that all negotiations between them had long since concluded. She had done her part in the transaction, first by allowing herself to be persuaded to become his wife and then by consenting to the procedures that had given rise to two strapping proofs of the vivacity of her reproductive apparatus. With the arrangement thus sealed, all that remained was for him to do his part by working without complaint for the term of his natural life to keep his dependants in their accustomed style. Nowhere was it stipulated that she must be his nursemaid in perpetuity. Did he imagine that she had no troubles of her own? She was so tired this afternoon that she literally could not stir from the sofa. She had spent hours ransacking Oxford Street for a hat to wear to the wedding of one of her dearest foes, and had then returned home to find the nanny quaking in the corner of the nursery while Herbert and Algernon pelted her with lead soldiers. Mrs Bell had no objection to high-spirited play but she could not abide the noises the girl was making, and so, closing the door, she had retired to the parlour to recover from her exertions. Now, as her husband sat in the armchair staring emptily before him, her keen animal instincts delivered a warning. He was about to forget himself and speak of his pain. He was going to tell her what weighed on his spirit. This, of course, could not be allowed – think of the precedent it would set – and so, knowing that a swift response was called for and marvelling at the inner fortitude that enabled her to make such an effort even in her exhausted condition, Mrs Bell searched her mind for a means to remind him of his place. A large, well-organised, much visited department of her mind was devoted to the archive of her husband's failures and transgressions, but she was put out to discover that he had not lately incriminated himself in any way fit for her purposes. Fortunately this small obstacle was no match for the resourcefulness of Amanda Bell née Lillywhite. If no particular offence was available for her to wield, she would have to reach instead for the general principle. For a woman of her accomplishments it was easily done: a simple matter of stiffening her posture on the sofa, permitting the line of her lips to harden and the angle of her chin to increase, and projecting a stony glare at the wall a little to the left of her husband's head. These measures took effect at once. Dr Bell blinked in confusion, sensing dimly that he was guilty of some domestic outrage. His earlier distress was swallowed up by the more pressing terror of not knowing what he had done to upset her, nor what it might cost him to regain her favour. He began to twist his handkerchief into knots. Mrs Bell smiled within. She had laboured long and hard to mould him into a husband deserving of the name, and at moments like this she felt that it had all been quite worth her while.

The narrative soon moved away from Mrs Bell, as if a few pages in her company were more than enough. Arthur didn't know what he was supposed to make of it. If the doctor character was sending him up in his professional capacity, then the scene with the wife was, now that he looked at it again, a thorough assassination of his private life. He ought to ask Louis why he was incapable of writing anything without slandering his friends. Why this compulsion to claw at those who cared for him? And perhaps a proper man would not be sitting here wondering about it: he'd already be marching in to the ward, calmly ablaze at the injury to the honour of his wife, inviting Louis to step outside, Queensberry rules.

He looked across the water at the row of houses opposite. He turned his head and looked into the green world. Then he leafed forward through the book and began to read the last section.

Jott's story now became a sequence of degradations. Having been expelled from the Golgotha Hospital with nothing but the ragged suit on his back and the handful of coins that had been in his pocket when he was admitted, he drifted back to the site of his former lodgings on Flood Street. *He was drawn by some idea of retrieving the trunk that had been the companion of his most tolerable hours. When he reached the spot he found a wasteland of rubble. The row had been demolished as per*

256

information supplied in Section One. Jott was chased away by a watchman's dog; he tried to buy a loaf of bread, but his personal appearance was such that no shopkeeper would serve him; he was robbed of his money by a small boy and harassed by a policeman; he drank from drainpipes, ate from dustbins and slept in doorways. Eventually he came to rest in Battersea Park. As the bell rang for the closing of the gates Jott lay under a bush, watching the shadows of the evening steal across the sky. He dozed, and woke to find himself surrounded by threatening figures: a freakish family consisting of a brutal old man, a haggard crone and an idiot youth, all of them as filthy and tattered as himself. They kicked and beat Jott, spat on him and made him beg for scraps of food. The following day they roamed the streets, where the good people of the city ignored the spectacle of three derelicts leading a fourth by a rope around the neck. At night they returned to the park, where they entertained themselves by forcing Jott to dance and beating him when he stumbled.

Rain speckled Arthur's hands, and pinpricks showed on the pages of the book for a moment before disappearing. The branches stirred above his head. He shrugged deeper into the collar of his coat. He didn't really see what Louis was getting at. Possibly the reader was supposed to feel sorry for Jott, but this didn't quite seem to be the point. The narrator recounted Jott's sufferings without comment, just as Jott suffered without complaint. The aim couldn't be satire, because how could Louis expect the reader to be indignant at an ordeal that was so obviously a fantasy, an exercise in unpleasantness for its own sake? And perhaps that was it. The story told of misery and degradation as if these were the most ordinary things in the world, and the implication of every sentence was that if you, the reader, thought otherwise – if you were so naïve as to be distressed by the book's view of life – then you were a fool.

Jott continued to be abused by his captors until one night they were driven out of their park by unseen assailants. Lost in the confusion, Jott went back to wandering the streets until, early one morning, he was found lying in the gutter by a kindly man. *Jott took him at first for a priest, but inspection revealed no collar nor cincture nor crucifix. The man might be clergy in spirit but was not so in fact. His mind at rest on this point if no other, Jott suffered himself to be helped to his feet.* The man, who did not seem offended by the stench, led Jott into a nearby house, showed him a basement room, invited him to rest on the cot and left him to take stock of his good fortune. *This basement was in every respect superior to the one on Flood Street, being smaller, warmer and without windows. Fully certified interment could hardly have been preferred.* Each day the man brought Jott a meal and a chamberpot, and left him to his own devices. The mystery of the man's motives was unfolded, if not exactly solved, in an odd passage in which he knelt by the cot and confessed, in a voice strained by emotion, that his political views were of a radical stripe, and most deeply held. He had struggled with his conscience, he said, and he could no longer bring himself to give charity to Jott when to do so was merely to perpetuate the system of which Jott's individual wretchedness was a function: when to do so was, in fact, to uphold injustice, slavery and massacre. Please don't think I'm being unkind, said the man, but you cannot stay here. Jott, mystified but not surprised, walked out of the house.

Arthur rubbed his thumb across the edges of the pages that were left. There weren't many. He'd finish the book, then walk back to meet Sarah at Front Arch. The story seemed to be flowing faster now as it moved towards the end. Jott wandered the city, hounded from place to place, growing ever more decrepit, until at last he found refuge in a collapsed shed in an abandoned industrial yard. He dragged himself into this shelter and lay there for days or weeks, no longer able to move, watching the rats playing in the yard, getting sustenance by sucking at the moss on a broken paving-slab across which brackish water flowed, occasionally trying to defecate or masturbate, without success. No one came to him. His greatest pleasure was coughing up a good clot of blood. As he died, presumably from some combination of starvation, exposure and pulmonary infection, the narrative drew away from his present circumstances into a vision of his early childhood. It was a happy memory. The young Jott walked along a stony strand, holding hands with his mother and looking at the sea. *With wonder he saw the sea colours and longed to know the words for what was beautiful and endless and always changing. He asked her: What colour is the sea?* His mother looked at him with contempt, and replied that the sea was grey.

The novel finished with an epilogue in which Jott's remains were discovered by workmen and then conveyed back into the hands of Dr Bell, thanks to a receipt from the Golgotha Hospital storage cupboard that was found in a pocket of the ragged suit. Bell made the identification, conducted the autopsy and had the remains incinerated at the hospital mortuary. As the exhaust began to rise from the furnace chimney, the doctor and the coroner took a turn in the mortuary garden, Dr Bell reflecting with compassion on the sad waste of human potential, the coroner laying a hand on his shoulder and saying that no doctor could have done more for his patient. Then they went to play tennis, a friendly but hard-fought match in which Bell beat the coroner by three sets to two.

Arthur shut the book and looked at his watch. It was almost a quarter to four, but if he moved quickly he could be at Front Arch on time. They were going to walk over to Baggot Street together. Louis was due to leave the hospital this afternoon, and the plan, agreed yesterday, was that Arthur and Sarah would escort him down to Dalkey to be reunited with his family. He would then have a confession to make, because all week he had insisted that his mother and brother must not be told he was in hospital. It was better this way, he said: they would assume that his absence meant he had gone off on a spree in disreputable company, and although this would cause them much pain it was preferable to what would happen if his mother knew he had been laid low by a cerebral event. Arthur didn't like being sworn to silence, but he supposed Louis knew best when it came to Mrs Molyneux; or rather it was apparent that he didn't know best, but no good could come of interfering. The family must conduct itself in its own way. In any case Louis had promised that once he could claim the danger was past he would tell her the whole story. He only asked that he be allowed to do it at the time of his choosing, and that Arthur and Sarah come with him for moral support.

Arthur crossed from Lower Leeson Street into Stephen's Green, retracing his steps at a smart pace, unbuttoning his coat as he walked. The copy of *Jott* knocked against his hip. He didn't know what he was going to say to Louis. Perhaps he needn't say anything: they could simply avoid the topic of the book. He'd absorb the insult without a fight. It was the method he knew best. Louis could hardly be unaware that the book as a whole read as a methodical attack on every principle by which Arthur chose to live. The Dr Bell business was bad enough, but the story of Jott's trials after leaving the hospital was even more of an accusation, because it seemed that in some way Jott's demise was meant to be a perverse triumph for his way of looking at things: he had to suffer and die in order to condemn the world and all those hypocritical creatures who, like Dr Bell, were content to live in it. This was not a new story to Arthur, who in Trinity days had often heard Louis discourse on his own helpless integrity, complaining that he could not adapt himself to the dishonesty of everyone around him. I can't give them the lies they want, he said. I can only be as I am. At the time Arthur had murmured in admiration and reassurance, but even then he'd felt that Louis was overdoing it. He wasn't lamenting, he was bragging, and the implication was that Arthur, who had a normal capacity for inauthenticity and could subdue himself to convention as well as the next man, had been judged and found to be second rate. Nothing out of the ordinary, no doubt, as adolescent posturing went, but on the evidence of *Jott* Louis's attitude had not changed since those days. The book wanted its reader to feel that the world was a wasteland in which meaningless suffering held sway, and that the only honourable course of action was to reject the entire mess.

Well, maybe Louis was right. He had no shortage of evidence to make his case. The morning after they got back from Wexford Sarah bought an *Irish Times* on Abbey Street and showed Arthur the headline: a town in northern Spain had been destroyed in an aerial attack. They stopped in the middle of the pavement to read the report. The town, which had been the most ancient in the Basque country and had contained no military targets, had been bombarded for three and a quarter hours during a busy market day. A fleet of aeroplanes including Junkers and Heinkel bombers had unloaded thousand-pound bombs, two-pounder incendiary projectiles and hand grenades on the town while Heinkel fighters flew low to machine-gun those of the civilian population who had taken refuge in the fields. The town, home to seven thousand inhabitants and three thousand refugees, was completely obliterated, together with villages and farmhouses inside a five-mile radius. The number of victims was unknown, but the attackers' strategy had been calculated to cause as many casualties as possible, using successive waves of bombing to stampede the townspeople and machine-gunning to drive them back under cover, where further bombing could trap them in burning wreckage. The reporter was an eyewitness who had seen the houses falling into red debris. The raid was unparalleled in military history, according to the report, in that it had no military objective and was intended solely to demoralise the civil population through mass slaughter.

Holding the newspaper between them, they exclaimed softly. It was odd that reading about something like this could so closely resemble a pleasurable experience. Even as you agreed with your wife that it was too awful, even as rightful outrage and sympathetic horror and misgivings for the future of Europe twined together in your chest, you had another feeling as well. There was a thrill of excitement, like the nervous glee of a boy unwrapping his birthday present. Part of it was sadism, possibly; part of it was simple relief, the sense that although this has happened we ourselves are safe and well and need not trouble about the news. But then there was the stranger and more complicated relief that came with the sheer fact of a dreadful thing having occurred, as if by moving from the realm of the possible into that of the actual it had released us from suspense. And even beyond that, there was the purer joy of discovering something about the world, because to learn of a new form of horror was to glimpse reality as it came into being – was to hear yourself say So this is how it is, and this is how the future is to be, and now we know. And perhaps this meant that Louis was right. Perhaps his book was a vision foretelling that the future was to be one single great big new-fangled atrocity, and perhaps the annihilation of a townful of civilians with firebombs and machine guns was of only incidental relevance to this. Perhaps the book was right, and the heart of the evil was a complacent little deracinated godless Irish Quaker of a head doctor who let himself off rather too easily and set altogether too much store by his profession and had put on a bit of weight lately and still got tetchy with his parents at the age of thirty-two and had embraced his wife lazily last night and had eaten a good breakfast this morning and could read about the massacre of innocent people by fascists with a cosy thrill. But then how was he supposed to respond?

As he and Sarah had continued along Abbey Street that morning, heading for the daily visit to Louis, they had been silent for a minute or two. There was a shyness between them that had not been there before they read the report in the newspaper. They picked their way carefully across the silence, first by telling one another that the news was awful and then by addressing the questions of exactly how bad it was, how such a thing was possible, why it had happened and what it all meant. Soon they were at ease with one another again. But it would continue to happen: shyness would always be there, ready to fall between them, as he knew it would do a few moments from now. In a few moments – he was approaching the corner of Grafton Street and Nassau Street – they would meet at Front Arch and would find that over these hours of separation they had taken different courses, each unknown to the other, so that they must reach across and close the gap. She would probably be wondering what he made of Louis's book; or truer to say that she already knew, but would be waiting to see how he carried off his feelings on the subject. It would always be like this, he saw. Every time they met after being apart, every word they spoke after being silent, they would have to overcome the embarrassment of revealing themselves to one another yet again. She would ask him if he'd got through the whole thing, he'd say that he had, and they'd go from there, so that by the time they had walked through college and around Merrion Square back to Baggot Street they would be in agreement, close allies, holding hands and walking in step. They would be ready to meet Louis, then, to try and close *that* gap, the next and wider gap.

Louis did ask a lot. He had made his accusation – his peculiar, oblique accusation over one hundred and seventy-five pages – and now it was Arthur's turn to say something in reply, because until he did there would be a different kind of silence between them, a treacherous kind. He could feel it already, deepening, becoming harder to break the longer it went on. He'd always hated the idea that he was shy, had hated knowing at Donard that he was the sort who couldn't be on easy terms with the other boys, but at the same time he'd thought of the shyness as a virtue, a sign that he was finer and truer than the others. It might be time to think instead that what counted was not being shy but being brave enough to overcome it. Perhaps that was what Louis was asking. Arthur must hear how compromised and conventional he was, how small his scope and foolish his morality and self-serving his good impulses, and then he must decide what he had to say about that.

He thought of William Walker, sitting in a day room on General Ward One at Cranfield Park Lunatic Asylum, lost among the mad people.

He walked along College Green, peering through the railings to see if he could spot her among the people waiting at Front Arch. Louis would have to let him do it in his own way. First let him find Sarah, because it was with her that he needed to begin: they would meet, break the silence and remember that the world begins with the person in front of you. Think of it that way. The world poses impossible questions and the future is in darkness, you have no claim on health or peace or the way that you feel things ought to be, you are required to live without knowing what comes next, you must carry on in hope as best you can, and you must begin by attending to one another. Which was why, as they walked to collect Louis from the hospital, his hand would be in hers and their feet would swing in step.

And there she was.

They walked along the seafront in silence. They were walking abreast, Arthur in the middle, Louis to his right and Sarah nearest the strand, with nothing between her and the breaking waves but a low wall, a descending slope of boulders and a stretch of shingle and bladderwrack. Dublin had a habit of turning its back on the sea, so that if you kept to the central districts you'd never know you were in a maritime city, but go far enough into the suburbs that straggled down the coast and gaps opened between buildings through which you could glimpse gulls and wherries, rock pools and long mirrors of wet sand. Since leaving the hospital they had walked through Sandymount, Booterstown and Blackrock, but it was only now, as they neared Dun Laoghaire, that they had emerged into full view of Dublin Bay.

Louis was determined to walk all the way from Baggot Street to Dalkey. He had been cooped up for long enough, he'd said as they set off: he needed to stretch his legs, and besides he was in no great hurry to get back home. He was only putting off the inevitable, he knew, but if you weren't going to put off the inevitable then what were you doing on this planet? Arthur had been less keen to come all the way on foot, but when he had turned to Sarah in the hospital foyer she had been in favour, saying it was about time she joined in one of these heroic walks of theirs. So far she seemed to like it, showing no signs of flagging although they had been walking for an hour and a half. There was half as far again to go, and evening was drawing on: across the bay the factory chimneys were getting ready to merge with the sky. Nor did Sarah mind the silence, though it had gone unbroken since Ballsbridge. She was walking with her hands deep in the side pockets of her winter coat, sometimes coming close beside Arthur so that their upper arms bumped and at other times drifting away towards the seafront wall. Because the silence was not hers to worry about she could move in it easily, in the rhythm of feet and breaking waves, even if it lasted all the way to the Molyneux front door.

Arthur couldn't feel that way himself. It was the same as ever: let a silence carry on long enough and it began to reveal new and unpredictable qualities. Its hidden dimensions unfolded, its buried structures appeared, so that now it was dusty and empty, now taut with strain, now crowded with the words that were not being said. And now Louis was walking beside him like a conscript on a route march, morose and mechanical, eyes downcast. It might be that he wasn't up to this exertion. Possibly Arthur should have forbidden it, doctor's orders, no attempting to walk halfway across Dublin the minute you get out of hospital after a medical crisis for which no explanation has yet been found. Nor, it seemed, was one likely to be forthcoming. As Louis was getting his things together on the ward, Arthur had slipped out and found Dr Nolan walking along a corridor with a cup and saucer in his hands. Nolan slurped his tea, clinked the china and said what Arthur had known he was going to say. They were still completely in the dark as to the nature of Louis's episode, and no professional opinion could be formed about its causes, its effects or the chances of its happening again. All they could say was that Louis had been kept in for a generous period, that no further symptoms had presented themselves and that he must now continue on his way. They must accept that they didn't know what had been the matter with him that night. If they were lucky they would never find out. Balancing the cup on its saucer, Nolan touched a knuckle to his forehead and gave a little tap. No knowing what goes on up there, more often than not, when you get right down to it. He angled himself closer to Arthur. As if you need telling!

Arthur glanced at Sarah, who crimped her eyes at him, a coded smile. Louis was oblivious, sunk in brooding, less than two feet away but beyond reach, tramping forward with his face locked in a frown as if he were alone on the path. Since leaving the hospital Arthur had not been thinking much about what Nolan had said, or in fact about anything that had happened over the eight days since he had found the note in his pigeon hole at the Bradshaw, but now the implications were settling on him. From now on he would never be free of guilt over Louis's infirmity. He would always be watching and waiting for the worst to happen. The silence dragged at his limbs so that for a few paces it was all he could do to keep moving. He saw the mistake he had made. It was a mistake he had been making for many years without interruption: he had been making it when he introduced Louis to Walker, and when he recommended the analysis with Venn, and when he sat up listening to Louis through all those nights in Trinity, and at Donard when he allowed himself to become a willing sidekick. He had been making it since the day they met. Long ago he asked for your help, and you helped him, so that now and forever you are responsible for what goes on inside that skull, for the electricity that pulses through the troubled brain. At such pains to help and to understand, and perfectly incapable of doing either. They would always be like this, Arthur and Louis, walking side by side, together but apart, with no way out of the silence.

And yet Sarah was walking at Arthur's other elbow. She looked out to sea as she walked, holding her head high to feel the breeze off the bay but perhaps also to sense the currents of the silence as it flowed, because now it was beginning to flow more freely again, still changing and unfolding, and this, Arthur realised, was because silence between the three of them was different from a silence of only two. Arthur and Louis might be locked into a silence that they couldn't escape, but Sarah was there as well, and she felt it differently, because she

268

could see – to her amusement, Arthur knew – that the two of them were just a pair of old schoolfriends who were still shy of one another after all these years, and that if Louis was being more than usually morose this evening it was because he was nervous.

As they had walked from Front Arch to Baggot Street, Arthur and Sarah had talked a little about the book. Sarah felt there wasn't much to say. She saw what he meant, of course, about the bit with the doctor and the wife and all that, but she didn't see why it should upset them. Louis had written what he felt he needed to, and as far as she was concerned he was welcome. It wasn't especially her kind of thing. She had said as much to Louis on the first day they visited the hospital, when Arthur had gone out to speak to the doctor.

They walked on, their shoes scraping on the path, the dusk violet. It was strange that Louis minded what Arthur or anyone else thought of his book, and perhaps he himself had been surprised to find that he did: perhaps for all the talk down the years of the artist's obligation to exploit and betray all around him for the sake of his work, of how incapable he was of the smallest human compromise, he was finding that he had given away a little more than he'd intended. He had given away an advantage, because if, unexpectedly, he was in suspense about what Arthur was going to say about *Jott*, if he was concerned about the effect it might have on their friendship, then all Arthur had to do was let the silence continue. If he said nothing it would be impossible for Louis to bring up the subject, and Arthur would be the one with the upper hand for a change, the one whose unknowable thoughts cast great shadows across every conversation.

The silence had turned itself on Louis now, as possible

moves turn themselves on a threatened piece. His eyes were still fixed on the path and his face was still set in its frown, but he had sensed the shift. His pace was slowing, his feet dragging. He fell behind, and finally they turned to see that he had come to a stop on the footpath some thirty yards back.

They watched him. He stood with his head bowed and his arms hanging by his sides, showing no sign that he intended to move again. And this, Arthur realised, was the move he was making. He had sensed the shift in the silence, and rather than continue at a disadvantage he was prepared to resign. It was an effective measure, Arthur couldn't deny: already he could feel the urge to hurry back to Louis and say something placatory and foolish and half dishonest about the book, to give in and embarrass himself rather than let the suspense continue.

Instead he looked at Sarah. They were free to walk on without Louis, and if they did that then they need never trouble themselves with him again. Leave him standing here in silence, trapped in his own machinations. Forget about seeing him safely home: go for a drink in a nice seaside pub, then stroll a little on the strand and catch the bus back to the guest house. Tomorrow, the ferry, the train and everything else that was to come. There was justification enough. Louis had taken all Arthur had given him and had twisted it into complicated untruth, and if he really did want to know Arthur's feelings about this he would never be satisfied, because some things are too difficult to put into words. Better surely to call this the end of the matter. After all the false endings, there would be no better chance to make a true one.

The light was going. Sarah stood with her hands deep in her pockets. A vessel sounded its horn in the bay. Arthur walked back to Louis, laid a hand on his shoulder and kept it there until the head lifted and the grey eyes turned towards him, full of doubt. They began to walk again.

The silence was loosening now, releasing its grip on Louis and opening to become an avenue that ran clear ahead of them as they left the seafront and turned inland towards Sandycove, still walking three abreast, following the streets that would lead them to a house that Arthur knew from long ago. There was more silence ahead, he thought, but they would reach the end of it if they kept walking.

Acknowledgments

To Caoileann, all my love and thanks, always. Odhrán, Sadhbh and Oisín: thank you for everything.

For unfailing help and support, deep thanks to my parents Dan and Jenny, to my brothers James and Andrew, and to Jane Anderson.

Thank you, Nina Allan, Christopher Priest and Mark Richards, for helping this book into the world.

Thank you Ronan Crowley, Michelle Ryan, Darran McCann, Bryan Radley, Tom Clarke, Tom Sperlinger, Deborah Friedell, Hilary Hammond.

Thank you Mima and Windsor Chorlton, Toby and Pippa Thompson, Lily Chorlton, Holly Hofer, Jim and Bernie Curry.